Trav•

...uld have

...y were on a first date...flirting. ...na revealed about herself, his admiration for her grew.

He suddenly wished he had met her at some other point in his life, instead of this desperate moment. When was the last time he'd flirted with a woman? Had to be Judith.

Had he ever even known what it felt like to simply enjoy the company of a woman? He'd spent his youth staying alive, keeping his brother on track. Then there was the army, prison, his business...and Judith. Nothing about his ex-wife had been simple. Every encounter with her had been fraught with the stress of trying to meet her expectations.

His heart ached unexpectedly with what could never be—not with Elena, and probably not with anyone. By the time he got out of prison this time, he'd be an old man, and Elena would be married to someone else with a houseful of children, even grandchildren.

Another Project Justice story where fighting injustice can lead to finding love!

Dear Reader,

Being kidnapped would have to be in my top five fears. Maybe I've watched too many serial killer true crime shows. But I wanted to do a book where the heroine was kidnapped, tapping into my own primal emotions.

The kidnapping romance plot is an oldie but a goodie; the trick is to make it fresh for modern readers. I chose to place most of my focus on what happens *after* the hostage situation ends. How do two people who had such an unpromising start ever forge a relationship?

I have to give credit to my feisty heroine, Elena, for going after what she wants despite everyone in her world telling her she's wrong. I'm not sure I'd be as determined, or as forgiving. But then, if I wrote about a heroine who was me, it might not make a very good book. (I don't have much drama in my life!)

Hope you enjoy Elenas and Travis's adventure!

Kara Lennox

In This Together

—

Kara Lennox

⟨H⟩ **HARLEQUIN**® SUPER ROMANCE®

Recycling programs
for this product may
not exist in your area.

ISBN-13: 978-0-373-60804-1

IN THIS TOGETHER

Copyright © 2013 by Karen Leabo

Printed in U.S.A.

ABOUT THE AUTHOR

Kara Lennox has earned her living at various times as an art director, typesetter, textbook editor and reporter. She's worked in a boutique, a health club and an ad agency. She's been an antiques dealer, an artist and even a blackjack dealer. But no work has ever made her happier than writing romance novels. To date, she has written more than sixty books. Kara is a recent transplant to Southern California. When not writing, she indulges in an ever-changing array of hobbies. Her latest passions are bird-watching, long-distance bicycling, vintage jewelry and, by necessity, do-it-yourself home renovation. She loves to hear from readers. You can find her at www.karalennox.com.

Books by Kara Lennox

HARLEQUIN SUPERROMANCE

HARLEQUIN AMERICAN ROMANCE

#Project Justice
*Blond Justice
**Firehouse 59
***Second Sons

Other titles by this author available in ebook format.

CHAPTER ONE

TRAVIS RIGGS LOOKED up at the imposing wrought-iron gate, and for the first time in his life he knew what the word *awe* truly meant. Who the hell had a gate like this? Who *needed* a gate like this? What was Daniel Logan protecting? This ostentatious show of wealth didn't jibe with the Daniel Logan he'd heard about, the one who'd spent six years on death row for a murder he didn't commit, the one who'd devoted his life to helping other men and women who'd been falsely convicted of serious crimes.

He wondered if this was some wild-goose chase.

Still, Travis had come too far to turn back. Whoever Daniel Logan was, he was the last hope for saving Eric. Travis had put on his best shirt and his newest pair of jeans, the ones that weren't yet paint spattered. His work boots weren't exactly classy, but it was that or beat-up athletic shoes. He didn't have much call for dressing up in his normal life.

Taking a deep breath, he pushed the buzzer.

"Yes, may I help you?" The husky female voice was unexpected. Whoever she was, she had an accent, not strong but exotic nonetheless. A picture came into his mind of a sultry Spanish flamenco dancer.

"Yes, my name is Travis Riggs. I've come to see Daniel Logan."

"Do you have an appointment?"

"No, I'm sorry, I don't." Every time he thought about his unsuccessful phone calls to Project Justice, his blood boiled. *I'm sorry, you'll have to fill out the online form.* No matter what he said, he got the same response. Even when he'd gone in person to the foundation's physical address in downtown Houston, he still couldn't get anywhere. An elderly dragon of a woman had barred his way and insisted the online form was the only method open to him.

"I'm very sorry," the flamenco dancer said, "but Mr. Logan's schedule is full. To see him, you have to have an appointment."

"I tried to make an appointment." Travis kept a death grip on his temper. "But they kept telling me I had to go online and fill out a form."

"Oh…you're here because of Project Justice?"

"Yes, ma'am." If he could just keep the mystery woman from cutting him off, he was sure he could talk his way through this impenetrable gate. He was hopeless with online forms, but he could be very persuasive with women. Younger ones, anyway.

"So, may I ask why you didn't fill out the form?"

"I did. At least, I think I did." He'd gone to the public library to use their computer, but computer skills weren't his strong suit. "I got stuck in a loop that kept taking me back to the same page, and then I kept getting these error messages..." By the time his thirty minutes were up, he'd been ready to bash his head through the computer screen. He'd hit the submit button, but he still wasn't sure exactly what he'd submitted.

"I'm sorry you had such a bad experience." The funny thing was she actually sounded like she was sorry. "Maybe you could get someone to help you?"

Like who? All of his many friends? He'd pretty much lost touch with everybody he'd ever been close to, except Eric. Eric was the one constant in his life. And he was not going to abandon his cause. Ever.

"With all due respect, ma'am, I've kind of run out of options. I'm up against a deadline. My brother's going to lose his little girl." Travis realized then there was a security camera above him. The woman with the sexy voice was probably watching his every move, yet he had no idea what she looked like.

"You have a friend or loved one who is in prison?" she asked, sounding curious.

"Yes, ma'am. My little brother, Eric. I can promise you on a stack of Bibles he didn't do it. He would never kill his wife. He loved her. He never raised a hand to her, and he certainly would never do what they said he did."

"Has he exhausted his appeals? Is he on death row?"

"He was sentenced to life in prison without parole.

And he's still appealing—but like I said, he's about to lose his daughter. She's going to be adopted by her horrid foster parents. MacKenzie is the only link he has to Tammy. I have to do something. It's not fair."

Travis had intended to keep his emotions out of it. But every time he thought about MacKenzie moving on to new parents, calling some other people Mommy and Daddy, his throat closed up and his eyes burned. Eric had been the best father in the world. From the time baby MacKenzie had come home from the hospital, Eric had changed her diapers and fed her, helped with 2:00 a.m. feedings, gone with Tammy to take the baby for doctor visits. The sun had risen and set with that little girl. And now he couldn't even see her, except for sporadic and very brief visits with a glass partition between them.

"Just a minute," Ms. Sexy Voice said. "I will talk to Mr. Logan and see if he can spare a few minutes. Your brother is Eric? Eric Riggs?"

"Yes." She probably recognized the case. The entire trial had been televised on some cable station.

"Please be patient. Sometimes it takes a while to pin Daniel down to a conversation."

Travis would be patient. He would stand outside this house all day and all night if he had to. But somebody had to listen to him.

ELENA MARQUEZ TURNED OFF the mic, but she continued to regard their visitor on the monitor. He was a man of uncommon handsomeness—not like a pretty-boy movie star, but more like a cowboy riding the fences—dark, glossy hair, rugged, tanned. A face of harsh planes and angles that somehow fit together pleasingly.

But the world was full of handsome men. It was the emotion in his voice—and on his face—that moved her. Normally, if some stranger came to the gate, security turned them away—period. Daniel Logan, with his extreme wealth, was a target for all kinds of kooks and terrorists. Today, however, Elena was sitting in for their regular security guy while he was on his lunch break. They were short staffed; it was holiday season, and the flu was running rampant among the employees. She'd just gotten over it herself.

She would talk to Daniel.

Abandoning her post by the front-gate monitor, she made her way through the house to the elevator, then descended to Daniel's lair. That's what everyone called it. Down here he had his office, which looked something like NASA's Mission Control. He sat in the middle of a horseshoe-shaped desk he'd had custom-made out of some exotic wood. A minimum of three computers lined up on the desk. Then he had TV screens all around on the walls, tuned to the news and weather channels. And he always had at least three or four cell phones—why anyone needed to have that many, she wasn't sure. He only had one mouth, but she supposed he could text with one, talk with another and check email with the third.

When he wanted to take a break, he had his own fully equipped workout room. There was even a dining patio with faux sunlight that looked as if it could have been transported from a Tuscan sidewalk café.

Daniel's commanding voice drifted toward her as she strode down the hall. "I can see this is something I have to take care of myself. Give me an hour." He sounded thoroughly vexed about something, so this probably wasn't the best time to approach him with a request. But what choice did she have?

He was hanging up the phone as she rounded the corner and tapped on his open office door. "Daniel, can I have a word with you?"

"You can have ten words, as long as you can walk and talk at the same time." He stood and went to the antique armoire in the corner, where he had several sets of clothes on hangers—suits, tennis clothes, polo clothes. He grabbed one of the suits at random, pulled it out and hung it on the door. Then he started peeling his clothes off.

Elena was used to this sort of thing from him. She turned around and faced the wall. "Is something wrong?" *Dumb question, Elena.* Of course something was wrong. And she'd just wasted three of her ten words. She never knew if Daniel was serious about things like that. She'd always had a hard time deciphering his dry sense of humor.

"You could say that. There's a possible leak in Reactor Number Four."

"Oh, no." That was all Daniel needed—some kind of radioactive leak in the new power plant Logan Oil had recently acquired. *Logan Energy,* she reminded herself. The corporation had changed its name as it refocused on alternate forms of energy.

"I'm almost positive it's an equipment malfunction and not an actual leak," he said, more to himself than her. "But it's something I feel the need to micromanage."

"Understandable. But, Daniel, there's a man here who really needs to talk to you."

"You'll have to reschedule his appointment. Is it that guy about the intern program?"

"No, he's coming later. This man doesn't have an appointment. But—"

"They why are we even talking about him? Tell him to make an appointment."

"He tried, but apparently the online form tripped him up, and Daniel, he seems so desperate. I feel you should listen to him."

"Desperate about what? You can turn around."

She did. He was in the process of tucking a crisp white shirt into his suit pants. Without being asked, she searched in the bottom of the armoire for an appropriate pair of shoes. It was one of the things she was good at—anticipating his needs. She enjoyed her job, but it was demanding, and she was always glad that, at the end of the workday, she could clock out and his wife, Jamie, could take over. Not that he ordered Jamie around the way he did Elena.

"His brother is in prison for killing his wife, and—"

"This is about Project Justice? Did you tell him to go online—"

"He said he's done that. But he had trouble with the form, and there's a deadline involved—"

"Death row?" Daniel knotted his tie without even using a mirror.

"No. Life in prison. But—"

"An impending execution is the only excuse for anybody not going through the proper channels. Elena, you know the rules. Frankly, I'm surprised that you're bothering me with this."

She felt properly chastised. But if Daniel could just talk to him for five minutes... Okay, she was pulling out the big guns. "I'd consider it a personal favor." She didn't ask him for much. He worked her hard, but he also paid her well and demonstrated his concern for her well-being every day.

That made Daniel stop. "Elena. I can't today. This isn't an ordinary crisis. If we can't get the new power plant on line, on schedule, it will cost us millions of dollars. And if this is more than a gauge malfunction—well, it could be a lot worse."

Logan Energy's foray into alternative energies was a gamble, but Daniel thought it unwise to keep all his eggs in the fossil fuel basket. He wanted to do his part to reduce carbon emissions, too. Naturally he was more anxious than usual.

"Tell this man that if he can't manage the form on his own—though frankly a trained monkey could do it—he can ask for assistance. If someone really needs Project Justice's help, they'll persevere." With that, Daniel strode toward the stairs, leaving her in his wake. "Call Randall and have him get the Town Car ready."

Clearly this conversation was over.

She hated the thought of going back to Travis Riggs and telling him that a meeting with Daniel was impossible. It made her boss sound so unfeeling, when really he wasn't. He just had so many demands on his time that he couldn't accommodate everyone; he had to set priorities.

Well, Elena wasn't going to give Travis the bad news over the intercom. That was just too cold. She understood what it was like to be desperate. At a tender age, she'd experienced the real risk of her father going to prison simply for speaking his mind. How much worse must it have been for Eric Riggs's little girl to lose her father to incarceration?

Brandon, one of Daniel's security guys, had come back from lunch, and now she could take her lunch hour. She threw a blazer on over her dress and exited the house through the massive front door. She made her way down the driveway, belatedly recalling that cobblestones and high heels didn't mix very well. She ended up taking off her shoes and walking in her bare feet. As she approached, she saw he was still standing there. How long would he have waited?

TRAVIS WAS GETTING himself worked up. Who did this guy think he was, making him stand at the gates like this, not even letting him onto the property? Travis wasn't some criminal planning to steal the silverware.

Daniel was probably inside his climate-controlled mansion finishing off his filet mignon and caviar lunch, planning whether to spend his afternoon playing polo or tennis. Travis had heard that he actually owned his own string of polo ponies, like freaking Prince Charles or something.

Who cared about some poor schmuck standing out in the street? Let him wait. How long did it take to ask someone whether he could see a guy for five minutes? If Daniel was going to turn down Travis's request, why couldn't he just do it already? Then Travis could move on to his next strategy.

He wasn't sure what that strategy would be, but he wasn't giving up. Maybe he would go to the media, point out how cold and heartless the supposedly philanthropic Daniel Logan really was.

He saw a flash of blue coming toward him and refocused his eyes. It was a woman in a blue dress and a blue jacket. Carrying her shoes. A tall, shapely woman with long, golden-brown hair and the bearing of a queen. Could it be? Could this be the owner of that incredible, exotic voice from the intercom?

The closer she got, the more sure he became. Her

looks were as exotic as her voice. Was she Brazilian, maybe?

She raised her hand in a little wave, but he was too transfixed to wave back.

"Mr. Riggs?"

"Still here." He was amazed his voice sounded so normal. "You're letting me in?"

"No. I'm letting myself out." She unlocked the gate with some kind of magnetic card plus a numeric code she quickly typed in on a keypad. The gates began to open, swinging almost silently inward. As soon as the gap between the gates was wide enough, she slid through. The moment she was through, the gates halted and then reversed direction.

"What's going on?" he asked. Her behavior seemed strange, to say the least.

"I wanted to talk to you face-to-face. I'm Elena Marquez, Daniel's personal assistant."

"You could have let me in, instead of walking all the way down here. What is it, a quarter mile?"

She ignored the question. "The staff isn't allowed to let anyone onto the property who doesn't have security clearance."

That told him all he needed to know. "Son of a bitch. He's not going to listen."

"Please, try to understand. He's got a lot on his plate right now."

"Oh, and I don't? My whole family's been torn apart."

"I'm sorry."

"Some lowlife is out there walking free while my brother rots in prison. His little girl is so traumatized she won't talk about what happened, and she's about to be adopted by a couple of loons who actually *like* it that she hardly talks. I think the only reason they want her is because she's going to inherit a bunch of money from her great-grandmother."

"I'm sorry."

"Yeah? Well, sorry doesn't cut it. I'll stand out here all day and all night. I'll chain myself to these damn ridiculous gates." He gestured toward the wrought-iron monstrosities. "What kind of ego-maniac has front gates with their six-foot initials worked into the design?"

"Daniel didn't do that—his father did. Look, Mr. Riggs, I wouldn't recommend that you take up some kind of vigil here. It won't work. Daniel takes a dim view of people who use extreme tactics to try to pressure him into doing something. The result will be the opposite of what you want. He'll have you arrested for trespassing."

Travis was so frustrated that he could have easily put his fist through the stone column he stood next to. But all that would accomplish was a broken hand, which would mean he couldn't work. He settled for giving one of the shrubs a vicious kick. It broke off at the ground, leaving a raw stub.

Elena's eyes widened. "Excuse me, but there's no reason to destroy private property."

"Will you have me arrested for that, too? Why

don't you go back to your insulated little world with your manicured shrubs and your Rolls-Royces?" He reached into his pocket and pulled out a twenty-dollar bill. He wasn't exactly in a financial position that he could afford to throw money around, but there was the matter of the bush he'd just killed.

He held it out to her. "This ought to cover the dead shrub."

"I don't want your money."

"Take it. I don't want it on my conscience." After he'd left prison, he'd sworn he would never break the law again.

Not unless he had no other choice.

Hell, he shouldn't be taking this out on Daniel's underling. It probably wasn't her fault. Unless…unless she'd never actually talked to him in the first place. With that thought, his frustration rose again. What did it take to get his message across? All he wanted was an audience. A few minutes. He didn't think he was asking too much, yet this woman did.

He had to get out of there, before he said or did something he'd regret.

Travis had parked his truck on the street. Although it was in top running condition, it was old, and there was so much paint spattered on it that the original color was impossible to tell. He'd parked off to the side because he hadn't wanted the high-and-mighty Daniel Logan to see it, to realize Travis was a working-class guy. How stupid, to be ashamed of his truck.

"You haven't heard the end of this," he said as he pulled his keys out of his pocket. "Maybe the *Chronicle* or one of the TV stations will be interested in how Daniel Logan acts when he's not in the public eye."

"Oh, no, Mr. Riggs, please, please don't do that." She hobbled after him, still in her stocking feet. The concrete was strewn with sharp gravel, and it must have hurt, but she didn't seem to notice. "You really don't want to get on Daniel's bad side. Don't get me wrong, he's a good man—compassionate, really— and he helps a lot of people. But if you cross him, he can be a dangerous enemy. Bad publicity only harms Project Justice's reputation, and then everyone has to waste resources doing damage control. It won't help anyone, least of all you."

"Did they teach you that speech at spin school?"

"I... Excuse me?"

"I was just thinking you sounded a lot like a PR spokesperson just now, spouting some carefully worded sound bite intended to appeal to my emotions. Well, lady, I'm not getting help anyway. What have I got to lose?"

"Just don't do anything rash," she begged as they reached his truck. "Think about it overnight. You do have other options."

"Oh, really? What might those be?"

"Well, the online form—"

"I *tried* that, remember?"

"You didn't try hard enough, apparently. People

fill that form out every day. Somehow, *they* manage to do it."

Oh, that was it. He'd reached his tolerance for this bullshit.

"So, Daniel won't respond to pressure tactics, huh? Well, I'd like to see him ignore this." He opened his truck's rigid cargo cover and, in one swift motion, he scooped the woman up and thrust her into the truck's bed. He got the fleeting impression of her soft, womanly body against his, a photo-flash image of the look of surprise and hurt on her face.

And fear.

"Duck," he said. Then he slammed the cargo cover down and locked it.

CHAPTER TWO

IT TOOK ELENA'S brain a few long, terrifying seconds to realize what had just happened. She'd been abducted. Kidnapped. That seemingly nice man, who moments earlier she had sympathized with, had just thrown her into the back of his truck like so much dirty laundry.

Her heart hammered in her ears and her breath came in quick, short gaps. *Okay, okay.* She had to calm down and think clearly. She had to take stock of her situation and then formulate a plan.

First off, was she injured? She knew from her freshman biology class at Saint Thomas University that adrenaline could mask pain, and judging from how fast her heart was beating, her body had been flooded with the stuff. But she didn't think she was seriously injured. In fact, though Travis had practically thrown her into his truck, she distinctly remembered her head cushioned against his muscular forearm even as the rest of her landed with a thunk on the carpeted truck bed.

Her hip hurt. She felt around with her hand and realized she'd landed on a tool of some kind—a wrench, she decided, as she explored the cold steel item with her fingers. She shoved it out of the way.

Her prison was utterly dark. Although the vehicle was a pickup truck, it had a cargo cover. One made of granite, apparently, because it wouldn't budge no matter how she kicked and shoved.

The truck was moving fast—at least it seemed that way. Travis took a corner on two wheels, and a slew of tools slid against Elena. She shoved them aside, irritated. "Hey, watch the driving," she yelled.

"Doing the best I can," he yelled back, his voice muffled but understandable.

Dios mío, he could hear her! She kicked against the cargo cover. "Let me out! You let me out of here right now!"

"Simmer down back there."

"Hijo de puta!" she yelled, because she couldn't think of anything else. "Daniel is going to kick your ass."

He muttered something that sounded like, "I don't doubt it."

So the cargo cover didn't come off. Maybe she could get the tailgate open? Didn't modern vehicles have latches that could be worked from the inside? Granted, this truck was probably ten years old, but that counted as modern in her book. Her uncle Cesar still drove a 1976 Monte Carlo.

She felt around for a latch and found something near her elbow that was lumpy and bumpy, but no matter which way she pressed and squeezed, she couldn't make any parts move.

She had to face it: she wasn't escaping from the truck. She needed a new plan.

Travis was taking her someplace. Where? Before hiring her as his assistant, Daniel had required Elena to take a personal self-defense course for just this reason. He was a powerful man, and some people hated him and might try to get to him through her. Plus, she was an attractive woman, he'd said in a matter-of-fact, nonflirtatious way, and she needed to be able to fend off unwanted advances.

She'd been the worst student in the class. Her attempts to defend herself against her well-padded "attackers" had been pathetic. But she remembered her instructor stressing one thing: never let an assailant get you into his vehicle. If he did, your chances of survival diminished considerably.

That depressing thought wasn't helpful. What if Travis was driving her to some isolated woods, where he intended to rape her, murder her and bury her in a shallow grave?

Her one chance was to fight back—before he tied her up with duct tape and put a plastic bag over her head and skinned her alive— Oh, *Dios,* she had to stop watching those true-crime shows. She absolutely refused to believe Travis was the skinning-alive type of guy. He was a man who loved his brother, and he'd done something out of desperation. She'd seen that in his eyes. She hadn't seen the dead eyes of a psychopathic serial killer, right?

Still, she wouldn't just meekly go along with whatever his plans were. She'd fight back. Her best weapon was surprise—and tears. She hated the idea of using tears to manipulate a man, but like it or not, she'd found that when she cried, men would bend over backward to do whatever it took to make her stop.

She was too terrified to actually cry right at that moment, but she could do a good job faking it. She started in with a few sniffles, a quiet sob or two; then she started bawling like a hungry calf.

"Hey. Hey, stop that!" Travis objected.

"I d-don't w-want to d-die!"

"Did anyone say anything about dying?"

That was good news at least. "I'll do whatever you say—just don't hurt me." She kept sniveling, though not quite as loudly as before. When he finally got to wherever he was taking her, he would expect to find a terrified, cowed, cooperative hostage. Her hand closed around the wrench. Was he in for a surprise.

ONCE TRAVIS WAS a couple of miles from Daniel Logan's estate and on the freeway with a lot of other cars, he could breathe again. There were no red lights or sirens behind him.

He couldn't believe what he'd just done. Had he lost his mind completely? Kidnapping was a felony. With his record, he would end up in prison for sure, and a good, long stint this time, in a state penitentiary. Not the cushy county lockup.

For a second he wavered. His brother wouldn't want…Hell, no going back now. He'd done it. Might as well make it count for something.

He wasn't sure his actions hadn't been caught on video, but his car had been parked some distance from the gate, so he might have lucked out. Of course, Daniel would know soon enough that his pretty employee had been kidnapped. But Travis wanted to orchestrate exactly when and how Daniel found out. First, he had to stash Elena someplace where she couldn't escape and where her screams for help wouldn't be heard. He couldn't take her home— that was the first place the police would look.

Travis thought about it for a few minutes until the perfect solution came to him. There was a house he'd recently started work on, a foreclosed property in a five-year-old gated community just off Bissonet in swanky Bellaire. The former owners had trashed the place before vacating—out of frustration and spite, he supposed. It had to be tough, losing your home and everything you put into it. The developer had hired Travis to fix it up before they put it on the market.

The house, on picturesquely named Marigold Circle, sat on a double lot in a cul-de-sac and backed up to a creek. There were no close neighbors. The walls were thick, the windows triple-glass thermals. You could set off a bomb inside and no one would hear. Anyway, this wasn't the kind of neighborhood where people gave a crap what their neighbors did. Most people there didn't even know their neighbors' names.

Another advantage of this location was that it couldn't be connected to Travis by any paper trail. He didn't write anything down. His schedule, the address of the house, everything was in his head. He hadn't yet received any written work orders. His client was logged into his phone, but so were a hundred other contacts the police would have to check out.

He only needed one day, maybe two. If this harebrained plan hadn't worked by then, it wasn't going to work at all. Either way, he'd be off to jail when it was over.

Travis had a passkey to get him through the neighborhood gate. He entered the back way, where there wasn't a guard. The fewer people who saw him here, the better.

The trickiest part would be getting Elena from the truck to the house. The garage wasn't accessible; the former owners had stripped the house of everything valuable that wasn't nailed down, and some things that were, including the garage door opener. The door was too heavy to lift manually.

Travis pulled around to the back of the house. Elena had gone awfully quiet; he was worried about her. Though he'd tried not to be too rough with her when he'd grabbed her, he'd been in an awful hurry.

What if she'd hit her head when he was driving so crazy, making all those sharp turns?

He got out and unlocked the hatch, then slowly opened it. "Elena?"

Suddenly something flew straight at his face. A crescent wrench? He tried to duck, but it whacked him on the forehead and he was stunned for a moment. Unfortunately, during that moment, his hostage rolled out of the truck, gained her feet and started running and screaming for help.

Travis was after her like a dog after a rabbit. She hadn't gone five steps before he grabbed her and clamped a hand over her mouth.

"No, no, Elena, shhh!"

She tried to bite his hand as he dragged her toward the back door. God, she was all sharp elbows and heels and…and breasts. Yes, as he'd grappled with her, trying to get a more secure grip on her, he'd accidentally copped a feel. *Nice. Let's add sexual assault to the charges.*

She grabbed on to the door frame as he tried to pull her inside. A brief tug-of-war ensued, but her muscles were no match for his and her grip gave way. They both tumbled into the hallway onto a damnably hard tile floor. He took the brunt of the fall.

"Would you just knock it off? You're only making things worse for yourself."

"I'm supposed to just let you kidnap me?"

He wanted to reassure her that she was in no danger, that he'd never harmed a woman in his life and he wasn't about to start with her. But he resisted the temptation. He needed to keep her scared and cooperative.

Somehow he regained his feet. Before she could wiggle out of his grasp he leaned down, placed his shoulder against her midsection and hoisted her up into a fireman's hold.

She was still kicking and screaming, but her arms were flailing against his back where they couldn't do much damage, and he had a firm arm around her legs. He also had an enticing view of her rounded bottom, but he felt guilty as hell about his attraction to a woman he was using in such an ill way.

What to do with her now? He didn't want to tie her up. That seemed so unnecessarily cruel, so Snidely Whiplash. He needed to lock her up in a room with no windows, so she couldn't escape or break a window and scream for help. The walk-in pantry could work. With a chair, and maybe a pillow and blanket, she wouldn't be too uncomfortable. He carried her into the kitchen.

Damn it. One of the pantry doors was broken. Even if he latched it from the outside, Elena could probably collapse the door if she threw herself against it a few times. And what if she needed to go to the bathroom?

Then he had a thought. The master bath—it was huge. Luxurious. And it had no windows except the skylights, which were far too high for her to break.

Elena's movements had all but stopped. "The blood is rushing to my head. Figure out where you're going to put me and do it already."

Hmm. She didn't really sound that scared anymore. In fact, she sounded mad. Had she seen through him? Had she figured out he wouldn't hurt her?

He carried her through the living room, where red paint stained the carpet and someone had defaced the marble fireplace with a hammer and chisel.

"What happened to this place?" Elena didn't sound like a terrified hostage should.

He didn't answer. He didn't want to get chummy with the woman. He didn't want to get to know her. If he started to see her as a person, rather than part of the system keeping his brother in prison, he would find it impossible to mistreat her like this.

"This isn't your house, is it?" she tried again. "Hey, you know, this is really uncomfortable. Maybe you could let me walk. I won't try to run again. Obviously, I can't get away from you."

She was trying to lull him into a false sense of security. He'd give her credit—she wasn't stupid. He suspected the tears and hysteria had been calculated to manipulate him, too. Well, no dice. He wasn't falling for it.

The master suite was down a short hallway off the living room. This was the first room Travis had worked on, and it was pretty much finished. He'd replaced several sections of the hardwood floor, which the former owners had gouged with an ax, and installed a new light fixture. The walls had required a gallon of paint to get rid of stains left by permanent markers. Now that he'd repainted it in the neutral off-white his client had requested, it didn't look half-bad.

The bathroom was in pretty good shape, except for a chunk broken out of the sink, probably with a sledgehammer. Travis was going to try his hand at porcelain repair rather than replace the whole sink. He'd heard about a new product that produced amazing results.

Hell, why was he even thinking about that? He'd never get the chance to finish this job. He'd be in jail.

Travis set Elena down. She balled up her fist and hit him in the shoulder, rightfully pissed off. But as she shook off the pain in her own hand—it had probably hurt her more than it had hurt him—her face instantly transformed from anger to dismay.

"You're bleeding!" She sounded horrified.

"What?"

"Look at your face!" She stood aside so he could go to the mirror and look, and damned if he didn't almost do it. She would have slipped out the door right behind him.

Instead, he put his hand to his forehead and felt

moisture. When he drew it back, his fingers were indeed covered with blood.

"Well, what do you expect when you throw a wrench at someone?" He realized now that his forehead still throbbed where the wrench had hit him.

"You are not making me feel one bit guilty. I would have hit you with a hundred wrenches if I'd had them." She winced. "Does it hurt?"

"What do you think?" He caught his reflection in the glass shower enclosure; he did look like a horror movie victim. *Revenge of the Wrench Throwers*. He probably should clean the cut and patch it up. Lord only knew what sort of germs had been lurking on that wrench.

He joined Elena in the luxurious bathroom and closed the door. Then he sat down on the carpet with his back to the door. She would have to go through him to get out.

"How about you see if the people who used to live here left anything behind in the way of first-aid supplies." The guy who'd hired Travis said the former owners had moved out in the middle of the night, taking whatever they could haul or carry that was valuable but leaving behind some cheap furnishings. Travis had already cleared out most of the furniture and sold it to a used furniture dealer.

So maybe the former owners had left something useful.

"You think I'm going to play nurse?" Elena huffed. "Think again."

"You don't have to play nurse. Just hand me the stuff. I'll do it myself. The sooner you help me, the sooner I'll leave you alone and go take care of business—the business that will get you released."

"Fine." She went to the linen cupboard first and found a clean washcloth, which she soaked with warm water and handed to him. "You can use that to clean off the blood, at least."

He scrubbed his face and neck with the washcloth while she rummaged around in the cabinets and drawers. Then he gingerly dabbed at the cut. Now that his adrenaline had spent itself, he was feeling the pain. She'd really walloped him. He was lucky she hadn't knocked him unconscious.

"If you find any aspirin," he said, "I'll start with that."

"Aspirin will make you bleed more." She handed him a bottle of Tylenol. "Try that."

"Thanks." He shook out a couple of the pills and swallowed them dry.

"I was going to get you some water. But I don't see a glass."

"It's okay. What *did* you find? Any first-aid cream or bandages?" What he needed was stitches. The cut was still bleeding.

"Found some alcohol."

Not what he was hoping for. That would burn like hellfire. But he supposed he better bite the bullet and use it if he didn't want an infection.

"What else?"

"You're in luck. Butterfly bandages."

Except how was he supposed to apply them to himself?

She dumped everything she'd found on the floor beside him, including some cotton balls. Then she closed the lid on the toilet and sat down, her arms folded, pointedly ignoring him.

He started with the alcohol, soaking a cotton ball and swabbing the cut. He did his best to remain stoic, because his ego wouldn't allow him to cry like a baby in front of a woman. But she had to hear his sharp intake of breath. It was like being branded.

"I hope it hurts terribly," she said.

"It does. Thank you for your concern."

She peeked at him out of the corner of her eye. "Good." But she looked worried. And as he tried to apply a butterfly bandage, squeezing the cut closed with one hand and maneuvering the bandage with the other, she frowned at his ineptitude. The cut ran close to his hairline, making it even more difficult.

She stood up and took off her jacket. "Oh, for pity's sake, just let me do it."

He should have said no. Letting Elena get her hands on his injured self when she seemed to enjoy his pain wasn't a logical move. But blood was dripping down his forehead and he wondered if the injury was more serious than he'd thought. And he certainly wasn't having any luck himself. He'd already wrecked two of the four available butterflies.

Elena brought a box of tissues with her and knelt

beside him. She used a wad of tissues to wipe away the blood, and then quickly, efficiently closed the cut with the butterflies.

"It's not too bad, only about an inch long." She sounded like a concerned nurse. "It's not bleeding very much now. I'm going to put this big bandage on it, but you might want to apply pressure for a little longer."

"Okay."

She did as promised. She had surprisingly gentle hands. Her breasts were right at his eye level, and he studied them leisurely. Not overly large, but not small, either, they were about the size of large, ripe peaches. Her blue dress was fairly modest, not displaying much in the way of cleavage, but he could still see the outline of those luscious breasts. She smelled good, too, like cinnamon and nutmeg.

If he focused on the pleasant sights and scents of Elena, he found that his head didn't hurt too much.

"I get the feeling you've patched up people before," he said, hoping to get her talking. Her voice was pleasant, too—as long as she wasn't yelling at him.

"When I was younger, I had to deal with lots of injuries. My dad and older brothers would come home from the sugarcane fields with scratches and cuts, and my mother and grandmother and I would get out the iodine."

"Iodine. Now that stuff hurts."

"It was what we had on hand."

"Was this in Mexico?"

"No, idiot. Cuba. You can't tell a Mexican accent from Cuban?" Then she rattled off something that he actually understood. He'd picked up some Spanish from working construction, and from when he was incarcerated, too.

"I might be ignorant, but I'm not a pig," he said.

"So, you understand Spanish. Am I supposed to be impressed? There, your wretched head is fixed for now. I think you'll live, unfortunately."

Her tone sounded closer to teasing than hateful, which pleased him no end. God, he was stupid, looking for crumbs of good humor from a woman he'd kidnapped. He was stupid for being attracted to her, too, but no one had ever accused him of being smart.

He'd been an idiot to shove Elena into his truck. More than likely, his ploy would only succeed in landing him in prison and wouldn't help Eric at all. But nothing else had worked. This plan was all he had, and he was determined to get as much out of it as he could.

As Elena gathered up the trash and threw it into a wastebasket, Travis pushed himself to his feet. His eyes swam for a moment, but then the world righted itself.

"I'll be back in a few minutes. You can't escape from here, and no one can hear you, so your best bet is to just stay calm. If your boss is a reasonable man, he'll give me what I want, and I'll let you go."

"And if he doesn't give you what you want? I

doubt he will. Daniel doesn't negotiate with people like you."

"I'm willing to bet your welfare is important enough to him that he will."

And if he doesn't?

He would let her go anyway, of course. Then he would turn himself in and take his lumps.

CHAPTER THREE

"WAIT. CAN'T WE talk about—"

Travis slipped out the door and slammed it in her face. He couldn't listen to her. He couldn't look into those chocolate-brown eyes without feeling his resolve softening. It was time to contact Daniel Logan.

The bedroom was empty except for one straight-back chair in a corner. Travis remembered dragging it in there to stand on so he could open an air-conditioning vent. One of the chair's slats was broken, which was why he hadn't tried to sell it.

He could fix it; he hated throwing away perfectly good stuff that could be repaired and provide many more years of service.

The broken slat wouldn't affect the use he put it to. He grabbed it and shoved it under the bathroom doorknob.

"Don't leave me in here!" Elena screamed at him through the door. "Please, please, I can't stand it."

He turned resolutely and walked out the door.

He'd turned his cell phone off the minute he'd nabbed Elena so he couldn't be located by the phone's ping. He wasn't sure how fast Daniel Logan could mobilize whatever people and resources he had, but probably pretty damn fast. The guy was powerful. Still, it was possible Elena hadn't even been missed yet. If she had a lot of autonomy on the job, her absence might not be unusual.

Travis got in his truck and drove. He'd been driving for twenty minutes before he realized he should have gotten Daniel's private number from Elena. The only number Travis had was for Project Justice. Well, that would have to do.

Once he was miles away from the repo'd house, in some nameless, nondescript neighborhood, he pulled over, got out his cell, turned it on, took a deep breath and dialed.

"Project Justice, how may I direct your call today?" The woman who answered had a tone of voice that didn't match the polite words. She sounded like an older lady—probably that dragon who'd manned the front desk the time he'd dropped in at their offices, hoping to convince someone to listen to him.

Celeste, that was her name. "Good afternoon, Celeste. My name is Travis Riggs." There was no point in trying to hide his identity. "Please listen carefully, as I'll only say this once. I've kidnapped Daniel Logan's assistant, Elena."

"You did what?" Celeste shrieked.

God, the woman could shatter eardrums. "Please, don't talk. Just listen. She's safe and unhurt—for now. My demands are simple. Project Justice must take on the case of Eric Riggs, my brother, who was unjustly convicted of his wife's murder. Have Daniel Logan personally call this number and leave a message, indicating that he agrees. Have him provide me with this detail—What piece of the victim's jewelry went missing?—to convince me he really did investigate the case. When he does that, I will return Elena unharmed and turn myself in to the authorities. Do you understand?"

"Now, you listen here, young man. Daniel Logan doesn't negotiate with—"

"Do you understand?"

There was a long pause before Celeste answered. "Perfectly."

"I'll check my messages in twenty-four hours." He disconnected and turned off his phone. Despite the cool fall weather, he was sweating. He opened the window and cursed. Making that call had sickened him. But he had to keep thinking about Eric, sitting in that six-by-eight jail cell. And little MacKenzie, who was so traumatized by her mother's death that she had withdrawn from the world. Now her father was gone, too.

Travis could have accepted temporary custody of MacKenzie. His brother had tried to get him to do just that; MacKenzie seemed fond of her uncle Trav, and there weren't any other relatives except Tammy's aged grandmother, who was in a home. But at the time decisions were being made, Travis had thought MacKenzie would be better off with foster parents who could spend time with her and help her adjust. A single construction worker who worked seven days a week—and who intended to spend any spare time he had helping Eric prove his innocence—wasn't a fit guardian for a three-year-old.

Even if Travis had been willing to take MacKenzie, Social Services probably would have nixed the idea. Ex-cons were hardly considered prime parent material.

Now he wished he'd at least tried to take responsibility for his niece. Her foster parents were moneygrubbing lowlifes who only wanted to adopt MacKenzie so they could get hold of her future assets. Eric had been financially comfortable when Tammy was murdered, but Tammy came from serious money. When that aged grandmother died, her wealth would pass directly to MacKenzie. Without a trust fund in place, her "parents" would get control of the money.

Travis's own brief experience as a foster kid had been positive, and he'd based his decision on that. He hadn't counted on the foster parents from hell.

Travis got his truck moving again. He needed to get back to Elena. It just now occurred to him that if something happened to Travis—say, a fatal car accident—no one would know where to find his hostage. It could be months before anyone went through that house. She could starve to death.

He didn't take another full breath until he pulled

onto Marigold Circle and everything looked quiet and peaceful. No cop cars or news crews lurked in the cul-de-sac. Even as he pulled around to the back of the house, he half expected cops to spring out of hiding, guns drawn, as he exited his vehicle. But nothing happened.

He let himself in the back door. *Hi, honey, I'm home.*

ELENA TOOK STOCK of her situation once again, as it had evolved. *It could be a lot worse,* she conceded. She had no serious injuries; she hadn't been molested. And as far as prison cells went, this one wasn't bad. The sink provided running water, the toilet worked and she could even take a whirlpool bath if she wanted to.

But there was no way out. The door wouldn't budge; she'd thrown all of her weight against it several times and nothing had happened. She couldn't reach the skylights, and even if she could, she doubted they would break easily. She'd found a can of hairspray and had attempted to throw it with enough force to break the glass, but those windows were designed to withstand hail. Even if she broke one, what then? She couldn't magically fly up to it and escape.

She wondered what Daniel would do when he found out she'd been abducted. He was loyal to his own people; she couldn't believe he would allow her to be killed just to make a point that he didn't negotiate with criminals. And Travis wasn't asking for the world; he only wanted someone to take on his brother's case. But currently Daniel was dealing with something more urgent than his personal assistant's life. What if the new Logan power plant was in imminent danger of a meltdown? That was the sort of global disaster that would definitely take precedence over one person's welfare.

If Daniel didn't respond to Travis, would Travis understand why?

She heard a door open and close and immediately got to her feet and went to the door. "Help! Help me, please! I'm trapped in the bathroom!" It was probably Travis, returning from wherever he'd gone. But just in case it wasn't…"Help!" she shouted again, slamming her palms against the door. Her right hand still hurt where she'd hit Travis's shoulder.

"I'm back." It was Travis's voice. She slumped with disappointment even as her heart lifted slightly. It was really odd, but despite everything, she still felt sympathetic to Travis's cause—more than when she'd first listened to his story. Was this what they called Stockholm Syndrome, when a hostage started to feel affection for her captor? Surely it wouldn't happen this quickly.

"Hey," she yelled. "Are you going to feed me? Because I skipped lunch. While I was supposed to be eating lunch, I was trying to get you some time with Daniel."

"And I appreciate that. Really, I do," he said.

"I'll get you something to eat. Sorry, I hadn't even thought about food. I guess when your stomach is tied up in knots you don't notice if you're hungry or not."

"Well, I do. And I'm hungry."

"I'll see what the people who lived here left behind in the way of food."

Great. It sounded like she was in for a tasty meal of stale saltines, and maybe a can of cold soup if she was lucky. Travis didn't seem the type who could whip up a four-star meal out of nothing.

She waited a long time. She stood, she sat, she recited poetry to herself, verses memorized years ago in school. "Listen, my children, and you shall hear…" When she ran out of poems, she paced the bathroom, counting the steps from one end to the other and back, and then multiplying by each circuit she made. How long did it take to check the pantry? Maybe he'd gone out for fast food.

She was almost to five thousand steps when an incredible smell reached her nostrils. What was that? Oregano? Garlic?

Travis tapped on her door. "I brought some food."

"Are you waiting for me to give you permission to enter?" she asked incredulously. "I'm a prisoner, not a princess."

"Just because I'm a kidnapper doesn't mean I don't have any manners." He opened the door and entered the bathroom, quickly closing the door behind him, but at that moment she probably wouldn't have run even if she could have. She wanted to know what was on the tray, covered by the dishcloth. It smelled amazing.

He looked around, trying to figure out where to set it down.

"On the vanity," she suggested. Earlier, she'd found a sponge and some bathroom cleaner under the sink and had given the place a thorough scrub. If she was going to be held prisoner, at least her cell would be clean. "What is that?"

"Lasagna."

"Like, a store-brand frozen-dinner kind, or the homemade kind that someone froze the leftovers?"

"Does it matter? I already had a taste of it. It's not half-bad." He set the tray down on the pink marble vanity and whisked the cloth off. He'd served her a good-size square of the lasagna on a china plate with a knife, fork, spoon and cloth napkin. There was also a serving of broccoli. A cold soft drink and a glass full of ice completed the picture.

"You forgot the vase with a rosebud."

"Huh?"

She turned her head so he couldn't see her smile. "Never mind. This looks delicious." Then she added a grudging, "Thanks."

"Holding you hostage is bad enough. I don't intend to mistreat you while you're in my custody." He gestured toward the tray. "Go ahead. Sorry there's not a chair."

She didn't care. She ate standing up.

"Whoever lived here sure could cook," she said after a few hasty bites had dampened the worst of her hunger. She slowed down so she could appreciate the subtle spices and tangy tomato sauce. "Is there more of this?"

"This isn't enough?"

"For later, I mean."

"Oh. Yeah, there's a whole pan."

"Tell Daniel he can take his time meeting your demands."

When he looked at her like she'd gone raving mad, she shrugged. "I'm kidding, of course." She toyed with a broccoli floret. It wasn't as good as the fresh stuff Cora always served at Daniel's table, but with a little bit of lemon butter on it, it wasn't terrible. "So what's going on? Did you talk to Daniel?"

"I didn't have his number. I called Project Justice. Figured they'd get him a message."

She took that news with some alarm. "Depends. Who'd you talk to?"

"Celeste. The dragon lady?"

"Oh, I know who Celeste is," she said grimly.

"You don't think she'll get word to Daniel?"

"She might. Or she might try to launch some kind of pseudo-SWAT-team rescue on her own. You never know about Celeste. I took a road trip with her once to Louisiana. Made the mistake of letting her drive."

Travis laughed. "That bad?"

"She wanted to stop at a bayou crossing and look

for an alligator because she needed a new pair of boots. And she wasn't kidding."

"She doesn't strike me as a fool. She'll do what needs to be done."

"I wish I shared your certainty. When will you know?"

"I gave Daniel twenty-four hours to leave an answer on my voice mail. All he has to do is convince me he's looked into the case."

"That's it? He just has to say, 'Travis, you're right. There's been a miscarriage of justice. I'm going to make everything right for your brother'?"

"That's a start. I also demanded proof he really has looked into the case. He'll have to provide a detail that's never been released to the public."

"Not to blow holes in your plan, Travis, but Daniel can learn every detail about that case, inside and out, in about ten minutes. He has teams of researchers who can get the information in front of him so that he can provide the details you want."

"That's good. That's all I'm asking for. That, and his word that he'll take on Eric's case, that he'll assign investigators and give it his best shot. I understand Daniel is a man of his word."

"Well, he is that."

"I believe once he looks into it, he'll see what I'm talking about. He'll see Eric really was railroaded by an overzealous D.A. and a gutless defense attorney."

"You do realize Daniel is married to the Houston D.A., right?"

"I know. The trial took place well before she took office."

They fell silent for a few minutes. Elena finished up her soft drink. The cola was cold and sweet. She didn't normally drink soft drinks because of the sugar; she'd forgotten how good they were.

"Doesn't it bother you that even if you free your brother, you'll take his place in prison?"

"Eric's life is worth saving."

"And yours isn't?"

"Believe me, I don't want to toss my life away. But Eric is my little brother. I promised our mother I would take care of him."

The emotion in his voice was impossible to miss. He loved his brother. How could Elena continue to think of Travis as a villain when he was so devoted to his family?

She quickly changed the subject. "Why are you hanging here, watching me eat?" she asked when she was done. She blotted her mouth with the napkin.

"Actually, I'm keeping an eye on you. That plate is pretty heavy, and I haven't forgotten the damage you did with a wrench."

"Not to mention the knife and the fork," she pointed out. "The knife is rather dull, but a fork in your jugular would hurt a lot more than the wrench did."

He actually turned pale as his hand went protectively to his throat. Clearly this man hadn't ever taken anyone hostage before. He didn't know the first thing about it.

If she actually believed her life was in danger, she would use any means available—knife, fork, fingernails, teeth. But she didn't. And she wouldn't.

"Before Daniel makes a single concession, he's going to want to know I'm alive. How are you going to prove that to him?"

"I've thought of that. I'm going to have you record a message for him. I'll send it to him as a text attachment."

"You can do that?"

"What, you think I'm too stupid to master some pretty basic cell phone functions?"

"Stupid? No." That wasn't the word she had in mind. A little crazy, maybe. "It's just that…you said you had trouble with the Project Justice online form. I assumed that meant you weren't very…you know, tech savvy."

"I'm not when it comes to computers and…typing." He shuddered as he said the word. "But voice recordings—that, I figured out."

That seemed a little strange to Elena. The first thing most people figured out with a new phone is how to send a text or take a picture. "You can read and write, though…right?"

"Not my strong suit."

She thought back to his difficulty with the form. "Do you have a learning disability?" she couldn't help asking.

"Dysphasia, dyslexia, dysgraphia, attention deficit disorder… Take your pick. Counselors have labeled me with all kinds of big words over the years. Including 'just plain pigheaded.' So who the hell knows?"

No wonder the computer application had defeated him. But why was she concerning herself with that? Travis had a cell phone! It was probably in his pocket right now. Yes, she could see the rectangular outline on his thigh. His taut, muscular thigh. *Dios,* the man had a good body.

Elena had spent most of her youth around men who engaged in intense physical labor, day in and day out, either cutting sugarcane or working in the oil fields. All of her male relatives and family friends were strong and muscular. But Travis gave new meaning to the term "hard body."

How humiliating to have to admit that she found her kidnapper handsome. And sexy. And how strange that, in the span of a couple of hours, she'd gone from terrified to… Well, she wasn't afraid of him. He might be a desperate man, but deep down he was gentle, and he wasn't going to hurt her.

"Tell me about your brother," she said. "We've got some time to kill. Since I am a pawn in your little power play, I'd like to know why you are so positive that your brother is innocent."

He looked at her like she was crazy. "Because he's my brother. I practically raised him. As kids, we were together constantly. When the state wanted to split us up into different foster homes, we kicked up such a fuss that they found someone who would take both of us."

Foster care. It sounded like he didn't have an ideal childhood, then.

"Don't go looking at me like I'm some sort of charity case. It wasn't like that. Our mom was a good mom. But she went through a rough patch when she didn't have a job. We were in foster care for only about six months."

"So you were very close to your brother when you were children. But people change, you know."

"I'm still close to him. I spent a lot of time with him and Tammy. Eric loved her and MacKenzie more than anything in the world. He would have died for either of them without a second thought. There is no way he killed her, under any circumstances. No way."

Elena's heart ached for him. Whatever faults he had, Travis did love his brother. That was apparent.

"I believe you," she said softly. "But Project Justice requires more than belief, because it takes more than that to get a case overturned." Although Elena didn't work directly for Project Justice, she'd learned a thing or two about how the foundation operated just from being Daniel's assistant. "There has to be some kind of evidence that's been overlooked or ignored—like a witness that was never interviewed or physical clues that weren't properly analyzed—that sort of thing.

"Do you have anything like that in your brother's case?"

"Not exactly. But I think there's evidence that could be developed. There is one element of the case that was never brought to light."

"And what is that?"

"Tammy was having an affair."

"And this wasn't brought up during the trial?"

"It was never investigated at all."

"You think the man she cheated with might have killed her?"

"It's an obvious theory that should be ruled out, don't you think? Because the evidence they had on Eric was all circumstantial. There was no sign of forced entry into the house, Eric didn't have an alibi, and they'd had an argument earlier in the day. In the absence of any other suspect, Eric looked guilty."

As he went over some of the facts of the case, Elena started to remember more about it. Although she'd never been much interested in news coverage about violent crime before she'd started working for Daniel, since she'd been in his employ she'd started watching true-crime shows. Tammy Riggs's murder was the kind of sensational event that attracted attention—well-to-do lawyer stabs his beautiful blond wife to death in the kitchen while their toddler is in the house.

"The daughter—MacKenzie, is that her name?"

Travis smiled fondly. "Yeah."

"She was home when her mother was killed?"

He nodded. "She was only three. Eric came home and found MacKenzie there with Tammy… her mother's blood all over her clothes. But she was never able to tell what happened. Now that she's six years old, she says she doesn't remember, that she didn't see what happened. She might have been in another room, asleep." Travis shrugged.

Elena nodded. "Project Justice has a psychologist on staff. She's a nationally recognized expert on hypnotic regression and recovering lost memories."

"You see? I know Project Justice can help. If only they'll take on the case."

Elena was very afraid that, no matter what Travis did, the foundation wouldn't take on the case. There were many deserving cases, and Project Justice had only so many investigators, so many resources. That's why the application process was important, so that the most urgent cases, the most obvious miscarriages of justice, were given priority.

Daniel would never cave in to Travis's tactics, because it would send out the wrong message. Other desperate people might resort to violence if the tactic worked for Travis.

The best Travis could hope for was that this stunt would attract media attention.

"If Tammy was having an affair," Elena said, "why didn't the police look into it?"

"Because they didn't know about it. Eric absolutely refused to believe it was true, and he refused to even bring up the possibility. His lawyer told me to keep my theories to myself because even the suggestion of cheating would give Travis a strong motive for murder."

"And you knew about it…how?"

"I saw the signs. I know what it looks like when a woman is cheating." He said this with no small amount of bitterness, indicating to Elena that some woman had cheated on Travis in his past. "But Eric was blind to it. Tammy was a saint. She could do no wrong—especially after she was dead—and that was that."

"So I take it Eric is not in favor of looking for the man his wife was cheating with."

"He wasn't. Not for a long time. But now that he's had time to think about it, and MacKenzie is about to get new parents—he says he won't oppose me. He still doesn't believe his wife was unfaithful, though."

Elena had to admit, it was an intriguing case. Under other circumstances, Daniel—who had final say on which cases the foundation took on—would have at least done some preliminary digging around.

"The fact that MacKenzie's about to be adopted is bad enough," he said. "But the foster parents who are adopting her—they don't take care of her properly. They just ignore her. And I think they take away the clothes and toys I give her…. Hell, I don't know why I'm telling you this."

Elena knew: because she was willing to listen. She got the feeling no one had actually listened to his story before…at least nobody with an open mind.

He picked up the tray, apparently intending to take all those potential weapons out of Elena's reach. As he did, her empty soda can rolled off the tray and onto the floor.

"I'll get it." She leaned down at the same time he did. She bumped her head on his shoulder, and everything on the tray spilled to the ground. "Oh, I'm sorry, that was clumsy of me. Here, let me help."

What followed was an awkward dance as they both tried to pick up the fallen dishes, bumping into each other several times in the process.

"For God's sake, I'll get it, okay?" he groused. "Keep your hands off the fork."

She backed off and sat down on the closed toilet. Once he'd collected everything and put it back on the tray, he left her alone. She heard him wedge something under the doorknob, trapping her again.

She took a deep breath and reached under her thigh to the object she'd hidden there. All of that clumsy bumping together hadn't been entirely accidental on her part. As a six-year-old on the streets of Havana, she'd been a damn fine pickpocket.

She now had Travis's phone.

How soon before he missed it? How much time did she have? And what would she do with it, now that she had the chance to call for help?

CHAPTER FOUR

SHE HAD TO call someone. Of course she did. Travis Riggs had kidnapped her! What was she supposed to do, hand him back the phone with a polite, "Excuse me, I think you dropped this"?

Lord only knew what he might do when he found out he'd been pickpocketed. Thus far, he seemed pretty harmless. She didn't sense violence in him. But what did she know? Not everyone broadcasted their true natures. He was obviously unbalanced. One little thing could set him off like a firecracker.

She could call 911, but then she would have to do a lot of explaining. Travis had undoubtedly told Daniel not to call the police, and Daniel's natural inclination was to rely on his own resources first. All those years he'd spent fighting the murder charge against him had left him with a healthy skepticism toward law enforcement. He had a lot of respect for certain, individual cops. But for the institutions, he didn't.

Decision made. She'd call Daniel. With trembling fingers, she dialed the number.

He picked up almost before it rang. "Daniel

Logan. You listen to me. If I don't have Elena back unharmed within the hour, I will personally—"

"Daniel, it's me," she whispered. God, she'd never heard him so angry, and she'd heard Daniel angry plenty of times.

"Elena? Thank God. Where are you? Are you okay?"

"I'm fine. He hasn't hurt me and he's not going to. It's all bluff."

"Where are you?"

"I don't really know. Daniel, please listen, I don't have much time. Could you just give him what he wants?"

He paused just long enough that Elena knew he didn't have an easy answer for her. "I won't do anything to endanger you. If that were the only way to get you back unharmed—"

"He's not going to harm me." Well, she was pretty sure. "There's a child involved. His brother is going to lose his little girl forever. That's why he's so crazy. The wife, Tammy, she was having an affair that was never investigated."

"I will give him precisely what he asked for —no more, no less. And once I have you back safely, I will nail his ass to the wall so thoroughly he'll never see daylight again."

Oh, boy. Daniel was really, really bent out of shape. "How's the power plant?"

"Why are you asking me that? You've been kidnapped! Who cares about a power plant?"

"Everybody, if there's a radioactive leak."

"It was a false alarm. The safety team resolved it long before I got there."

"Oh, that's good."

"Keep talking, Elena. I'm going to work with his provider to see if we can triangulate your location."

"You don't have to do that. He's not going to hurt me."

"You think I should just roll over and do whatever he wants? Do you want every two-bit gangster out there with a friend or relative in prison to think they can get me to—"

"In this particular case, yes—give him what he wants. If you do find me, if you come in here with guns blazing, I'll be in more danger than I am now."

"You're being held hostage by a maniac. I don't think it could get much worse than that. You don't know this guy. You don't know what he's capable of. And I'm capable of conducting a proper hostage extraction, thank you very much."

Dios, he was in a snit. She'd made a mistake. She shouldn't have called Daniel. "I have to go. If he realizes I took his phone, he'll move me."

"I'll find you, Elena."

She turned off the phone, sick to her stomach. What if Daniel made good on his threat? She doubted Travis even had a gun, but she feared he might be dangerous when cornered, weapon or no. He could end up getting himself killed.

Her eyes burned with tears. Why was she like

this? She'd outsmarted her kidnapper; she'd gotten a message to Daniel. She should be elated. But she was frightened, and she felt as though she'd done something wrong. Really wrong.

Suddenly the bathroom door burst open, and if she'd been scared before, she was terrified now. Travis filled the door, looking very large, and if he could have shot lasers from his eyes, he probably would have. He looked like an avenging dark angel.

He came toward her, and for one horrible moment, she thought he was going to hit her. But he snatched the phone out of her hands.

"I didn't even turn it on," she said.

"You had my phone for five minutes and you didn't turn it on?"

All he had to do was check the call history to know she was lying. "Okay, yes, I turned it on, but I just wanted to tell Daniel I was okay. I asked him to give you what you want."

"I'll just bet you did." He took her arm. "Come on. We have to go."

"We do?"

"I suppose you think we should just sit here and wait for the cops to come and arrest me?"

She tried to reason with him as he dragged her through the house. "I didn't tell him where we were. I couldn't, because I have no idea."

"The cops can locate me by the GPS. They can get within a hundred feet, and once they do that, they'll figure out we're in the vacant house."

She knew that, but she was surprised he did. She'd assumed when he said he couldn't manage a simple online form that he wouldn't understand how the GPS tracker on a phone worked.

He took her through the back door. It was only a few feet to the truck, which was already open. No chance of her making a break for it, not that she'd have given herself even a small chance of escaping him. He was strong and fast. He'd recovered awful damn quickly after she'd bonked him with the wrench.

He pulled her to the rear of the truck.

"Oh, come on. Do I have to ride in the back again?"

"Of course not, princess. Your limo should be here in a few minutes. *Yes,* you have to get in the back. I know you think I'm stupid, but do you really think I'd put you up front with me where you can jump out at the first stop sign? Or open the window and scream for help?"

"I don't think you're stupid." She sighed as he opened the cargo cover and the tailgate.

"Will you get in, or do I have to stuff you in there? I don't want to hurt you. I really, really don't. But I'll do what has to be done not to get caught. Not yet."

She could fight him. He'd have a helluva time getting her into the back of the truck if she kicked and clawed and screamed, and maybe a neighbor would hear her this time. But in the end, she'd probably hurt herself worse than him. He'd get her inside the truck—no doubt about that—and be gone before the cops arrived.

She looked him in the eye and made sure he looked back. Then she gave him the evil eye, something her *abuela* had taught her. She'd reduced more than one grown man to quivering jelly with this look.

"I'm keeping score. I'll make you pay."

"I don't doubt it. Get it through your head, Elena. You can't talk me out of this. The only thing that matters is that someone gets Eric out of prison so he can get his little girl back and try to salvage what used to be a good and productive life."

She looked away. Then she sat on the tailgate and swung her legs up. Travis held her hand, helping her wedge herself into the truck bed as if he were assisting her into Cinderella's carriage.

"Oh, comfy." She patted a folded blanket he'd put in there so she'd have a cushion for her head. Just before he shut her in, she handed him his cell phone, which she'd pickpocketed again.

"Son of a bitch!"

"You might want to stop carrying it in your front pocket," she said sweetly.

"How did you do that? Do you moonlight as a magician or something?"

"Trade secret."

He closed the tailgate and cargo cover. The last she saw of him, right before it went dark, he had the strangest, most perplexed look on his face, as though he wasn't quite sure what to make of her.

She could have kept the phone. She could have turned it on again once she was out of his sight. His provider would track the pings and follow them right to whatever new location he drove to. But she hadn't.

Some part of her really didn't want Travis to get caught.

DANIEL HAD ASKED Randolph, his chauffeur, to drive him directly to the Project Justice offices downtown, where everyone had been put on notice. Elena had been kidnapped. And when it came to his people, no effort was too great.

Celeste was in her usual place at the front desk. A former Houston cop, she was the building's first line of defense—and a formidable one at that. Her wild-colored clothes and big dangly earrings were a deceiving affectation. No one got past her if she didn't want them to.

She got to her feet. "Daniel. Any word since she called?"

"No." It didn't surprise him that news of Elena's call had reached Celeste. She always seemed to know everything that was going on. "Celeste, thank you for your quick and decisive actions when the kidnapper called."

"I knew he was serious. I tangled with him once before, when he tried to get in here without an appointment."

"You've met him, then? What's he like. Tell me every detail you remember."

"He's over six feet, muscular build, working man's hands. Dark hair, kinda shaggy. Blue eyes. Nice looking, can't deny that. Any other time—"

"Irrelevant, Celeste."

"Right. He was very polite but insistent. And stubborn. He didn't want to take no for an answer, no matter how many times I explained that his first step was to fill out the online form. Once he realized I wasn't going to budge, he left. Not in a happy mood."

"Did he seem unbalanced?"

"No, not at all. He stated his case in very clear terms. I remember the case he was talking about, the Tammy Riggs murder."

Daniel remembered it, too, though not in great detail. He followed a lot of crimes, sensational or not.

"He had a sort of noble bearing. Looked me right in the eye. Never used any coarse language, didn't lose his temper."

"Thank you, Celeste. If any more calls come through from him, put them—"

"Directly through to the conference room. Yes, sir."

God, he loved Celeste. He suspected he was the only person in the world she addressed as "sir."

From the lobby, he went directly to the main conference room. He could hear the buzz of conversation behind the door before he opened it; his team was on the case.

Conversation stopped as he entered.

"Daniel." The speaker was Ford Hyatt, his most experienced investigator. "Any new developments?"

"Not on my end. Bring me up to speed." He pulled out a chair at the head of the long mahogany table. Usually he ran Project Justice meetings from home, via video conferencing. But for this matter, it was important to be there in person—if only to make sure his people knew this was no ordinary operation.

"We have copies of the security video from the front gate," said Mitch Delacroix, who was in charge of anything involving computers, video or audio.

"You caught the abduction on video?"

"Unfortunately no. Elena walked down the driveway and went outside the gate to talk to him."

Why had she done that? Elena was quite proficient at discouraging nuisance visitors. Then, she *had* seemed unusually troubled by the man's plight—not her usual ruthlessly efficient manner.

"What about his vehicle?"

"Also not caught on video."

Daniel made a mental note to add some extra surveillance cameras outside the gate to include more of the street in front of his house.

"We do have a vehicle description," Hyatt said. "Riggs owns a black 2001 Ford F-150 pickup."

"What else do we know about him?"

"Travis Brandon Riggs. Thirty-three years old. He and his brother, Eric, were raised by a single mother, now deceased. Father unknown. He did a short stint in foster care when he was ten. Dropped out of high school when he was sixteen. Since then he's worked in construction on and off. Three years in the army. Honorable discharge. Married to a Judith Evans, divorced a year later. Did a stint at the Harris County Jail for assault. Haven't found out the particulars yet, but I'm working on it."

So, he did have violent tendencies. That was bad news.

"No trouble since he got out—that was almost ten years ago. Currently he owns a small construction company doing home repairs, remodeling and renovation."

"Home address?"

"It's a one-bedroom apartment in Westridge, nothing special." Mitch brought up a picture of a blocky, 1970s-era building on the video screen. It was small but tidy—neatly trimmed lawn, freshly painted, freshly raked. "We've already got it under surveillance," Mitch continued. "He hasn't been there."

And he probably wouldn't be dumb enough to show his face there, either. He'd made no attempt to hide his identity, and he had to know there was a good chance the authorities or Project Justice people would come looking for him.

"Mitch. What's the word from Reynolds?" David Reynolds was Daniel's contact at Riggs's cell phone provider. For a hefty fee, he would check the GPS data and report back.

Daniel had already sent another investigator to

check out the first location, the place from which Riggs had made his first call, but it hadn't looked promising and had probably been only a temporary stopping point. Daniel was counting on Elena's call yielding more fruitful information.

"Reynolds is still working on it."

"Griffin," Daniel said, addressing another of his best, a former investigative reporter who had become one of his most skilled operatives, especially when it came to working undercover. "As soon as you have a location nailed down, I want you and Jillian to go there. Take the fake utility truck—uniforms should be inside it. Once you confirm it's the right place, we'll figure out our next move.

"Raleigh," he asked another senior investigator, who was also his top-dog lawyer, "are you ready to brief me on the Eric Riggs case? You know what I'm looking for—a piece of jewelry missing from the victim, a detail never released to the public." He needed something to appease Travis Riggs, to lull him into believing Daniel was knuckling under the pressure.

"It was a necklace," Raleigh said. "A gold locket."

Obviously Travis hadn't done his homework, or he'd know that Daniel did not knuckle under to anyone. He would do whatever it took to keep Elena safe, of course. But she said she didn't think she was in any danger. Daniel was banking on that being true. He just had to keep stringing Travis along until he made a mistake. And he would. When he did, his ass was Daniel's.

Mitch murmured something into his headset and then turned to Daniel. "We have the location nailed down to three houses in a subdivision in Timbergrove."

"Let's roll."

FORD HYATT, DRESSED in full SWAT-like gear, showed Daniel a satellite map on his phone. "It's these three houses, at the end of the cul-de-sac."

Daniel spoke into a radio. "Anyone have eyes on those houses?" Jillian and Griffin were already inside the complex in their fake utility truck.

"Affirmative," came Jillian's response. "We can rule two of them out. I've seen people going in and out, no kidnapper types. The third one appears unoccupied."

"That's our target, then. Hyatt, Kinkaid and I are right behind you."

Daniel and his two operatives were in a taxi with tinted windows. Daniel, behind the wheel, was dressed as your average cabdriver. Hyatt and Kinkaid were in back. Taxis seemed to have no trouble getting in and out of gated communities. Mitch simply faked a call from a resident to the guardhouse requesting a cab. Five minutes later, Daniel and his party were inside. The guard barely looked at them as they passed through. They would be on camera, if a question ever came up, but with shades and a hat,

Daniel wasn't recognizable, and the taxi's license plates wouldn't trace back to anything.

Moments later, he pulled up behind the utility truck and spoke into the radio again. "Griffin and Jillian, make entry at the rear." He didn't bother using code names; their communications were encrypted. "Hyatt and Kinkaid will come through the front. On my signal."

He watched as the utility truck slid into the driveway of the house in question, which did not appear lived in. That was good news. Less chance that they were breaking into the home of an innocent family.

Daniel gave Griffin and Jillian a few seconds to get situated and then signaled Hyatt and Kinkaid. They exited the taxi and ran noiselessly to the home's front porch. Daniel hoped to hell the neighbors didn't see; this was the sort of highly illegal maneuver that he and his people could get arrested for. He'd considered letting the police make the extraction, but no cops could mobilize as fast as Project Justice could. And this was Elena they were talking about.

Daniel remained in the taxi. He didn't have the same training as the others, and if he tried to play macho cop he could put himself and others in danger. But as soon as they had the kidnapper subdued, he would be there.

"On my signal," he said. "One, two, three, go."

Without hesitation, Hyatt broke the glass in the front door, reached in and opened the door, yelling out a warning to anyone who might be inside to get on the floor. They looked like cops and sounded like cops, but they never identified themselves as such. Posing as a cop brought additional criminal charges.

Daniel counted off the seconds as he listened to the shouting and banging door on the open channel of his radio. No sounds of gunfire, thank God. More good news.

"Clear… Clear… Clear…" That single word came through over and over again. Twenty seconds in, Daniel heard, "All clear." That meant he could go in. But he had a bad feeling as he sprinted across the front lawn and into the house.

Hyatt met him. "There's no one here. It appears the house is being renovated."

"Found something!" Jillian shouted from another part of the house. All eyes looked toward the hallway where she appeared, holding a blue piece of clothing.

"Elena's jacket. Damn." How close were they? By how many minutes had they missed rescuing Elena and taking Travis Riggs down? Ten? Five?

"There was also a small amount of blood in the bathroom," Jillian said, her eyes downcast. "And some blood-soaked tissues in the trash."

"Damn it! How much blood?"

"Enough to be concerned," Jillian replied.

Daniel sighed. "I hate to say it, but we're going to have to call in the authorities. What they lack in speed and precision, they make up for in sheer numbers. At this point, we have no idea where he might have taken her. The cops can get choppers in the air, monitor phones, bank accounts, credit cards." Project Justice could do all of those things, but they didn't have the number of people required to monitor it all. "Come on. Let's clear out of here before the real cops arrive."

CHAPTER FIVE

TRAVIS COULDN'T BELIEVE she'd gotten hold of his phone. Not once but twice! She must be a magician or a witch or something.

He hated it that he had to find a new safe house. That Bellaire McMansion had been perfect.

Travis sifted through various other possible locations, rejecting each one. Most of his recent job sites were occupied. He'd have to take to the country, find a place to camp. He had little food except the few cans and whatnot he'd grabbed from the kitchen and chucked into his backpack before putting Elena in the truck and heading out. He always carried a sleeping bag and a few essentials with him, but it was going to be rough. Although the climate in south Texas was almost always mild, it would get down into the fifties tonight—cool enough to be uncomfortable without a jacket.

He hadn't allowed Elena to retrieve her jacket, he realized. She'd taken it off and draped it over the side of the tub at some point.

Several camping spots came to mind, isolated places where you didn't have to register or reserve a space. A friend of Eric's had a hunting lease they'd used once, a few years ago. If they were lucky, they wouldn't run into anyone else. Elena wasn't likely to try to run away, not in her bare feet. The heels she'd been carrying when he'd kidnapped her were probably still in the truck, but she couldn't get far in those, either.

That was good. He hadn't wanted to tie her up. When he went to trial for this crime—and he would—he wanted Elena to testify that he'd shown some concern for her welfare. Photos of bruises and rope burns would make for damning evidence in court.

It took him more than an hour and a half to get to the hunting lease, north of Lake Conroe. He'd left the freeway long ago, following a series of increasingly smaller roads. At one point he'd pulled over and waited, scanning the horizon behind him for the telltale plume of dust rising from the road signaling the passage of a vehicle. But he wasn't being followed. For the time being, he was safe.

He hoped he remembered the turnoff. The sun was going down; in the dark, he'd never find it.

Wait, there was the dead tree, a black skeleton against sky the color of faded blue ink. Another five minutes and he'd have missed it in the dark.

He swung the truck onto the narrow dirt road. Though he'd slowed to five miles an hour, the bumps and ruts challenged the old vehicle's suspension. He shuddered to think of how uncomfortable Elena must be. What if one of his tools rolled into her and injured her?

If he had stopped to consider the consequences of his actions, he wouldn't be in this mess right now and neither would Elena. He'd thought he had mastered his troublesome impulsive streak years ago, but apparently he'd only temporarily stifled it.

It seemed he bumped along the dirt road for hours, but it was only a few minutes before the road widened to a turnaround spot. He was now on the hunting lease, and all appeared quiet—no signs of a campfire or recent tire tracks. He opened the window and stuck his head out to look up. The tree canopy was still pretty thick even though it was full-on autumn. No one would spot his truck from a helicopter. He couldn't smell any campfire smoke in the air.

He parked just off the road. Later he could camouflage the truck with some brush, but he doubted anyone would come along. Right now he needed to rescue Elena.

With the wrench-missile still firmly in his memory, he stood to the side as he opened the cargo cover and peeked in. She lay there placidly, staring up at him.

"It's about time. I was almost asphyxiated in there from the exhaust fumes."

Oh, hell, he hadn't even thought about that. As slow as he'd been driving, the exhaust fumes wouldn't dissipate in the wind as they did at normal speeds.

"Lucky for you I didn't," she continued as she sat up. "Or you could share a cell with your brother." She looked around. "Where are we?"

"Where we won't be found. Please, please don't try to run. We're miles from civilization, and I'd catch you anyway. So save us both the aggravation."

He opened the tailgate, and she swung her legs out and stood. She'd found her shoes and put them on, he noticed, wondering if she'd been readying herself to sprint for freedom. If she tried to run out here in those heels, she'd break an ankle.

"Are we camping out?"

"Yup."

She sighed. "I really screwed myself over by stealing your phone. I could have spent the night in that nice bathroom, where at least I had a flush toilet. Now instead I get to relive scenes from *Friday the 13th*."

"Sorry about that, princess." He grabbed his flashlight from the glove box and rummaged around in his truck for anything that might be useful in the woods. He loaded up his backpack with a few additional food items he'd found, a small tarp, matches, a hatchet—

"What's that for?" she asked with some alarm. She stood quite close to him, watching his every move, apparently.

"Firewood."

"Oh. Isn't it risky, building a fire? What if someone sees it?"

"It's gonna be a small fire. And if I hear any helicopters, I'll douse it before they see it." It was a risk; she was right. But very slight. Even if an air search was mounted, they couldn't investigate every campfire they saw.

He just couldn't see camping without the small comfort of a fire. It was un-American.

He grabbed his sleeping bag and gave it to Elena to carry. "Let's go."

"I can't hike through the woods in heels. It's ridiculous."

She was right again, damn it. He set down the backpack. "Let me see your shoes."

"Why?" she asked suspiciously. "You aren't going to throw them away, are you? Because these are my favorite shoes. Do you know how hard it is to find a comfortable pair of heels?" But she took off one shoe and handed it to him.

He snapped off the heel and handed it back. "There. Flats."

Fortunately, he couldn't see the expression on her face. It had grown too dark. But he could feel the anger radiating from her.

"You are going to pay for that."

"I'll probably be in prison for twenty years. What can you do that's worse?"

"Castrate you." But she gave him the other shoe, and he made his alterations and handed it back. She put them back on without further comment.

Travis led the way into the woods, walking slowly,

beating aside the brush with his work boots so Elena's legs wouldn't get scratched. At least the weather wasn't horrible. Camping in August in south Texas could be brutal—you spent the whole night sweating and swatting mosquitos. But autumn was downright pleasant.

"How far do we have to go?"

"'Til I find the right spot."

Every few steps Travis paused and scanned around him with the flashlight. About the tenth time, he spotted the platform, a rudimentary wooden structure you could at least spread your sleeping bag on, keeping it off the damp ground. And the ground *was* damp. It had rained quite a bit in the last couple of weeks.

"Thank God," Elena groused when he announced they were stopping. "How did you even know this was here?"

"My brother and I camped here before, on a hunting trip."

"What did you hunt?"

"Deer. Supposedly."

She gasped softly. "You killed deer?"

He laughed. "We never even saw a deer. That hunting trip was just an excuse for a bunch of men to hang out without their wives, exercise bad hygiene, drink gallons of beer in the evenings and do the male-bonding thing. I was relieved I didn't have to kill Bambi's mother."

Travis set the flashlight down and pulled the tarp

out of the backpack, spreading it on the platform. Elena had already sat down on a corner of the platform. He took the sleeping bag from her and opened it, shook it out and spread it over the tarp.

"Your bed, princess."

"*My* bed?"

"Well, yeah. You didn't expect me to take the only sleeping bag for myself, did you?"

"Where are you going to sleep?"

"I'll manage." Truth was, he wouldn't sleep. He hadn't been sleeping well lately in general as he worried about how to help Eric. He'd like to blame the lack of sleep for his lapse in judgment, but that really wasn't much of an excuse.

"Is there going to be dinner?"

"Well, let's see…" He opened the backpack again and extracted the canned goods one by one. "Baked beans, chili con carne, carrots and…pumpkin pie filling."

"You set the bar pretty high with that lasagna, you know."

"Yeah." He sighed. "That'd be good."

"Baked beans. I can eat those cold."

"But you don't have to. I'll build a fire and we can heat this stuff right in the can. Weren't you ever a Girl Scout?"

"No. The places I grew up didn't have Girl Scouts."

Her voice had taken on an edge, and he decided not to pursue that line of conversation for now, though he was curious about her background. She'd said she was Cuban. Had she actually come from Cuba? Or was she of Cuban heritage but born here? Did people come here from Cuba anymore? He knew that at one time many Cubans had fled their homeland and entered the U.S. illegally and then were given asylum.

He made quick work of building a fire. Despite recent rain, there was plenty of dry wood to be found. He couldn't find any stones the right size to place around the fire, but he cleared enough space so nothing close by would catch. He used his pocketknife to slit the can labels and remove them, and the knife's can opener to open the chili and the beans.

The beans were ready first, steaming and burbling. He set the beans on a large, flat rock in front of Elena. "Ladies first. Be careful—the can is really hot." He pulled his pocketknife out and extracted the spoon, but he hesitated before handing it to Elena. "Please don't get ideas about stabbing me. It would make me grumpy."

"Duly noted. What else does that knife do? Does it have a parachute? Maybe a bicycle?"

"It has all kinds of things—a screwdriver, a saw, a nail file—"

"Well, that's useful."

"Scissors, tweezers, toothpick, corkscrew—"

"If only we had a bottle of wine."

"I could go for a six-pack myself." Of course she was a wine drinker. Judith had tried to get him to drink wine, but after hours of instruction, he still couldn't tell a fine Bordeaux from a cheap Merlot.

Elena held out her hand.

Reluctantly, he handed her the knife. If she went for the blade, he could get to her before she could fold it out, but he really didn't want to go there.

She gave him a knowing look. "You're never going to let go of that wrench episode, are you?"

"Not until the scar heals."

He enjoyed the playful conversation way more than he should have. It was almost as if they were on a first date…flirting. With each snippet she revealed about herself, his admiration for her grew. How many women in her position would have the smarts and the gumption to fight back the way she had?

He suddenly fervently wished he had met her at some other point in his life, instead of this desperate moment. When was the last time he'd flirted with a woman? Had to be Judith. That women had soured him on the entire fair sex. Before her, he had loved women. Couldn't get enough of them. After his spectacularly short and bad marriage, he had only interacted with women long enough to get them into bed, satisfying an occasional urge to feel human again.

Had he ever even known what it felt like to simply enjoy the company of a woman, to appreciate her beauty, her wit and those feminine ways that were so different from his own, so yin to his yang? He'd spent his youth staying alive, keeping his brother on track. Then there was the army, prison, his business…and Judith. Nothing about his ex-wife had been simple. Every encounter with her had been fraught with the stress of trying to meet her expectations.

His heart ached unexpectedly with what could never be—not with Elena and probably not with anyone. By the time he got out of prison, he'd be an old man, and Elena would be married to someone else with a houseful of children, even grandchildren.

"Do you ever want to get married?" he asked impulsively.

She looked at him curiously, her face a work of art in the flickering light of the fire. But she answered. "I hope I will someday. I have memories of when I was little, having these big family get-togethers with my older brothers and my parents, grandparents, ten or twenty cousins. Here, we have very close friends that we treat as family. So family is very important to me. My parents would be so happy if I gave them a dozen grandbabies. But I wouldn't get married just to have babies."

"You're holding out for love, huh?"

"It makes sense, right?" She spooned up some of the beans and blew on them. "Who wants to spend fifty or sixty years with someone they don't love?"

"The problem with marrying for love is feelings change."

"You sound as if you speak from experience."

She took a bite of the beans, chewed, swallowed and nodded toward the can. "These aren't too bad."

He supposed he had let a note of bitterness creep into his voice. He'd thought he was over being angry about the Judith thing, but maybe this reminder about all he didn't have—would never have—had stirred up some old, buried feelings. Ridiculous, really.

"I married for love. Felt like love, anyway, at first. But she thought I was someone else—or that she could make me into someone different, someone better. I guess I was a pretty hard case, because she gave up, moved on to greener pastures. I kept trying to make her happy, and, meanwhile, she was lining up her next project."

"I'm sorry. I guess it must be hard to believe in love after an experience like that. But I've seen real love, lasting love, so I know it's out there. My parents have been married more than forty years, and my mother's eyes still light up whenever my father walks into the room. He still gives her flowers for no reason, just because."

Travis must have looked skeptical, because she added, "What about your brother? I know it ended tragically, but didn't he love his wife?"

"He did, and I used to think she loved him, until I realized she was cheating."

"Oh. Right. You mentioned that." She returned her attention to the baked beans.

It wasn't that he didn't believe in true love and

happy endings; it was just that such perfect pairings were exceedingly rare. Certainly didn't happen for his mother. His father hadn't even stuck around long enough to see Eric born.

The temperature was dropping. The chili was steaming now, so he used a folded T-shirt from his car as a pot holder, took the can off the fire and set it on the flat rock.

Elena offered the spoon to him. It seemed oddly intimate, sharing one spoon. But he could see she hadn't eaten much.

"I'll wait until you're done."

"No, really. I've had enough."

He accepted the spoon and then dug into the chili. It wasn't too bad. "This stuff reminds me of child-hood. You know, that chili they served in school cafeterias?" The school lunch programs had pro-vided Eric and him at least one good meal a day.... Sometimes the only meal they got.

"I wouldn't know. I always brought my lunch."

She'd probably had a lunchbox with some Dis-ney princess on it. He smiled at the thought. "Want to try it?"

"Sure. Might as well broaden my horizons."

When he presented her with the can of chili, like a waiter at a four-star restaurant presenting a sir-loin steak, she took the spoon and helped herself to a hefty bite.

"So, you never eat canned food?" Though Travis knew how to cook, these days he seldom bothered with anything more elaborate than a can of soup or tuna fish.

"Daniel doesn't allow canned food in his house. Everything is made fresh. And my mother cooks everything from scratch."

"Something about being out in the woods makes even canned stuff taste better. When you're hiking or canoeing, a peanut butter sandwich can be ecstasy."

She was staring at him. He turned away from her self-consciously.

"You're very handsome when you smile. You should do it more often."

"Don't have much to smile about lately. You about done with that?"

"Oh, yeah. I forgot for a moment that I'm hogging the only spoon." She handed the utensil back to him. Now that her hunger was satisfied, she might have more incentive to threaten him with the knife, so he was relieved she didn't try anything.

Elena surrendered her spot next to the rock, and Travis took it over. The ground was still warm where her bottom had rested, and he enjoyed the sensation, the secondhand contact with such an attractive part of her body.

Wow, he was obviously hard up.

He finished up the chili and the beans and set the cans aside. There was no trash bag, but he would carry the trash out when they left. Just because he was a desperate felon was no reason to litter.

"You want dessert? The canned pumpkin might be tasty. Or I have some granola bars."

"No, thanks. I'm full. I have to, um, use the bathroom."

He'd been dreading this moment. Once out of his sight, she could run. It might seem the smart thing to do, from her angle. But they were a long way from help. She might find her way to the road in the dark, but he would catch up to her if she did that. And if she went deeper into the woods she might elude him, but she risked wandering all night and becoming hopelessly lost. With no jacket, no proper shoes and no water, she could come to harm.

But what else could he do? He wasn't going to stand over her while she peed behind a bush. The situation would be humiliating for both of them, and her friendly, cooperative mood would come to an abrupt end.

"Don't go far."

"Can I take the flashlight?"

"Nope."

"Great. You better hope a snake doesn't get me."

"Snakes are hibernating this time of year."

With a backward malevolent glance at him, she stalked off into the darkness. Travis took a couple of bites of the pumpkin, but it had a chemical aftertaste—too many preservatives, or maybe it simply tasted of the can. He listened to the sounds of the woods at night. It was peaceful here, just him and Elena and the crickets.

And the coyotes. A long, mournful cry drifted on the night breeze—a coyote seeking its mate. Soon another cry joined the first, then a third. They weren't too far off; maybe a mile.

Elena hurried back to the campsite, her feet crunching noisily in the leaves. "What is that?"

"Uh, coyote?"

"It's enough to chill my blood." She looked around fearfully, as if carnivorous monsters might appear from any direction at any minute. "They sound close."

He opened his mouth to reassure her that they were safe, that the coyotes were just calling to each other and wouldn't bother them. Humans were far too big to be prey for a small critter like a coyote unless the animals were really desperate.

But then he realized he could use her fear and ignorance of the woods to his advantage. If she was afraid of coyotes, she was less likely to wander off in the night and try to escape.

He looked around, feigning worry. "They are close. And they sound hungry. They howl like that when they're hungry."

"Do you have a gun?"

"A gun? No. Why would you even think that?"

"Well, you're a kidnapper. I just thought you might have a gun."

"No. But they won't bother us so long as we keep the fire burning. Coyotes are afraid of...wood smoke."

Elena scurried back into the clearing, standing

close to the fire. "Do we have lots of firewood? Should we collect more?"

Travis eyed the meager pile of deadwood he'd collected, most of which had been lying around within twenty or thirty feet of their campsite. He'd been planning to let the fire die down; it wasn't so cold that they really needed the warmth. But after the whopping lies he'd just told, he was going to have to keep it burning. Well, he hadn't intended to sleep much tonight anyway.

"I'll go get more."

She picked up one of the smaller logs and held it, club fashion. "Don't go far. If I see anything move, I'll scream."

Now he felt a little bit guilty for making her so afraid. She hadn't shown that much fear toward him, and he had the capacity to do her a lot more harm than a scrawny coyote.

Travis spent about ten minutes collecting more wood, occasionally checking on Elena to make sure she wasn't pulling another fast one, using the distraction of the coyotes to get him out of the way so she could make a break for it. Then he moved the tarp to the ground closer to the fire and spread the sleeping bag on it again. "You can sleep here. It's not the Ritz, and you're probably used to a feather bed and silk comforter at Logan's house, but it shouldn't be too bad."

She shrugged. "I've slept in worse places."

"Really? When?"

She sat cross-legged on the sleeping bag and pulled one end of it around her shoulders for warmth. "How about in the bottom of a leaky dinghy?"

Yes, that sounded worse. "When did you—"

"Never mind. I shouldn't have brought it up. It's something I don't think about often, let alone talk about."

Now he was consumed with curiosity. She'd dropped a few hints that she hadn't always lived a privileged existence, but now he wondered how bad it had been.

"Elena, how did you learn to pick pockets?"

"It's a gift."

A pat answer. "So, you don't want to talk about that, either?"

She shook her head. The coyotes howled again, and she shivered.

"I promise not to let the coyotes get you, okay?"

Elena nodded, but she looked as if she didn't completely believe him.

"Is there anything you do want to talk about? It's kind of early to go to bed."

She hesitated, staring at him intently as if seeking to see beneath his skin. "Why are you willing to exchange places with your brother, to go to prison for him? Isn't your life worth saving, too?"

So, she didn't want to talk about bad times in her life, but *his* life was fair game? He supposed he could say no. But he didn't. "Look, I don't relish spending the next few decades behind bars. But

Eric… You'd have to know him. He was a special kid even before he could walk and talk. He had this wild, curly blond hair and inquisitive eyes, and as soon as he could talk, he wanted to know everything. His curiosity knew no bounds. He was smart, too—absorbed everything like a sponge. You'd tell him something once, he'd remember it. You'd show him how to do something and he'd pick it up immediately, and pretty soon he'd be doing it better than you. I taught him how to tie his shoes in five minutes.

"He made straight As in school. The teachers loved him. The other kids loved him. Yet nothing ever went to his head. He was exceptional in every way, and he knew it, but he still managed to somehow be humble.

"The girls were all over him, but he always treated them nice. He had a few different girlfriends over the years, but he was loyal to each one while he was with her.

"He got a full-ride scholarship to Stanford, and then he went to law school. He was courted by some pretty big law firms, but he didn't want to leave Houston, so he went with a smaller firm. He could have been a very successful trial lawyer—he was something to watch in the courtroom. But he chose real estate law instead because he didn't like the confrontational aspect of the courtroom or the unsavory nature of dealing with criminals. He's basically too nice to be that kind of lawyer.

"When he met Tammy, he was positive she was the one. They seemed to be the golden couple living the perfect life. They had a gorgeous home, and when MacKenzie was born it was the icing on the cake.

"Eric didn't have a malicious bone in his body. I never once in my whole life saw him lose his temper. Which is why it's so ludicrous that he would kill Tammy.

"We used to go fishing as kids, but I noticed that Eric never baited his hook right. He was hoping a turtle would steal his bait so he wouldn't have to catch anything—so he wouldn't have to clean it. That was how much he hated knives. Can't see him picking up a knife and stabbing someone."

"Did you testify at your brother's trial? As a character witness?"

"No. His attorney was afraid I'd do more harm than good, seeing as I'm an ex-con. He thought I would have no credibility."

A wariness came into her eyes. "Oh. You've been to prison?"

"Assault. It was self-defense, but I couldn't prove that, so I pled out. Did eighteen months."

"Excuse me for saying so, but Eric's lawyer was an ass. If a jury had heard what you just told me... Well, let's just say it would have made them think."

CHAPTER SIX

ELENA COULDN'T BELIEVE this was happening to her, but she was actually taking Travis's side. She'd always had strong feelings about the work Project Justice did. Her family had come to this country to find freedom and fairness, and it had appealed to her sense of honor that even when the justice system made a mistake, there was still recourse. Her family had left Cuba when they did because her father was being threatened with jail simply for expressing an opinion that wasn't popular with the government.

Her father had trained as a doctor, but for reasons Elena never fully understood, he hadn't been allowed to practice. Instead, his fine mind had gone to waste in the cane fields and his family had lived in a tin shack. And even that had been threatened.

Their first few years in America, they'd still been relatively poor. But they'd been free—free to speak their minds, to live and work where they wanted, and free from the constant threat of jail.

She was proud to work for the man who had created a foundation that defended people who'd been unfairly imprisoned.

But this was the first time she had been so up close and personal with the pain and devastation a false conviction wreaked on the prisoner's family. If her family had not left Cuba when they had, she could easily be the one left on the outside, mourning an innocent person's life being wasted behind bars. She could easily see herself in Travis's place—powerless to help, desperate to make someone—anyone—listen to reason.

Still, she couldn't overlook the fact that Travis had himself committed a crime. He'd kidnapped her and was still holding her against her will, though her will had weakened considerably over the past few hours.

How she felt didn't really matter, she supposed. The course had been set. Nothing would happen until tomorrow, when Travis checked his voice mail to find out Daniel's response.

The whole thing would be over before too long. Travis would let her go—she felt pretty sure about that. Then he would be arrested. But something good would come of it. Daniel would be forced to take a look at Eric's case. And when he realized Eric's lawyer had been weak, that he hadn't pursued certain avenues that he should have, that he hadn't let Travis testify, Daniel would have no choice but to do something. His conscience wouldn't let him ignore the situation, no matter what he said about proper channels and priorities.

And there was a child involved. Daniel had a soft spot for little ones, and unless Elena missed her guess, he would soon have one of his own. He and Jamie hadn't made any announcements, but Elena had noticed that these days Jamie often ate saltines for breakfast, and that some of her suits were a little tight across her formerly flat tummy.

Those damned coyotes howled again. It sounded like a whole pack of them now instead of just one or two. Tomorrow would be soon enough to deal with the repercussions of Travis's rash actions. First, she had to survive the night without getting eaten.

"Where are you going?" Elena asked in a panic when she noticed Travis walking away from the fire. He might be a kidnapper, but there was no one else around to protect her from hungry carnivores.

"I'm taking this trash farther away from here so it won't attract any unwanted visitors. Besides coyotes, we have to think of the raccoons, possums and skunks."

"Oh, great, give me more to worry about!"

He disappeared into the darkness, and she felt sick to her stomach at the idea that he could leave her alone out here. What if he just abandoned her and never came back, decided to make a run for it? He could get a pretty good head start while everyone was looking for him around Houston, assuming he was still holding her hostage. Would she die out here? Would some hiker or hunter find her bones years from now, picked clean and scattered by wild animals?

After a couple of minutes she couldn't stand it

anymore. "Travis?" She waited, didn't hear anything. "Travis!"

"What?" She still couldn't see him, but he wasn't far off.

"Oh, um, nothing, I just thought something was rustling the leaves, but I guess I was wrong." Now she felt really stupid. She'd die of embarrassment if he knew what a total coward she was.

"It was probably just me."

A moment later he reappeared, and she quietly sighed with relief. She was not cut out for this outdoorsy stuff. As a child, during the cane harvest she'd lived in rural areas, but she'd always preferred the city. Concrete and traffic noise were far more comforting to her than trees and crickets.

She would never get to sleep.

"Is it okay if I share that tarp with you?" he asked politely.

It struck her as funny that he was so concerned with her sensibilities. She shrugged. "Sure."

"You won't come after me, will you?"

"With what? My fingernails?"

"You could club me with a log."

"Then who would protect me from the coyotes? No, I'm resigned to my fate. I figure if you were going to do anything hideous to me, you'd have done it by now."

He sat down cross-legged on the tarp next to her. His body radiated its own heat, which she welcomed.

"You can go to sleep if you want," he said. "I'll stay awake and watch for coyotes."

"I'm not really sleepy. What time is it? Without a phone, I'm clueless."

"I don't know. I left my phone in the car so you wouldn't be tempted."

"We wouldn't get a signal out here anyway." She yawned. "It's probably earlier than it seems."

"When I was a kid, I learned how to tell the time by the stars."

"Were you a Boy Scout?"

"No, but Eric and I went camping sometimes. Eric had a book about the stars. He learned how to do it and taught me."

"You actually like the whole sleeping-under-the-stars thing?"

"Yeah. It was fun. Hiking, hot dogs, s'mores. What's not to like?"

"What's a s'more?"

"Oh, my God, you've never had a s'more? That's un-American."

"I'm from Cuba—sue me."

"You toast a marshmallow over an open fire until it's brown and crusty. Then you take a graham cracker, and you put a chocolate bar on it, and you squish the toasted marshmallow between the chocolate and a second graham cracker. And the chocolate melts and everything is all warm and gooey...."

Her mouth watered. "This is a traditional camping food?"

"Absolutely. You should try it sometime."

"I will. Next time I plan a camping trip. Which will be when they start making ice cubes in hell."

"Can't have that. You haven't lived until you've tried a s'more."

"Why is it called a s'more?"

He grinned. "I've never actually had to explain this to an adult before. Because after you eat one, you always want s'more."

She stared at him blankly.

"Some more?"

"Ohhhh. I'm not really stupid—it's just that sometimes the cultural references escape me."

"In a pinch, you can toast the marshmallow over the flame on a gas stove. I'll make one for you once we're back to civil—" He caught himself then looked supremely guilty. Of course he wouldn't make a s'more for her. He'd be in jail. They would never see each other again.

The realization made her eyes burn. Or maybe that was just the wood smoke.

It sounded as if Travis had lived a good life, for the most part, despite a few bad breaks. It made her uncomfortable to think of him in prison, where they undoubtedly did not have s'mores. She had heard that American prisons were like luxury resorts compared to Cuban prisons, but, still, nobody wanted to go there.

She kept her thoughts to herself. It was embarrassing enough to have such feelings for the man who'd grabbed her off the street and held her hostage. He didn't need to know.

Elena yawned again. Her back hurt from sitting unsupported for so long. She curled up inside the sleeping bag, resting her head on her folded arm and trying not to take up more than her half of the tarp.

"Oh, here. You can stretch out if you want—"

"No, no, really, I'm good. I always sleep curled up in a ball like this." Actually, she was more of a sprawler. She hadn't shared a bed since childhood, and at Daniel's she had her own queen-size pillow-top bed. She always went to sleep on "her side," and then migrated during the night, because in the morning she might find herself in the middle or diagonal or with her head at the foot and pillows strewn all over the place. But since she didn't plan on going to sleep, she didn't have to worry.

"So you didn't go camping when you were a kid," Travis said. "What did you do?"

"I did what poor kids do. Played in the street." Normally she didn't talk about this stuff, and she was amazed she'd let her guard down enough to tell him anything about her childhood. Most people looked at her, at her wardrobe and job, and assumed she'd grown up rich.

She wasn't sure what it was about Travis that made her drop her guard. Maybe it was his own candor with her. He seemed so alone in the world. She felt this ridiculous urge to share something of herself with him, to show him trust he didn't deserve.

"How did you end up working for a billionaire? Seems like a pretty big jump from street kid to… whatever it is you do for him. Gate guard?"

She laughed. "No, I'm not normally the gate guard. I was just filling in while the regular guy was at lunch. I'm Daniel's personal assistant. I keep his schedule, take phone calls, handle travel arrangements, do all those normal but annoying things that most people do for themselves, so that he can get on with the business of running his companies."

"How did you get that job?"

"I was working at Logan Oil before. That's how he knew me. When his previous assistant transferred to Project Justice, he asked me if I wanted the job. I jumped at the chance. Doubled my salary overnight, and I got to live on the estate. It's a hard job—the hours can be long and Daniel is demanding and he doesn't tolerate many mistakes. But I like it…sort of."

"Why only sort of?"

"It's not something I want to do the rest of my life. At some point, I want to…what's the expression? Do my own thing. Make my own mark in the world. Still, Daniel's a good boss. I mean, he's not my best friend, but I respect him."

"He's going to grind me into dust when this is through. There may not be enough left of me to put in jail."

"He'll calm down once I'm back." At least she

hoped he would. Daniel did not let people cross him without consequences.

"It doesn't matter. As long as he looks into Eric's case. That's all I care about."

"You know, if you'd asked me, I'd have helped you with the application. That would have been a whole lot easier than kidnapping me. In fact, I was about to offer to help when you grabbed me and threw me in your truck."

"Huh."

"Huh? That's it?"

"Assuming I believe you, it wouldn't be the first time I showed bad judgment. But why would you have helped me? I was a complete stranger to you."

"Your story got to me," she admitted. "Normally my job would have been to get rid of you. Daniel has no patience for people who show up without an appointment. But I could tell you were sincere, that you really did want to help your brother. That was why I talked to Daniel. That was why I came out there in person to talk to you. It seemed way too cold to tell you on the phone that Daniel couldn't see you."

"And I repaid your kindness by kidnapping you. Makes me a pretty big jerk."

But she *didn't* think he was jerk. This whole episode in her life was getting weirder by the minute.

Now the wood smoke was *really* burning her eyes. She closed them so they would stop stinging.

"How did you get to the States?" he asked. "Last

I heard, it's not so easy to emigrate from Cuba to the U.S."

"I'm done talking about me," she said gruffly, afraid of revealing even more of herself. Every little piece of herself she handed him gave him power over her. "Maybe I'll go to sleep now. Maybe things won't look quite as bleak in the morning—for either of us."

"That's a load of crap, and you know it."

"No, I don't know it. My mother is quite fond of saying how any situation will look better in the morning. Things always look bleaker in the night, when it's dark and you're tired. In the morning, the sun is rising and you have a fresh day ahead of you, a chance for a fresh start."

"Elena, I can't undo this."

"Maybe you can," she said drowsily. "Wait and see."

EARLIER, ELENA HAD said sleep would be impossible, but she dropped off quickly. For a long time, Travis stood guard over her, as he'd promised, protecting her from imagined dangers. He watched her sleep; she didn't stay in a little ball like she'd started. She tossed and turned and thrashed, throwing the sleeping bag off, then burrowing underneath it, sprawling like a hedonist, then curling up again.

Eventually she ended up using his thigh as a pillow. She would probably be horrified to find herself in such an intimate position with him, but she looked comfortable, so he left her there, despite the fact that her nearness had given him a raging hard-on. It was difficult to look at her, especially in such an unguarded state, without getting aroused.

He desperately needed sleep. The past couple of weeks he'd probably averaged four hours of rest per night as he'd tossed and turned, frustration churning in his gut over his outrage, his feeling of powerlessness and the unfairness of it all.

Especially when the date for MacKenzie's adoption hearing had been set.

Maybe he could still do something about that, he pondered. Eric's lawyer had wanted to keep Travis at arm's length from the criminal case, but that pompous ass wasn't involved in MacKenzie's adoption. Travis could go to the trial and speak up about the things he'd seen when he'd made unannounced visits to MacKenzie at her foster home. She hadn't been neglected in a physical way—she'd always been relatively well-groomed and wearing clean clothes. But the clothes were old, faded and ill-fitting, not the pretty new outfits Eric had bought for her—with Travis's help—on a regular basis as she grew. The hair ribbons and barrettes he'd given her weren't in evidence, either. In fact, MacKenzie's beautiful long hair had been cut short in an unprofessional manner.

More disturbing, though, was that he'd always found MacKenzie sitting alone, usually in some dark corner, clutching a stuffed animal. The other kids in the household would be running around, playing, watching TV, but MacKenzie didn't interact with them—or with anyone—and the parents didn't care. They always had some explanation about where the new clothes had gone—they were in the laundry, or MacKenzie had worn old clothes because she'd been making mud pies.

Travis suspected the new clothes—which had come from a high-end store per Eric's instructions— had been sold.

He deliberately turned his thoughts away from MacKenzie, because he always felt furious if he dwelled on the situation, and fury wasn't going to serve him right now. Emotions out of control were what had landed him in this situation.

Instead he thought about Elena, a much more pleasant subject. He wanted to know how she'd come to America, but she apparently didn't want to talk about it, and he had to respect her privacy. He, too, didn't like it when people poked and prodded him about private stuff, like some of the things he'd seen when he was in the army.

Elena looked almost like a child, so innocent and pure. He touched her hair, being careful not to wake her. In this light, her hair looked black, but with a few shiny gold highlights from the firelight. When he rubbed a strand between his thumb and finger, it felt soft and slick, full of health and vitality like the rest of her.

He imagined using his fingers to comb through her hair. How would it feel? He'd touched her a couple of times, when he'd lifted her in and out of the truck and when he'd carried her, but he hadn't paused long enough to catalogue the sensations in a way that he could remember them later.

She chose that moment to move in her sleep, curling up again and abandoning the thigh-pillow. *Thank God.*

Was she cold? He wished he had another blanket for her. The sleeping bag was an inexpensive one, not meant for cold weather. For him, in this climate, it was adequate. But maybe not for her.

He needed sleep. His eyes involuntarily closed.

After jerking awake a couple of times, he realized he was losing the battle. He lay down on his side of the tarp, trying to take up as little room as possible, and cradled his head on his arm. If he could just catch an hour or two, he'd be okay.

ELENA AWOKE IN the most deliciously warm cocoon. Still in the grips of the aftereffects of some wonderful dream, she kept her eyes closed and snuggled deeper into the covers and tried to reclaim sleep. But the harder she tried, the more she woke up.

That was when she realized she wasn't alone in her bed. Her body was plastered against another body—a hard, hot, male body. And she was not in her comfortable bed at Daniel's, or the squishy double bed of her childhood bedroom, where she still slept sometimes when she visited her parents.

She gasped as her mind flooded with memories.

She'd been kidnapped, taken to the woods. She'd gone to sleep curled up a safe distance from Travis, but now her body was draped over his in a more intimate way than she'd ever experienced. She must have unconsciously gravitated toward his heat during the night.

Not that she was totally without experience. She'd gone to college, after all, and she had done her share of experimenting, determined to throw off the ultraprotective restraints of her family and become a thoroughly modern American woman. But she'd never spent the whole night with a man. She'd never been in a relationship serious enough to warrant overnight privileges. Especially since she'd been working for Daniel, she hadn't had time for men.

She'd had no idea what she'd been missing.

It wasn't just the feel of all those hard muscles pressed against her. It was also the way he smelled— like pine needles and wood smoke and essence of male. She'd never smelled anything so heavenly.

Weighed down with guilt over her inappropriate feelings, she realized she needed to extricate herself from this situation before he woke. He *was* still asleep, she fervently hoped. Although the sky was turning from black to gray with the impending sunrise, it was still too dark for her to see his face clearly, but his breathing was slow and even, his body relaxed.

Elena was on her side next to him, her cheek resting on his shoulder, one arm and one leg thrown over him possessively. Her leg was positioned at a very strategic portion of his anatomy, and though he'd remained fully clothed, she could still tell he had an erection.

Lots of men had erections in the morning, or so she'd heard. It was no big deal. But she couldn't help the little thrill she got out of knowing she had aroused this powerful male animal.

She tried moving her leg first. But as she slowly lifted and straightened it, she realized Travis's arm was draped loosely around her. Her movements caused him to stir in his sleep, and his grip on her tightened. One of his hands rested on the top of her hip. Her dress had ridden up, and nothing stood between their skins except her thin silk panties.

Her stomach swooped and she felt hot, deep at the core of her being. What was happening to her? This was not right. She could not be having these feelings for the man who'd committed a serious crime against her.

He was a violent man. A criminal. Her father would kill her if she even dated such a man. Never mind what he'd do if he found out Travis had touched her in any intimate way.

But he hadn't, she reminded herself. She was the restless sleeper who was undoubtedly responsible for the way their bodies were pressed together like peanut butter on toast. And she was going to remedy the situation.

Moving inch by inch, she finally had her leg free

of him. Next she withdrew her arm. If she could just scooch down toward the foot of the sleeping bag, which was resting on top of them like a blanket, she might be able to escape this predicament with her dignity intact.

The second she started moving again, however, his hold on her tightened. "Where ya goin'?"

Oh, *mierda,* he was awake! Or was he? He was still breathing like he was asleep. Maybe she was some random girl in his dreams.

She tried moving again, but she realized there was no way she could manage to discreetly extricate herself. She gave up. This was ridiculous. None too gently she removed his hand from her back and sat up, throwing off the blanket.

His eyes flew open and he was instantly awake. He sat up, too. "What happened?"

Her face was as hot as the smoldering coals in their campfire. "We moved together. In our sleep. It was very embarrassing and I'm sorry. I was trying to move away without waking you, but I clearly did not succeed."

He nodded his understanding. There was enough light now that she could see his face. He was blushing. "Ahhh. That might explain the dream I was having." He flashed a wicked smile, and she knew he wanted her to ask what kind of dream, but she refused to give him the satisfaction.

She was already humiliated. He was making it

worse. "Excuse me," she huffed. "I'm going to find a little privacy."

"Aw, don't go away mad. I hope I didn't take liberties, but honest to God, I was asleep."

She found her shoes, what was left of them, and stalked away into the bushes, no longer worried about the coyotes. Let them come and eat her. At least it would end her shame.

Men looked at her and assumed she was, oh, what was the expression? Hot to trot? But she was really rather old-fashioned, and she didn't treat sexual matters lightly.

When she was younger, she and her parents and older brothers had lived in that awful tin shack with thin walls. She had often heard her parents having relations. Sometimes they would talk in low, intimate voices, exchanging words of love and some words she didn't understand. Sometimes they would laugh in a way they didn't do outside their bedroom.

Ignorant of this aspect of married life, she'd asked her mother about it. Her mama had explained that what she had overheard was a very special part of being married, and that when she was older and she had a husband, she would understand. Her mother had never made her feel that sex was wrong or bad. More like it was part of a sacred bond.

Though she hadn't waited until she was married to experience sex, her limited sexual encounters had made her realize that casual couplings and frantic dorm room assignations were a far cry from what her parents shared.

She wanted what they had. It had literally been years since she'd been with a man. She might feel a transient attraction to Travis, but that didn't mean she wanted to trade sexual banter with him. That simply wasn't her.

CHAPTER SEVEN

WHEN ELENA RETURNED to the campsite, Travis was stoking the fire again. He looked sexier than ever with his rumpled hair and a day's growth of beard.

Something smelled good. Travis wasn't just stoking the fire, he was cooking something in the tiniest aluminum frying pan she'd ever seen. Another small pot containing a dark liquid sat in the coals.

"Coffee?" she asked hopefully.

"Probably not the kind you're used to. Cuban coffee is in a category all to itself. This, unfortunately, is instant."

"I don't drink Cuban coffee. Nasty stuff." But she did drink a pricey blend made from freshly ground beans and filtered water. It was always ready and waiting in the kitchen when she got up. She was spoiled, she realized, although right now she would settle for anything warm that had a caffeine kick. "I'll take whatever you've got."

He poured some of the dark brew into an insulated coffee cup and handed it to her. "I have some powdered creamer if you're interested."

"No, that would just add insult to injury. I'll drink

it black." She blew on it and then took a tentative sip. "I've had worse. What are you cooking?"

"Pancakes."

"Seriously."

"I have some of that powdered baking stuff from a box. You just mix it with water." He used his knife blade to flip the pancake over.

"You can cook," she declared.

"Nothing fancy. I had to buy groceries and fix meals for Eric and me while my mom worked. I learned we could eat better if I made stuff myself rather than buying frozen pizza and such."

"That lasagna you served…"

"Yeah, I made it from scratch."

"Why didn't you just tell me?"

"I was trying to maintain my image as a big, bad kidnapper."

"And big, bad kidnappers don't wear aprons and whip up dinner. But you don't care if I know now?"

"Let's face it, we both know you're not in any danger. In fact, I'm completely ashamed by what I did. As soon as we're done eating, we're going to pack everything up, I'm going to drop you off back where I found you, then I'll turn myself in. What I did was wrong, not to mention stupid, and I'm sorry." He looked up at her. "I'm really sorry, Elena."

She looked away. Her eyes swam with tears. "So you did all this for nothing?"

"It wasn't going to work anyway. Like you said, Daniel Logan doesn't respond to pressure tactics. I brought Eric's case to his attention—that's the best I could hope for."

Somehow, this didn't sit well with her. She didn't like the idea of Travis giving up. She especially didn't like that he would go to jail when he hadn't hurt her, and he'd acted only out of love for his brother and niece.

"Thank you," she said as he handed her a single pancake. He then poured more batter into the frying pan.

"There's no butter, but the syrup is there." He pointed to the platform, where a jug of Aunt Jemima sat.

"Where did all these groceries come from?"

"I grabbed a few cans from that house before we left, and I had a few things in the truck."

Now that the pancake was slightly cooler, she rolled it up and ate it like a burrito. She didn't use the syrup because she didn't want sticky fingers or face, not when there was no way to wash properly. It was pretty tasty. Or maybe she was just really hungry. Half a can of baked beans and a spoonful of chili wasn't much of a dinner.

They sat on the edge of the platform, finished the simple breakfast and drank coffee while the sun came up and the woods came alive all around them. A light fog had formed during the night, giving everything a misty, magical look. Birds chirped and cooed and cawed; she caught sight of a flash of red flying from tree to tree.

"What are those red birds called? The ones with the pointy heads?"

"Cardinals. They're all over the place. I hear them calling."

"I should have figured you would know a lot about birds and stuff."

He shrugged. "Eric was interested in birds at one time. He taught me the names of a few of the common ones."

They didn't talk as they packed up their supplies. Travis shook out the sleeping bag and carefully rolled it up while she folded the tarp. He packed everything else into the backpack. The last thing he did was pour the rest of their water on the campfire.

"Before we go back…" Elena looked at Travis uncertainly. She felt as though she needed to say something, to let him know she was on his side, even if she didn't fully support his methods. But the right words wouldn't come.

"What? Is something wrong?"

"Unfortunately, a lot of things are wrong, and I can't fix them. But I wanted you to know…" She gave up and instead took a couple of steps closer to him, until they were nose to chin. She stood on her toes and brushed her lips against his.

She wasn't sure why she did it; maybe because she knew she'd never have another chance.

At first his only reaction was a sharp intake of air. But when she grabbed hold of his shoulders and gave him a proper kiss, teasing until his lips opened, he responded with obvious enthusiasm.

Still, it was a sweet kiss, a tentative exploration. He never touched her with his hands. When she pulled back, he looked as surprised as she felt. Her face suddenly went flush. Why had she done that? What was she thinking?

"I guess you're not the only one with impulse control issues," she murmured.

Travis shook his head. "You're very complicated, Elena."

With that, they left. Elena felt an inexplicable sense of sadness that they had to go back to the real world. The next few hours were going to be difficult for both of them.

He let Elena ride in the passenger seat this time. "Do you want me to take you back to the Logan place? Or maybe I should go straight to the closest police station."

"Neither. I want to call Daniel. I'm going to tell him it was all a setup, that I went with you willingly."

"What? No, Elena, you can't do that. Then we'll both get in trouble."

"I don't think so. I don't think Daniel will want to file charges against me. He'll be angry, for sure, but I'm too valuable to him as an assistant." She hoped. The job didn't require any particular education, just a knack for organization and anticipating Daniel's needs. She could be replaced. "And if he doesn't file a complaint with the police about me, he can't very well make charges stick against you."

"Why would you even want to do such a thing?"

"Because I know you aren't a bad person. And because kidnapping can result in a long prison term, and you don't deserve that simply because you want to help your brother. What you did was wrong, but I think you know that. You shouldn't suffer the rest of your life for one error in judgment."

"And I won't let you take the heat for something you didn't do. It's preposterous."

"Let me just call Daniel, okay? He's probably pretty upset, but I'll calm him down."

"My phone's in the glove box. Knock yourself out."

She opened the glove compartment. His phone sat on top of a stack of papers—vehicle registration, a maintenance folder and a thick stack of receipts bound with a rubber band. She powered it up. The moment she did, someone would figure out their location. She only had a short time to get this done. She dialed Daniel's private number as soon as she was able.

He answered before it even rang. "Logan," he barked.

"Daniel, it's me. Everything's fine. I'm fine."

"Elena. Thank God. I've got a team triangulating your location right now," he said urgently. "You have to keep this phone on as long as—"

"No, Daniel, no! Please don't do that. Travis is

taking me home right now. He's had a change of heart. He acted impulsively because he loves his brother and his niece. Please, if you haven't involved the police, don't do it. I'm fine, and there's no way Travis would hurt me."

"How do I know he's not pressuring you to say that? How do I know he doesn't have a gun to your head?"

"He doesn't! Travis doesn't even own a gun." She looked at him questioningly. "Do you?"

He shook his head.

"Then give me the correct code word."

"Oh. Of course!" Anyone who worked for Daniel knew the code words, which changed periodically. One was to communicate you were in real trouble. The other was to reassure that you were not in danger. "Macadamia."

Daniel breathed an audible sigh of relief. "Thank God. Where are you? If you're in a safe neighborhood, have Riggs let you out. Anywhere—a restaurant, a fire station—"

"That's not necessary. He's taking me home now. You don't have to worry."

"Let me talk to him."

"I don't think that's a good idea. Daniel, I want you to promise me something. Don't have Travis arrested. If you haven't involved law enforcement, don't. Please."

"Are you crazy? He kidnapped you!"

"It's not like he tried to extort money from you,"

she reasoned. "He just wanted you to help his brother. His heart's in the right place. Really, it is."

"I don't care. You can't just go around kidnapping people because you want someone to do something."

"I know that.... He knows that. I don't care. Promise me you won't have him arrested. Give me your word. If you don't, I can't come back."

"What, are the two of you going to make a break for Mexico?"

"Please be serious. I'm asking you as a personal favor. Sending Travis to jail isn't the right thing to do."

After a long pause, he finally replied. "All right. I give you my word." It sounded as if he said it with his jaw firmly clamped. "For now. But once you're home safe, if you can't convince me that guy shouldn't be underground the rest of his life, all bets are off."

"Thank you, Daniel. I will make it up to you." She hung up and powered down the phone—just in case. She trusted Daniel, but if he'd already sicced a team on them, it might take time to contact the team and turn things off.

"Just like that? All is forgiven?"

"I don't know that I'd go that far. But he said he wouldn't have you arrested on the spot, anyway. I'll have to convince him to make that permanent, but I think I can. He does listen to reason."

"I don't know what to say. No one's ever done

something this huge for me. And I have no idea why you're doing it."

"I'm not a hundred percent sure, either, to tell you the truth. I mean, you did throw me into the back of a pickup truck. Twice."

He winced. "I'm sorry."

"I'll have a great story to tell my children someday." Assuming she ever had children. Her mother was beginning to despair that Elena would ever get married. Of course, Elena's mama had married when she was fourteen. Things were a little different back in Cuba.

True to his word, Travis drove her straight toward Daniel's home. Elena found her tension mounting with every mile they drew closer. In some strange deranged way, she didn't want this episode to end. She would probably never see Travis again.

"I'm going to see what I can do for Eric," she said when they turned down Daniel's street. "The offer still stands—I'll help you with the application."

"You don't have to."

"I want to."

"But the adoption—"

"I know, but adoptions can be delayed. Applications can be expedited. Don't give up hope. Not yet."

For the first time since she'd met Travis, she saw something that resembled hope in his eyes. "Really? You'd really do that?"

"If Eric is innocent, he shouldn't be in prison, and

he shouldn't be separated from his daughter. Anyone can see the injustice in that."

"All right, then." He reached into the console and pulled out a business card for her. "My contact information is on there."

"I'll call you and let you know what I find out."

Five minutes later, Travis pulled up to those preposterous front gates. All appeared quiet. Too quiet.

The gate started to open. Someone was watching. "I'll get out here." She fumbled in her haste to unfasten the seat belt. This wasn't how she wanted to say goodbye to him, rushed and frantic. But she had a bad feeling about this. "Soon as I'm out, hit the gas," she said. "Don't look back."

She got out, slammed the door. She banged on the door with her hand. "Go!"

Before she could even get the single word out, a man leaped from behind a bush and grabbed her, dragging her away from the truck.

"Hey, what the hell—let me go!"

"I'm with the police," the man said. "You're safe now."

"If I'm safe, then why do you have me in a headlock?" But she was more concerned about what was happening to the truck—it was being swarmed by men and women in riot gear. Someone broke the driver's side window, and then Travis was being dragged out of the truck.

"On the ground! On the ground!" the cop shrieked in an adrenaline-fed, frenzied voice.

"No!" Elena shrieked. "What are you doing?"

"We got him!"

It was all over so quickly, Elena barely had time to blink. They had Travis in cuffs and back on his feet. His face was bleeding; he'd probably hit his head and reopened the cut on his forehead.

Travis shot her a venomous look. "Thanks a heap. You couldn't just let me turn myself in?"

"Shut up!" the cop bellowed. Then they were stuffing Travis into a Houston Police SUV and the SWAT guys were giving each other high fives.

"Get your hands off of me!" she yelled at the cop who still had her tightly in his grip. "I'm not under arrest, you moron." Maybe it wasn't smart to throw insults at a cop, but she was furious—beyond furious. This was not supposed to happen. And she knew exactly who to blame. Daniel had had plenty of time to call off the cops. He'd given her his word. How could he have done this?

Daniel himself appeared at the gate, looking harried and badly groomed, as if he'd slept in his clothes. She allowed herself half a second to be flattered that the thought of her being in danger had affected him so badly. Then the fury returned.

"Elena. Dear God, are you all right? Everyone's been so worried about you." He came toward her as if he might hug her. Daniel was not a hugger.

She gave him a cold stare, and he skidded to a stop. "Elena? *Are* you okay?"

"No, I am not okay. Daniel, you promised me no police."

He gave her a puzzled look.

"Never mind. I need a bath and some clean clothes."

"You must be starving. Let me have Cora—"

"No, I'm not hungry, actually. Travis kept me quite well fed." Maybe that was an exaggeration— one pancake and instant coffee was a far cry from the fresh berries, omelets and fancy pastries that were always on Daniel's breakfast table. But she wasn't about to admit that.

"All right. Do you… I mean, before you get cleaned up… I'm not quite sure how to ask this, so I'll just come out with it. Should you visit the hospital first?"

"Hospital? What on earth for?"

"He didn't, um…"

"Oh, *Dios mío,* no! He treated me gentle as a kitten." Was that what they all thought? That while he was trying to get attention for his brother's case, he was raping her?

If she didn't get away from Daniel in the next ten seconds, she was going to say something she regretted. "May I go, now? Sir?"

He looked even more puzzled by her behavior. "Yes, of course."

She stalked past him, down the long driveway, tripping several times on the awkward, heel-less shoes. But she couldn't take even the short time it would require to remove the shoes. She was about to lose it.

As soon as she was inside, a host of people greeted her—mostly household staff, a few Project Justice people. Jillian Baxter-Blake, who had been Daniel's assistant before Elena, ran up and hugged her.

"Oh, my God, we were so worried!"

"I'm fine. I'm fine," she said on a sob. "Just… I need some time alone." She ran out of the foyer and down the hall to the staircase. Someone called after her, but she ignored them.

DANIEL HAD CHOSEN to meet with her in the dining room. Hardly anyone ate in the formal dining room unless it was an important occasion, so at least Daniel attached some importance to their meeting.

She'd bathed, washed and dried her hair, put on makeup and dressed carefully in a long, gauzy skirt, a silk T-shirt and ballet flats—something that screamed she was not on the clock, because she wasn't.

Despite the fact that she'd said she wasn't hungry, a tray of tasty-looking snacks awaited her on the table. Her mouth watered just looking at the gourmet cheeses, fruits and pastries arranged artfully on the silver tray. She was tempted to ignore the food, but realized she was being petty, so she ate a few apple slices and three cubes of cheddar cheese. She felt better almost immediately—calmer, more centered.

"The police want to speak to you," Daniel said.

"I told them you needed some time, but I can't put them off too long."

"Oh, screw the police," she muttered.

"Elena!"

"Even if they were simply doing their duty, they did it with a bit too much zeal if you ask me. The cop who pulled me away from the car was far more violent toward me than Travis ever thought about being."

"Elena, I'm confused. Were you kidnapped or not?"

"Yes. But he only did it because—"

"His reasons are immaterial! He kidnapped you! It's not like he parked illegally or…or used his office photocopier for personal tasks."

"I know it looks bad—"

"He's a felon, did you know that? Spent eighteen months in the county jail for assault."

"Yes, I know. He told me. But I would bet he hasn't so much as stolen a paper clip since he got out."

"And you believe him."

"Yes, I do. We spent many hours together with nothing to do but talk, and he told me a lot of things. Mostly he talked about Eric. He loves his brother, and he has good reasons for believing Eric is innocent."

"That is a separate issue. Lots of people have loved ones in prison who are innocent, and they don't go around kidnapping people to resolve the issue."

"Yes, yes, I know. They go through proper channels. But Travis has a learning disability. Severe dyslexia or something like that—"

"And you believed that, too?"

Obviously Daniel thought she was the worst sort of gullible sap. She persevered with her argument. "That's why he struggled with the application. But that's not really the issue here, is it? The issue is you made a promise to me. You gave me your word you wouldn't have Travis arrested."

"It's not like I can order the police around—"

"I'm not stupid. You had to have told them where they could find Travis *after* I called you. *After* I told you he was bringing me back. Or do SWAT teams just hang out in your bushes on the off chance—"

"All right, yes, I told them about your phone call. But, Elena, I had to appear to agree with your terms because Travis might have been listening. If I'd refused you, he might not have brought you home. Surely you can see my reasoning."

"So you weren't really agreeing with me. You just pretended to agree as a means to an end."

"To save your life? That's not an acceptable reason?"

"My life was not in danger. You knew that! I gave you the safe code word, didn't I?"

"Well…I was worried."

"Do you think I would give you the safe code word if I was in danger?"

"Maybe you didn't realize the danger you were in."

She sighed. "So you don't trust my judgment."

"I always have before. But this incident was unprecedented."

"Face it, Daniel. You sicced the SWAT team on Travis because you felt personally violated by what he did. And you got your revenge. You also broke your promise to me."

He had no comeback. She'd nailed it.

"I will talk to the police," she continued. "But I won't press charges against Travis."

"So you actually want to see him walk? What kind of hold does he have on you?"

"Nothing. Except I judge him to be a good man who is trying to save his brother, and to keep his niece from being adopted by unscrupulous people. Sending Travis to jail would only compound the wrong that has been done to his brother. If you can't trust my judgment on this matter…" She wasn't even sure how to finish that sentence. Their professional relationship had been based on absolute trust. Could it ever be the same?

Daniel's mouth firmed as he looked out the window. He absently spread a cracker with brie cheese and a dab of pomegranate jelly, a treat he loved. "I guess we're done here."

"Are you firing me?"

Daniel looked slightly alarmed by her question. "No, of course not. But I think we both need to take a step back and…reflect."

She'd been ready to resign. It was a matter of principle. But Daniel was probably right about taking a step back. She needed some time to process all that had happened.

Something inside her had changed. She wasn't sure what, or why, but she felt that going back to work for Daniel as if nothing had happened would be impossible.

"I could use some time off," she said.

"Elena, of course. Take as long as you need."

"I think I'll go stay with my parents for a while." She needed to remove herself from the estate and everything associated with it, to get her head straight and her feet back on the ground. Her day spent with Travis had reminded her that there was a big world out there, filled with people who didn't have unlimited resources to deal with their problems.

She would be welcomed by her parents. Her mother had preserved her bedroom as a shrine to Elena's youth, on the off chance she would return home. Her parents were good people, well-meaning, but they smothered her with their overprotectiveness. She wouldn't stay there long, she reasoned. Just until she figured some things out.

"I'll have a car brought around to take you—"

"No, don't do that. I'm going to call a friend."

"If that's what you want."

She stood up. "Where do I need to go to talk to the police?"

"Central Division."

"Daniel, I know you have the power to have the

charges dropped against Travis. You're married to the district attorney. Couldn't you…just…"

"No, I couldn't. You know I don't try to influence Jamie's office for personal reasons."

Oh, please. That was a total lie. Everyone knew he had the D.A.'s ear. If he told her a case needed to be reopened, she listened to him. But, to be fair, he usually only did that when he was reasonably sure the alleged perpetrator was not guilty.

It had been worth a shot. She turned and headed for the door.

"Elena, for what it's worth, I don't blame you at all. You were the victim, and whatever happened while he had you tied up in some empty house—"

She turned. "He never tied me up! He cooked me lasagna! And pancakes!"

Daniel looked at her as if she were deranged. Oh, God, maybe she was.

"I have to go." She needed to get this interview with the police over with. And then she needed to find Travis a lawyer—a good lawyer, not some public defender just out of law school. On her way upstairs to grab her purse, she scrolled through the contacts on her phone. It was Saturday. Who might be free? Finally she settled on someone and dialed.

"Celeste, are you by any chance available to pick me up at Daniel's and take me downtown? The police want to interview me about my supposed ordeal."

"I'd be happy to. The Vette needs to get out of

the garage. But why doesn't Daniel give you a limo or something?"

"It's a long story. I'll explain it to you while we head downtown."

CHAPTER EIGHT

TRAVIS HAD NEVER been in an interrogation room before. When he'd been arrested after that fateful bar fight years ago, there'd been no question who had been responsible for the guy lying unconscious on the floor. More than a dozen people had witnessed the fight. At least half were ready to tell the truth of what had happened—that the other guy had thrown the first punch and Travis had merely defended himself. Unfortunately, the other half—buddies of the unconscious man—had been eager to tell the police the exact opposite, that Travis had attacked the guy for no reason.

Travis hadn't seen any point in trying to argue his way out of it. He'd taken a lousy plea bargain. Given the seriousness of the other guy's injuries, Travis had received two years and was released after eighteen months for good behavior. The sentence had been unusually harsh, but Travis hadn't done much to help himself. He'd been pretty torn up back then, still freshly postdivorce and not too far removed from his stint in the army, which hadn't left him in a positive frame of mind.

Eric had been furious with him for not calling him, for not asking him to find a good criminal defense attorney who could have gotten him off, or at least gotten him a lighter sentence.

Now, he didn't have Eric to call, and, like before, he didn't feel much like arguing. He'd done the deed, after all; no one could dispute that he'd kidnapped an innocent woman.

The only thing that stopped him from just pleading guilty and getting it over with was the knowledge that while he was behind bars, he would be of no help to Eric or MacKenzie.

Eric had told him the best thing to do if he was ever arrested for anything was to not say a word, just ask for a lawyer. So this time around, he was going to try to do the smart thing.

The two detectives who entered the cold, dismal, claustrophobic room looked ready for a fight. The older one smirked, as if he knew a secret that Travis didn't. The second one just looked deadly serious, like if it were up to him he'd just get a gun and shoot Travis now.

"So," the younger one began. "Why did you kidnap Elena Marquez?"

Travis took a deep breath. "I'm not saying anything without a lawyer present."

The two cops looked at each other. They couldn't hide their disappointment.

"Okay," said the older one. "Do you wish to hire your own counsel? Or would you like a public defender?"

A private criminal defense attorney would blow through what little savings Travis had in no time. Then again, he wouldn't have any use for the money if he was locked away in Huntsville for twenty years.

He thought about the court-appointed guy who'd handled his assault case. He'd looked like Howdy Doody with acne. He could have passed for a high schooler.

"I'll hire my own."

The younger detective looked up at the video camera in the corner and made a slashing motion across his throat. Then he looked at Travis with a superior half smile. "You think you're pretty smart, I guess. You know better than to answer questions without an attorney, at any rate."

"Pretty much anyone who watches TV knows that."

"You didn't know it back when you got nailed for knocking that guy out cold in a bar, did you? Back then, you spilled your guts."

Of course they would know about his criminal background. He knew what they were doing. They'd turned off the video, and now they were illegally continuing to question him without his attorney when he'd plainly asked for one. Anything he said now could still be used against him. They would just claim he'd said it in the paddy wagon on the way over.

Travis shrugged.

The young cop got in his face. "Tough guy. What

are you, about six-one, six-two? Maybe two hundred twenty pounds?"

Travis said nothing.

"That would make you about twice as big as Elena Marquez. Guess you moved on to easier victims than… Who was that guy you beat up?"

"You read the report. I'm sure you know his name."

Suddenly the cop came around the table, leaned down and put his face right in Travis's. "I hate guys like you—guys who victimize people who are smaller and weaker. Tell me, Riggs, did she struggle? Did she scream? Did it turn you on? She's hot, for sure. I hear Cuban women like it rough."

It was all Travis could manage not to smash the guy's face in. He gritted his teeth. He said nothing.

"Hey, Eddie," the older cop said, "knock it off. He asked for a lawyer."

The younger cop, who was apparently Eddie, stood up and straightened his tie. He glanced at the older man and murmured a foul word that indicated he didn't have much respect for his colleague. Travis was just glad when they both left. A few moments later, a uniformed cop led him to a holding cell.

They'd appropriated his truck and taken his cell phone when he'd been arrested, but now they gave the phone back. "You got one phone call," the cop said in a bored voice. "Make it a good one."

Hell, who was he going to call? Who knew a good criminal defense attorney?

He scrolled through his contacts. The letters and names swam together so he could hardly tell them apart; his reading problem got worse when he was tired or under stress, both of which were the case right now.

Then one name on the list jumped out: Paulie. Paulie was a guy Travis often called to do roofing; he had a brother who was in constant scrapes with the law.

In a matter of about thirty seconds, Paulie agreed to find him a good lawyer. He didn't even ask what Travis was in for and didn't sound all that surprised, either. "You got money to pay?" Paulie asked.

"Some. Not a lot. But it's a high-profile case," he added. "I'm accused of kidnapping a billionaire's personal assistant."

"That's messed up, man." Paulie sounded slightly awestruck.

The guard took Travis's phone back. He wondered if he'd ever see it again.

CELESTE DROVE AS if she was trying to qualify for the Indy 500. Her car was a late-model red Corvette with the most souped-up engine available. She burned rubber taking off from every stoplight, took every corner on two wheels and treated speed-limit signs as suggestions rather than the law.

But she wasn't sloppy. Elena released the death grip she had on the door handle after reminding herself that Celeste was actually pretty skillful behind the wheel—and why wouldn't she be? She'd driven a patrol car for God only knew how many years, and then Daniel had sent her to a special school to learn evasive driving techniques. He liked for all of his key people to be prepared for anything. He'd even talked about sending Elena to that driving school.

"So what's the scoop?" Celeste asked. "Why did Daniel take your car away?"

"That's not it. I'm taking a leave of absence."

"Really." She sounded shocked, and it was no wonder. Very few people ever left Daniel's employ, even temporarily. For one thing, he selected his employees carefully and rejected anyone with a sketchy work history. But mainly, working for Daniel Logan was everybody's dream job. He hired the best, and he paid them extremely well. The benefits were top-notch. So, yeah, Elena walking away, even temporarily, would surprise anyone who knew her.

It wasn't as if she could walk out and expect to find an equivalent job, especially since she was a no-body without any prestigious experience. She'd been running the Logan Oil day care center when Daniel had waved his magic wand over her and transformed her life.

"Celeste, Daniel lied to me. He betrayed my trust."

"That doesn't sound like Daniel."

Elena knew Celeste was fiercely loyal to Daniel. After a lifetime of being overlooked as a female cop, turned down for promotion to detective again and again, she'd been on the verge of retirement and resigned to life as a senior, tending her garden and wondering what could have been, when Daniel had given her a chance at a second career. He'd seen her worth—she was tough and scary and smart, if a tad unconventional. She was Project Justice's first line of defense.

"Look, I don't want to talk Daniel down. Whatever he did, he thought it was the right thing. But he should have trusted me—" Her voice broke, and she clamped her mouth shut.

"Men can be clueless sometimes, even Daniel. You're not nursing some kind of crush on him, are you? 'Cause I can guarantee you he's utterly devoted to—"

"Oh, God no. That's not it at all." She wouldn't admit that her crush was on her kidnapper. "Celeste, how much trouble can I get in for lying to the police?"

"Depends. Did you commit a crime?"

"No. But I don't want Travis Riggs to go to prison."

"Well…you don't have to lie. You can simply refuse to talk about certain things, and you can make it clear you will not appear in court to testify against Travis. Without your testimony, I doubt they'll bother to even formally charge him."

"Really?" Could it be that simple?

"Yeah. They have enough people to prosecute without taking on an iffy case like that."

"Even if Daniel wants him behind bars?"

"Daniel has a lot of influence, true, but it wouldn't

do much for his image if he ended up on record trying to put someone *in* prison instead of the other way around."

"I never even thought of that. Celeste, you are so smart. Thank you."

"My pleasure. But I hope you'll repair your tiff with Daniel. He needs you. Frankly, no one thought Jillian could be replaced, but you've stepped up to the plate."

"Thanks. Things just feel a little strange right now."

Celeste was willing to go in with her to talk to the cops, but Elena politely declined the offer as she climbed out of the low-slung car. "It might look odd, me showing up with someone from Project Justice when I haven't committed a crime."

"How will you get home?"

She leaned into the open passenger window. "I'll call my dad."

"Okay, but I'm around if you need me. Since I'm near downtown, I think I'll do a little shopping. There's a fantastic African market here where I can pick up amazingly fresh, exotic squashes, right off the boat." She hit the gas, tires screeching right in front of a stopped patrol car, but the cops ignored her.

Elena's stomach swooped as she entered Houston Police headquarters on Reisner Street, in the shadow of the downtown skyline. As a child, she'd had it instilled in her that cops were bad. They could arrest you on a whim, and you could be convicted without a fair trial and spend the rest of your life on a chain gang—for nothing. They had no Project Justice in Cuba. Cops in America were different—in general, better—but some of them were still entranced with their own macho images. Power could go to anyone's head. Where the police were concerned, you had to be careful.

They were waiting for her. She didn't have to introduce herself or explain anything; a young, female uniformed officer met her almost before she cleared the doorway.

"Ms. Marquez, thank you for coming in. First, I want to say that everyone here admires your bravery—"

"What bravery?" she asked in all honesty. It wasn't as if she'd chosen to be kidnapped. But she didn't say anything else; she wasn't going to admit that she ever *was* kidnapped.

The cop looked at her quizzically. "Um, come right this way. The detectives are waiting for you."

She was taken to what was undeniably an interrogation room. Right now, they were treating her as a guest. One cop offered her coffee, and another asked if she wanted a snack from the vending machine or maybe a sandwich from the deli down the street.

"No, thanks. I'd just like to get on with this."

"Of course, Ms. Marquez," a guy in a suit said. He must have been the detective. "We understand. You've been through a terrible ordeal—"

"No, I haven't." All conversation stopped. Everyone froze and stared at her. "It wasn't that bad, okay?"

They gave her a chair. They brought her water. And then they started in with the questions.

Recalling Celeste's advice, to every question she answered with some version of "I'd really rather not talk about it."

"Ms. Marquez," the young detective said. His eyes were filled with phony sympathy. "I know this must have been traumatic for you, but we need information in order to put your attacker—"

"Attacker? Where did you get that? I was never attacked."

"Then why don't you tell us what did happen?"

Ah, they'd tricked her. "Look, it wasn't traumatic, okay? I know you think something horrible happened to me, but it didn't. Regardless of appearances, I do not feel as if a crime was committed against me."

"So, you weren't kidnapped?"

"I…don't want to talk about that."

"That's not going to sound very convincing to a jury."

"I don't plan to speak to any juries."

"But don't you want your att—I mean, Mr. Riggs—don't you want him locked up where he can't commit any more crimes?"

"No."

The young detective remained quiet, thinking for

a few moments. He conferred softly with an older detective and then came back at her with more questions. "Ms. Marquez, did you cooperate with Mr. Riggs to…to make it look as if you'd been kidnapped in order to—"

"You mean did Travis and I cook up a fake kidnapping scheme? No. Absolutely not. I never met him before yesterday."

"So when you called Daniel Logan and told him you were being held hostage—"

"I never said that. Not in those words."

"But you did call Daniel Logan."

"Yes."

"According to him, you reported you were being held against your will."

"I don't recall precisely what I said to him, but if that's what he told you, then I'm sure that's what he understood to be true."

"But it wasn't true? You weren't being held hostage?"

"I don't want to talk about that. And if you continue in this confrontational manner, I'll be forced to end this interview and retain an attorney." She knew that was the thing cops hated more than anything— getting attorneys involved in any sort of questioning, even that of a witness.

"So you're saying that you won't testify to the fact that you were kidnapped?"

"No, I won't."

"Listen, if Riggs is exerting any kind of pressure

on you—if he threatened you or your family or even your dog, you need to let us know. We can offer protection."

"He didn't pressure me. He didn't threaten me. We never even talked about what I might or might not tell the police."

They took another couple of stabs at her—speaking in soft, conciliatory tones so Elena wouldn't consider them confrontational—but once they realized they were getting nowhere with her, they let her go.

The young detective—Eddie Peck, his name was—couldn't resist one parting shot. "If I find out you and Riggs cooperated to pull some kind of fraud on your boss, I will nail you to the wall."

"You won't find evidence of that because it didn't happen." She turned and walked out, never looking back, though she could feel a dozen cops' eyes drilling into the back of her head. She didn't take a full breath until she was outside in the sunshine. She walked half a block from the police station and then dialed her parents' number.

WHEN TRAVIS'S DEFENSE lawyer finally appeared, she wasn't what he expected. For one thing, he'd been picturing a male, which was sexist of him, he knew. But what he got was a polished young woman, probably close to his own age, with honey-colored hair pulled back in a bun and stylish glasses. She had a curvy figure, a healthy, farm-girl complexion and a sweet smile.

"Well, good afternoon, Mr. Riggs," she said. "I'm Megan Ramsey."

"Is it? A good afternoon, I mean."

"Actually, it is. No formal charges will be filed against you. You'll be free to go shortly."

"Wow. You work fast." She had to be kidding.

"Fortunately, I didn't have to do anything. Just thought I'd introduce myself and give you the good news."

"You're telling the truth?"

"Yes, of course. I wouldn't lie about something like that. There's a serious lack of evidence. Apparently your alleged victim refuses to say one word against you."

"Really."

"Yeah. There's a little bit of paperwork to fill out, and then they'll spring you."

"What did she say? Elena, I mean."

"I don't know the particulars. Just that she didn't give them enough to make the charges stick."

"What about Logan? He couldn't push some magic buttons?" Travis got a chill when he recalled how angry Daniel Logan had been with him. The emotion had been a tangible thing, wafting over the cellular network.

"We live in a democracy, Mr. Riggs. Absent of rampant corruption. One man can't buy another man's fate in the justice system."

"Still young enough to be idealistic," he said with a smile.

"Not idealistic. Just optimistic. I have faith in people."

Almost immediately, a guard appeared with keys. He looked disapproving but didn't say a word as he unlocked the door of the holding cell. The door swung open and Travis stepped out, though he was almost afraid everyone would burst out laughing and push him back inside, yelling "April Fools'."

Megan escorted him out. "Thanks. If anything, you know, happens—if they gather more evidence or something and toss me back in here, can I call you?"

"Of course." She handed him a business card.

"What do I owe you for today?"

"I'll send a bill. But don't worry, I'll give you my first-timer discount."

He really didn't know what to think. This just seemed too good to be true. One thing was for sure; he would be eternally grateful he'd decided not to mouth off to that smug bastard detective.

"Where do I pick up my truck?" he asked as the guy in the property room returned his belt, his wallet and his phone to him.

"There's a claim ticket in the envelope," the bored cop said. "Go to the impound lot."

"And where is that?"

The guy rattled off an address that was at least two miles away. *Great.* He had no cash in his wallet. He'd have to hoof it, he supposed.

He said goodbye to Megan, then kept his head down as he left the station. The weather had cooled off while he'd been incarcerated; a blue norther had blown through during the past few hours, and the temperature had dropped twenty degrees. He'd been perfectly comfortable in a T-shirt earlier, but now he was freezing. Ah, well, it hardly ever got really cold in Houston. He'd survive.

He stood in front of the police station, looking down the street one way, then the other, trying to orient himself. Suddenly his heart stopped. Was he seeing things? No, that was definitely Elena, sitting on the hood of a parked car, her arms folded against the brisk wind. Waiting for someone or something, it looked like.

A compulsion to move toward her overtook him. He wanted to thank her. He wanted to ask her what the heck she was doing, because if she hadn't given the cops the evidence they needed to make a case against him, then she'd lied. Granted, he and Elena had come to an understanding over the twenty-four hours they were together, but was it enough of an understanding to cause her to lie?

He actually took a couple of steps toward her, and then he stopped himself. If he was truly grateful, he needed to just stay the hell away from her.

Besides, someone might be watching him. Maybe this was a trap. What if Elena was wearing a wire, and they just needed him to admit to something....

No. Elena wouldn't do that to him. If she wanted

him to go down for kidnapping her, all she needed was to tell the truth.

Resolutely, he turned away from her. But then he turned back. He couldn't resist. Just one more look. She was so pretty, sitting there in that billowy skirt blowing in the wind, her hair whipping around her face. He wanted to remember her. Aside from MacKenzie, she was the one pure thing he'd come into contact with in a long time.

Just as he started to look away, she swiveled her head and saw him. She froze. He froze. She stood up. Then she waved. Just a slight wiggle of her fingers, really, as if she was unsure how he'd take it.

He waved back and smiled.

She took one step toward him, then another.

Christ, he didn't think they should be seen talking to each right in front of police headquarters. He headed toward her, walking briskly until they met on the sidewalk.

CHAPTER NINE

"ELENA." HER NAME came out a hoarse whisper.

"Did you post bail, or…"

"They let me go. Lack of evidence. Thanks to you, I imagine."

"Really? I didn't think—"

"You shouldn't have lied. But I'm grateful. Really, really grateful. I don't deserve—"

"I didn't lie. Everything I said was true. I just didn't tell them the parts they wanted to hear." She flashed an impish smile. "That's what Celeste told me to do."

"Celeste? The dragon lady?"

"Don't call her that. She's an amazing woman, much smarter than most people give her credit for."

"If you say so. Um, I just wanted to say thank you. And now I'm going to get the hell out of your life and stay there. I'm really glad I chose you to kidnap, Elena."

"Oddly enough, I'm glad you did, too."

A shiny silver SUV pulled up to the curb. Elena looked over almost guiltily. "Oh, that's my ride. Where are you headed?" She looked around. "Where's your truck?"

"Impound lot. I'm on my way to get it."

"We'll give you a ride."

"That's okay."

"Don't be ridiculous. It's freezing, and you don't have a jacket."

"I'll be fine."

Whoever was in that truck tapped on the horn. Not a loud blast, just a polite I'm-here-in-case-you-didn't-notice beep. She looked over anxiously.

"I insist."

He knew he shouldn't. He needed to stay out of her life. But somehow, the words wouldn't come out of his mouth. She dragged him to the truck and opened the passenger door. "Don't say anything about... He doesn't know," she whispered.

"Elena!" An older man behind the wheel greeted Elena with a big smile.

"Papa. Thank you so much for picking me up."

"Of course, *pequeña*. Anytime. But how come your rich boss doesn't send a car?"

"Um, long story. Papa, this is my friend Travis. He needs a ride, too. Where are you going, Travis?"

"Market and Texas Street."

"Oh, that is not far," the older man behind the wheel said. His accent was thick. "Climb in."

"Thank you, sir."

Elena started to get in back, but Travis shook his head. He felt more comfortable letting her sit next to her father and carry the conversation. After hesitating a moment, Elena nodded and got in the front.

Elena's father reached between the seats and offered his hand. "Elmer Marquez." His hand was surprisingly smooth for a field-worker's. Isn't that what Elena had said he did for a living? Something about cane fields, but that was back in Cuba. Maybe he did something different here.

"Travis Riggs."

"How do you know my daughter?" he asked lightly, though Travis sensed a certain edge under the seemingly friendly question.

"I, um, met her when I went to Daniel Logan's house for a meeting." That was the truth, as far as it went.

"He had an interesting story to tell," Elena said. "He's trying to help his brother to regain custody of his little girl."

"Does Mr. Logan get involved in that type of thing?" Elmer asked, sounding genuinely interested.

"As it turns out, not this time," Elena said drily. "But anyway, that's how I met Travis."

"What about you, *pequeña*? You need me to take you back to River Oaks?"

She hesitated. "No, actually.... I thought maybe I could go home. To the house. Your house, I mean." She seemed flustered.

"Of course! Your mama will be happy. She's making a big pot of *congri*. Now I won't have to eat the whole thing by myself. How about you, Travis?"

Elmer asked. "Hungry? You haven't tasted heaven 'til you've had my wife's *congri*."

Travis was about to say he wasn't hungry, but just then his stomach growled.

Elmer laughed. "Well, I guess that settles it."

"Yes, Travis, you must come to our home and have dinner. I bet you're starving. I had a tasty but very small breakfast this morning and no lunch."

"Ah, I'd like to, but—"

"Houston is playing Tulane," Elmer said in a voice intended to tempt.

Travis sensed Elmer was desperate for some male companionship to watch football with. Maybe when Elena and her mother got together, they ganged up on him. "Yeah, okay. For a little while, anyway."

"Whenever you want, I can run you where you need to go. Or Elena can." He winked at Elena, and she grinned.

Travis was surprised when Elmer drove them to a fancy neighborhood on the fringes of Memorial Park, near downtown. Their house was a huge colonial, bigger even than the one Travis was renovating. The front yard was professionally landscaped and maintained. Elmer stopped in the circular driveway, and they all climbed a short flight of steps to the columned front porch. A pinecone wreath the size of a Mack truck tire adorned the oak front door.

Helluva home for a Cuban immigrant farmworker.

Elena's brow furrowed slightly as she glanced over at Travis. He probably hadn't hidden his surprise very well. But, really, the Marquez family wealth and how they acquired it was none of his business.

Still…he'd been sure Elena came from humble roots, like him. Had she made up all that stuff about playing in the street in Cuba? Almost drowning in a leaky dinghy? Patching up relatives who worked in sugarcane fields?

He wouldn't blame her. She'd probably thought she would never see him again after they parted ways. Sharing a meal with her family the day after he'd kidnapped her was an eventuality neither of them could have envisioned. He still wasn't sure how it had happened. Any second now, he expected to hear the *Twilight Zone* music.

As they entered the house, Travis became acutely aware of his clothes, and the fact that he hadn't had a shower today. Elena had obviously bathed and put on fresh clothes. He, on the other hand, was about as fresh as day-old dog food. What he wouldn't give for a hot shower and a razor. He must be giving Elena's father the worst sort of first impression.

He forgot about bathing and clothes as the most heavenly scent greeted them. Someone was cooking—someone who really knew how to cook. The blend of spices and grilling meat made his mouth water.

"Rosalie, we have company!" Elmer announced happily as he led the way into a great room that featured plump leather furniture and a big-screen TV.

A half wall separated the great room from a bright, roomy kitchen decorated in primary colors, where a petite, chubby woman waved a greeting. Her thick black hair was pulled back in a bun, and she wore a flowered dress covered with an apron.

Her face blossomed into a smile when she spotted Elena. "*Pequeña,* what a surprise!" The two women met in a doorway between the two rooms and embraced warmly. "You never come to see us anymore."

"Mama, I was here last weekend," Elena chided.

"And you brought a friend? You could have warned me!" She patted her hair self-consciously. "I could have at least put on a nicer dress."

"You look fine, *Señora* Marquez." Travis walked toward her, his hand extended. When she girlishly placed her hand in his, he leaned over and kissed it. "My name's Travis."

"Please, call me Rosalie," she said.

"Rosalie, the stove?" her husband reminded her gently. "Dinner?"

"Oh, right. *Señor* Travis, you are staying for dinner, *sí?*"

"Your husband was kind enough to invite me." He wished he could have brought something to contribute to the meal—a pie, or cornbread at least.

"Of course he's staying for dinner," Elena said. "Travis, I know you're hungry. We eat early on weekends, so it's not that much time out of your day."

"Then it's settled," Rosalie said before Travis

could even nod. "We'll eat in about half an hour." She bustled back to the stove, where a tall, stainless steel stockpot simmered, apparently the source of the delectable odor.

Elmer had already edged into his leather recliner and grabbed the remote. "Elena, why don't you get me and your friend a couple of cervezas, eh?"

"Of course, Papa."

Travis parked himself at the end of a sofa. This was more than awkward. Why had he said yes? What force had taken over his brain? But he'd been helpless to deny Elena. If he could just make himself relax, it might be nice to watch football, drink beer and pretend the past twenty-four hours had never happened.

He couldn't…could he?

Travis stood, on the verge of making some excuse and leaving. He could pretend to receive an urgent call. But then his stomach grumbled again, and he inhaled that heavenly scent. His knees bent, and he found himself sitting.

The Marquez household moved all around him. Elmer switched channels until he found the game he wanted; Elena disappeared and reappeared with two cold bottles of beer in hand.

"Travis? You can sit closer to the TV if you want." She indicated a second chair, closer to her father's.

"Actually, I need to clean up."

"Oh, of course!" She found a couple of coasters and set the beers down on a large square coffee table. "It's right this way."

She took him down the hall to a guest bathroom that smelled like potpourri. The pastel hand towels looked too pretty to use. The vanity was an expensive, custom marble number, not something you picked up at Home Depot. He'd installed a few of these, and he knew how much they cost. The light fixture was expensive, too.

A memory flashed through his mind of the first time he'd visited his ex-wife's family home. His jaw had repeatedly hit the floor as he'd ogled all the signs of wealth. He'd known she hadn't grown up poor, like him, but that was the first time he'd realized how vastly different their backgrounds were.

She'd seemed to enjoy his reaction. He should have realized then what her expectations were, what she was used to. He should have run far and fast. But he'd been too bedazzled.

He liked to think he was smarter now. He had no idea why Elena was being so civil to him, but did that really matter? He could see he'd taken a huge misstep coming here. Now he simply had to gracefully extricate himself, and that was that.

She turned and headed back toward the living room, but he stopped her. "Elena." He might not get another chance to speak privately with her. "Why are you doing this?"

"Doing what?" she asked innocently.

"Being so nice to me. Introducing me to your parents, for God's sake. You know as well as I do if they heard how we really met, your father would kill me."

"You needed a ride. You're hungry. And you need a safe place to regroup for a couple of hours, at least."

"All of which is not your problem."

"I'm making it my problem, okay?"

He really, really didn't understand this. But he let it go, because he sensed he wasn't going to get an answer that was any clearer. Not right now.

"What did you tell the police?"

"I didn't lie. But I told them I didn't want to talk about what happened and that I wouldn't support any attempt to try you for any crimes. That's all."

She turned and left.

That's all?

He turned on the hot water and removed his shirt. He really wanted to hop in that blue-tiled shower, but that would be taking advantage of the Marquez's hospitality. He did wash pretty thoroughly in the sink, however. They'd given him a toothbrush and toothpaste at the jail.

Clean clothes would have been nice, but he had to settle for his stale shirt. He would stay long enough to be polite. He would eat some of Rosalie's dinner, because to refuse would insult her. Then, for sure, he was getting out of Elena's life—for good this time.

"ELENA, I NEED help in the kitchen."

Elena would rather have stayed in the living room with the men, watching football. Not because she didn't like helping in the kitchen—she did—but because she knew her mother was going to grill her about Travis. Still, she couldn't say no.

"Coming, Mama."

"Elena!" her mother scolded in a strident whisper once the two women were alone in the kitchen. "You didn't tell me you were seeing anyone. Here, chop that onion."

Elena dutifully began work on the large white onion, chopping the top and bottom off and peeling it. "I'm not 'seeing' him, not like you think. I barely know him."

"Then why do you look at him with hunger in your eyes? And that is no ordinary hunger, no."

Did she look at Travis in some particular way? It was scary to think she was so transparent. "He's a very good-looking man," Elena conceded. "It's kind of hard *not* to look at him."

"I can't argue with you there. Is he married? I didn't see a ring."

"No, he's not married. Actually, he's divorced." Elena thought that would cool her mother's interest in Travis.

"Ah, well. When a girl gets to be your age, it's hard to find an available man who hasn't been married before. She was probably a bad wife."

"Whatever. Don't start planning the wedding yet. He has no interest in me…that way."

"You obviously don't see what I see. There is interest."

"Mama!" Elena laughed. "You see what you want to see. And you act like I'm too old to find a husband and I should just settle. I keep telling you, girls don't often get married so young in this country." Sometimes her mother acted as if she'd just set foot in the United States.

"Well, it wouldn't hurt you to at least think about it. This Travis, he is a good man, I think."

Maybe she should tell her mother that Travis had served time in prison. *That* would sour her opinion of him. But she couldn't bring herself to trash Travis's image. A lot of people no doubt looked down on Travis because of his stint in prison, never mind that he'd served his debt to society, that he was a different man now. He didn't need her adding to his grief.

The onion was chopped, and Rosalie took it and added it to the pot. She always added some at the last minute, so the *congri*—basically, black beans and rice—had a little bite.

"You make the plantains. You probably never have any reason to cook since all your meals are fixed for you at that mansion, but Travis needs to know you *can* cook. When he tastes the fried plantains, he will be yours forever."

Elena laughed at the thought of a man falling in

love with her because of fried plantains. "Anyone can fix this dish. It's simple."

"Men don't have to know that. How do you think I got your father to marry me?"

"Plantains?"

"No, it was my *caldosa*. But we don't have time for that today." *Caldosa* was a thick soup made with various tubers and meats, and with Rosalie it was an all-day affair.

Elena began peeling the bananalike fruits. "Actually, Travis can cook. He made me lasagna."

"Aha!" Rosalie pointed her wooden spoon at Elena. "You *have* been dating him."

"No, I haven't. Anyway, I thought you wanted me to marry a Cuban man."

"When you were prime marriageable age, sure, I wanted a Cuban son-in-law. You could have had your pick of a dozen suitors, but you were determined to go to college and have a career. Now the good ones are married to other women. Anyway, I don't really care as long as you marry a man who's good to you. You know that."

"Mama, really, stop playing matchmaker. This isn't going to work. Travis is just an acquaintance."

Rosalie didn't argue, just gave her a knowing look. "I'm going to set the table in the dining room. As soon as you're done with those plantains, we can serve."

A few minutes later, Elena and her mother carried dishes to the table and called in the men. They were deep into a conversation about how to fix a slab foundation that had started to settle and cause cracks. Elena's father could easily have hired someone to do work on the house, but he liked to do things himself.

"Rosalie," Elena's father said, "Travis owns his own construction company. Did you know that?"

"Of course I did," Rosalie said smugly. "Elena told me all about it. She was very impressed with the work you do."

Elena gave her mother a warning look, but Rosalie pretended not to see it. Travis was going to think her mother was crazy. Or that Elena herself was.

"He said he could show me how to repair the foundation without calling one of those rip-off slab repair companies."

"Oh, that would be wonderful! Elmer is getting tired of fixing the cracks in the walls."

Oh, boy. She'd thought asking Travis to dinner was the right thing to do, the nice, decent thing. But now they were getting in deep. What would happen if her parents found out Travis had kidnapped her? Sure, Elmer was all smiles now, but if he thought Elena had been wronged or compromised or... Well, he could be pretty fierce.

"This looks wonderful, Rosalie," Travis said. "Do you cook like this every day?"

"Oh, most days even more. Most weekends we grill meat—chicken, beef, pork, lamb, *cabrito*. But with the weather turning nasty, we decided not to today. This is mostly leftovers."

"They look a lot better than my leftovers do." Travis eyed the grilled pork. He was practically flirting with her mother, though Elena didn't think it was calculated. He really was just being nice.

They all sat down, Elmer said the blessing and then Rosalie began piling food on Travis's plate as if he was the only one who was hungry. Elena was pretty darn hungry herself. All she'd had to eat all day was that pancake and a few nibbles at Daniel's.

She smiled at the memory of Travis somehow coming up with an appetizing breakfast under such primitive conditions. He'd done it to please her.

After everyone had been served, Travis took a bite of black beans and rice and then closed his eyes in apparent ecstasy. "Oh, Rosalie. These are the best rice and beans I've ever tasted."

Elena tried not to grin, but she couldn't help it. Travis Riggs—when he wasn't trying to kidnap her or worrying about his brother—was funny, engaging and clearly intelligent despite his obvious reading and writing difficulties. He was relaxed but still respectful around her parents, engaging them in conversation but not trying to impress them.

"It's the spices," her mother said. "I have my own blend. My mother used it, my grandmother..."

"You should open a restaurant." Travis ate heartily. He cleaned his plate, and when Rosalie forced seconds on him, he ate those, too.

"Who won the football game?" Elena asked. When she'd joined her mother in the kitchen, the game had been in the last few minutes. She didn't really care, just wanted to keep the conversation going—and on neutral ground.

"Houston," Travis answered in a way that told her he really wasn't rooting for one team or the other. He'd just watched the game to be sociable.

During commercials, Travis had asked about the house—how old was it, what improvements had they made. Her dad was handy—he could fix or build just about anything—so they had that to talk about. The conversation about the foundation must have happened after she'd left.

"Save room for dessert," Rosalie said. "Elena made fried plantains—it's her specialty. She used to make them every day when she lived at home."

Elena had never realized what a good liar her mother was. Before this meal was over, Rosalie would have Travis convinced Elena was the Cuban Julia Child.

"Do you like plantains?" Elena asked him. "Don't feel like you have to eat them."

"Of course I'll eat them."

"Working at that big mansion, she doesn't get much of a chance to cook," Rosalie went on. "But if she had her own kitchen, and people to cook for, she'd cook more."

Not even Elena's most stern look could stop her mother from embellishing Elena's stellar qualifications as a wife. Later, when she had a chance, she would apologize to Travis for putting him in such an uncomfortable position.

Then again, he didn't look too uncomfortable. He devoured the plantains with the same enthusiasm he'd shown the rest of the meal.

"These are great," he said between bites. "Can you buy plantains at the grocery store?"

"The Fiesta Mart," Elena answered. "They have a good selection of foods we Cuban ladies like to cook with."

"I'll have to remember that."

When the meal was over, Travis offered to help clear the table, but Rosalie shooed him away. "You are a guest in my house. Put down that dish." She said it so sternly, Travis immediately obeyed.

He didn't stay long after the meal. Elmer asked him a few more questions about home repairs, but then Travis insisted he really needed to go.

"Of course. I don't mean to keep you." He pulled his car keys from his pocket and handed them to Travis. "Take my SUV, and take Elena with you. She'll drive it home. My, um, sciatica is acting up."

"Since when do you have sciatica?" Elena asked. And since when did he let Elena drive his SUV?

"Oh, you know, one of those things. Getting older. It's not serious."

"I understand it can be very painful," Travis said. Elmer shrugged.

"Well, I better get going. Thanks again for the ride

and the hospitality. I enjoyed myself." He sounded surprised but sincere.

"Come back anytime."

Rosalie came bustling out of the kitchen. "Yes, Travis, please feel free to visit anytime. It's a pleasure for me to cook for more than just two people."

"I still think you should open a restaurant." He shook hands with Elmer, and he squeezed Rosalie's hand. Elena thought her mother was on the verge of hugging him, which really would have been too much, but she refrained.

Elena said nothing until they were in the truck. "Well, you certainly charmed them."

"They charmed me," he countered. "Your parents are very nice people."

"They are. But I know you didn't mean to get roped in to spending all afternoon with us. When they get revved up, they're a force of nature. It's best just to go along."

"I didn't mind." He put the SUV in gear and carefully pulled out of the driveway. "In fact, I can't remember the last time I actually watched football or enjoyed a meal like that."

"Yes, well, they came on a little strong. My mother seems to think we're…you know, involved…despite the fact that I assured her we are just acquaintances who only met recently."

"She liked me, though," he said with a wink.

"A little too much. She's probably planning our wedding as we speak. All that business about me being such a great cook—so not true. But she believes she caught my dad with her cooking, and the same should work for me."

Travis laughed. "Well, I think she's a gem. Truthfully, ever since Eric was arrested, my life has been consumed with trying to get him out of jail. And working. I couldn't afford to lose my business."

"I'm sorry the kidnapping thing didn't work for you. Although your brother's case *was* brought to Daniel's attention. You can bet he knows everything there is to know about it by now."

"Really?"

"And it's hard for him to walk away when he knows someone is in prison who shouldn't be."

"He won't do me any favors."

"He won't do it for you. If he does anything, it'll be because it's the right thing to do. He tries to do the right thing." Even though he had behaved like a snake in the grass. She couldn't forget that.

They were silent for a time as Travis drove them back downtown. Elena struggled with what to say.

"I'm still willing to help you with the online application form."

"I think that's a lost cause now. MacKenzie's adoption hearing is next week."

"So, you'll go and testify as to what you saw. Surely if the judge thinks there is any chance your niece is being neglected, they'll look into it."

"They won't believe me," he stated flatly. "They

see me as an ex-con, blindly loyal to my murderer brother. If I speak out against the Stovers—the foster parents—they'll just hate me, and they'll never let me see MacKenzie again."

Elena could understand how the risk might stop him from even trying.

"Do they let you see her now?"

"Yes, but only because they have to. I'm her next of kin. They never let me see her alone—to make sure she doesn't tell me what's really going on there, I'm sure. I think she's a little bit afraid of them."

"When she's adopted, they might not let you see her anyway, even if you don't testify against them."

"Can they do that?"

"I think so. You won't legally be her next of kin anymore."

"Damn. I hadn't even considered that possibility."

"At the very least, you should talk to a family law lawyer. Someone who can look at things objectively."

Travis made a face. He'd probably had his fill of lawyers during Eric's arrest and trial ordeals. But then he nodded. "You're right. You know a lot about this kind of stuff."

"It's hard to see alternative solutions to a problem when you're so close to it, that's all," she said modestly.

They'd reached Texas and Market Street. Travis pulled up to the curb. "Thanks for everything, Elena. But it's over now, okay?"

She looked like she wanted to challenge him, but in the end she nodded brusquely. "If that's what you want."

"Go back to your life. Forget you met me." He unfastened his seat belt, opened the door and stepped down to the curb, hunching against the cold wind as he slammed the door.

She quickly climbed over the console to the driver's seat and opened the window. "I can't go back to my old life," she called after him.

He stopped and turned. "Why not?"

"Because it wouldn't be the same. I'm different than I was yesterday. I feel differently about Daniel, about my job. I'm afraid the change can't be undone."

She closed the window, pulled the seat forward, put on her seat belt and drove away.

CHAPTER TEN

TRAVIS STARED AFTER the receding taillights of Elmer Marquez's SUV, still puzzling over Elena's revelation. Had she quit her job? Or was she planning to? All because her boss had called in a SWAT team to take Travis down? He had a hard time comprehending that or believing it was true.

Elena loved her job. Last night, she'd waxed eloquent for almost an hour on how grateful she was to Daniel Logan for giving her such a great opportunity. She had practically glowed when talking about Daniel—not a sexual glow, he'd decided, but an aura that came from the depth of her admiration for the man.

She respected him and the work he did.

And the pay—she'd said her paycheck was more than twice what she would have earned anywhere else doing similar work, though she'd pointed out the job was unique. Her family in Cuba depended on the money she sent to them. Because of her, their lives were more comfortable.

Clearly her parents were doing okay financially.

Was it possible Elena supported their lifestyle, too? Was her salary *that* generous?

He hoped she came to her senses before she did something she'd regret—like quit her shockingly lucrative job.

Something strange was going on with Elena. Why had she lied to the police? All she'd had to do was tell the cops what they wanted to hear—that he had violently abducted her from in front of her home, thrown her into the back of his truck and kept her locked up against her will for almost twenty-four hours. All she needed to do was tell them the truth.

If she'd done that, he wouldn't be standing on the street right now, free.

He couldn't let her give up her high-paying job out of some misguided defense of him. He would talk to her and convince her that whatever problems she had with Daniel were fixable.

First things first. His truck. Then a shower. Then he wanted to go see MacKenzie, even if it was just for a few minutes. Talking about her had made him worry about her again.

After that, a good night's sleep. Then he would figure out what to do.

JOHN AND BEA STOVER, MacKenzie's foster parents, lived in Timbergrove, just a block away from Eric's house, though on a street that wasn't quite as swanky. Eric had known them slightly, but apparently Bea and Tammy had been friends. The Stovers had a house full of foster children, and they also provided day care on a casual basis to lots of neighborhood kids—including MacKenzie.

After Tammy's murder and Eric's arrest, the Stovers had come forward, volunteering to take in MacKenzie. Letting them do so had seemed the prudent thing to do at the time; MacKenzie had been so traumatized, and she was at least familiar with the Stovers and their home.

It was almost seven by the time Travis pulled his truck into the Stovers' driveway. They wouldn't be pleased to see him; they preferred if he scheduled his visits—so they could make sure everything looked hunky-dory, Travis guessed.

The Stovers were probably sensitive to criticism about how they took care of all those kids. He'd tried not to blame them too much…at first. It took a special kind of person to agree to take on other people's kids, and with such a houseful, of course things weren't going to be perfect. Belongings were going to be misplaced, and clothes would get dirty. But the Stovers' excuses as to why MacKenzie's things always went missing were starting to wear a little thin.

Her foster siblings made no attempt to engage her, and the parents didn't seem to mind that MacKenzie was so quiet, that she spent a lot of time just sitting and staring. But anytime he mentioned that MacKenzie's behavior seemed unhealthy, they brushed away his concerns. *She's just tired. The therapist said not to push her.*

Bea answered the door when Travis rang the bell. She was a roundish woman—not fat, exactly, just soft and rather shapeless, but she was always stylishly dressed, her blond hair perfectly styled, makeup fresh. Whatever care she gave the kids, she never seemed to get dirty or rumpled doing it.

She pursed her lips in displeasure. "Travis. What are you doing here?"

"I know I should have called. I just… I really wanted to see her. Just for a few minutes."

"We're in the middle of dinner…."

Travis could hear kids laughing, dishes clanking, one child crying. Probably hard to keep them all happy at the same time.

"I can wait 'til you're done." He didn't want to mess up the family's routine too much—if there was a routine.

"Oh, I guess it's okay. MacKenzie's done eating anyway. Honestly, she eats like a bird, that one." Bea turned and headed for the kitchen, and Travis stepped inside, shutting the door behind him.

MacKenzie's appetite never used to be an issue. She used to eat whatever she was served without complaint. "Is that a problem?" Travis asked. "Should she see a doctor?"

"In my experience, kids eat when they're hungry. If she picks at her dinner, she'll eat a healthy breakfast. No need to worry."

Travis didn't necessarily agree. But what did he know? He didn't have kids. He'd been given his chance to take in MacKenzie and he'd turned it down. The idea of being the child's sole supporter, the one she depended on for everything—that was too frightening to contemplate.

Did he even have a right to criticize the Stovers?

"MacKenzie, your uncle is here to see you," Bea said.

John Stover looked up sharply as Travis entered the large, eat-in kitchen where the family was gathered around a table that wasn't quite big enough for all of them.

"At this hour?" Stover said.

MacKenzie looked worriedly from Travis to her foster father.

"Just for a few minutes," Travis said.

"Okay. But her bedtime is at eight. And she needs a bath first."

"Understood."

When John nodded to MacKenzie, she slid out of her chair and went to Travis. Travis leaned down and held out his arms. She went into them easily enough, and he gave her a good hug. "That one's from your dad," he whispered in her ear. "And this one's from me."

MacKenzie hugged him back, her tense little body relaxing in the embrace.

"Let's go into the living room where it's a little quieter." He let her go and took her hand. Bea stood up from the table. "John, can you handle the kitchen cleanup? I need to pay some bills before bedtime."

"Sure, honey."

Bea followed Travis and MacKenzie into the living room and sat down at a small desk in the corner, switching on a reading light.

It was always like this. They never left him and MacKenzie completely alone. He wondered if they were worried about what he might do to her...or what she might tell him about what actually went on in that house.

"Hey, MacKenzie," Travis said. "Do you want to have a tea party?" Eric had bought MacKenzie a beautiful, high-quality doll-size tea set for her birthday a couple of months earlier, and Travis had delivered it to her. The little girl had seemed delighted with her gift but hadn't wanted to play with it. She'd sat with it in her lap, staring at the colorful dishes behind the clear plastic window in the box as if they were priceless artifacts at a museum.

MacKenzie nodded and ran to her room. After a couple of minutes she returned, looking stricken. "I can't find it."

"That's okay—we can do it another day." The last thing he wanted to do was upset her.

"But I put it in my closet. Now it's not there." She must have been pretty upset. She usually didn't speak up this much.

"MacKenzie, honey," Bea said. "You probably just forgot where you put it. Or someone might have moved it—you know how crazy things are in this house sometimes. Don't worry. It'll turn up."

Bea sounded like the soul of concern, a loving, patient mother. But MacKenzie didn't appear comforted. In fact, she shot her foster mother a brief, mutinous look, as if she wanted to argue but didn't dare.

Okay, this went beyond disorganization. Travis understood that sometimes toys were shared or misplaced, but the tea set had been a special gift. A child ought to have some things that were hers alone.

Travis was beginning to think there was more going on here than just a little girl who misplaced her things. Eric insisted MacKenzie had plenty of good-quality clothes that fit well; he didn't want her to be known as "that poor foster kid" at school. But right now, she was wearing a pair of faded green stretch pants that were too big and a striped T-shirt that was too small and frayed at the cuffs.

"MacKenzie, why don't you show your uncle how you can write your letters?" Bea suggested.

"You're writing now?" Travis asked, not having to fake being impressed. MacKenzie was a smart kid. She might be quiet and withdrawn at home, but she was doing well in school.

MacKenzie nodded. She opened a notebook that was on the coffee table, picked up a pencil and plopped down on the floor. Leaning over the paper, she laboriously drew some letters into the notebook and showed them to Travis.

"That spells 'cat'!" Travis beamed. Before long,

she would be reading and writing better than he could. "Can you spell 'dog'?"

She nodded and printed the word for him, fastidiously working between the lines of the ruled paper.

"That is really good. Hey, do you want to read to me?"

She nodded, went to a crowded bookcase and pulled out a well-worn book of fairy tales. It was well beyond her reading level. She handed Travis the book and sat on the sofa.

Clearly she wanted Travis to read to *her*.

Reading wasn't his strong suit, but for MacKenzie, he'd try. His voice was halting, and a couple of times, the kid actually helped him sound out a word and they figured it out together. She seemed to like helping him read.

"MacKenzie, it's time for your bath," Bea said after they'd been at it for about ten minutes. She looked apologetically at Travis. "With so many kids, and a small hot water heater, we have to stick to our schedule. I'm sure you understand."

"Sure." Travis gave MacKenzie another hug. "I'll be back to visit next week at our regular time, okay?"

She nodded. "Uncle Trav, when's Daddy getting out of jail?"

Unfortunately, there was no shielding MacKenzie from the truth of where her father was. Everyone knew, including her foster siblings. Travis had gone to great pains to emphasize that Eric hadn't done anything wrong, that it was all a mistake they were trying to straighten out, and MacKenzie accepted that.

But every time he visited, she asked the same question.

"I don't know, MacKenzie. Soon, I hope. I'm doing everything I can to help your dad. Meanwhile, he loves to get your letters. We'll write him another one next time I come, okay? Maybe you can color a picture for him."

She nodded. Last time she'd drawn a picture. She'd made stick figures portraying herself, her mommy and daddy and even the dog.

The dog had disappeared; during the chaos of the police investigating the crime scene, someone had left the gate open and it had run away. Eric had tried like hell to find it, even while mourning his wife, but poor little Pixie never came back. Everyone and everything MacKenzie had held dear had been taken from her.

As Travis made his way to his truck, a boy of about twelve fell into step beside him. "I know what happened to MacKenzie's tea set."

"Yeah?" The kid was MacKenzie's foster brother. "You're Wesley, right?"

"Yeah, that's right." He seemed surprised Travis would remember his name. "The Stovers sell MacKenzie's stuff online. Any time any of us gets something good, the Stovers take it from us. And they say if we tell, the state will take us away."

"So why are you telling?"

"'Cause I'm sick of this place. It's not bad, as far as foster homes go. We get enough to eat. But I'm sick of all the lies. And MacKenzie—they're mean to her. She's a scared little kid, y'know? And they take advantage. I'm just sick of it. Check eBay if you don't believe me."

"WHY DIDN'T YOU tell me this before?" Missy Kelso, MacKenzie's social worker, looked at Travis over the top of her large black glasses. "I assumed everything was fine at the Stover house. I mean, I know they have a lot of kids they're responsible for, but the kids always seem relatively happy, they're always clean, they have healthy food in the fridge…"

"Well, it hasn't been like that when I've been there. MacKenzie's father provides lots of clothes and toys for his daughter, which I've delivered on many occasions, but they seem to disappear. I've asked MacKenzie what happened to them, and she doesn't know."

The social worker shrugged. "Kids lose toys."

"Not MacKenzie. She's a very careful, meticulous child. She was always a little fashion plate—she wanted the bows in her hair just so. She would never willingly wear the faded, badly fitting clothes I've seen her in unless she had no choice. And they cut her hair off."

"Long hair can be a chore to take care of."

"There's always a reason, always an excuse. But

I'm telling you, things aren't what they seem in that house. Maybe they know when you're coming to visit somehow and…and spiff things up."

"Why would they move to adopt MacKenzie if they didn't love her?" Missy asked. "They'll lose the money from the state that they receive for her care."

"Because MacKenzie is rich. Or she will be. Her great-grandmother is loaded, and MacKenzie is her sole heir now that Tammy is gone. I'm telling you, I see dollar signs in the eyes of those people."

"You're not just…exaggerating because *you* want custody, are you?"

"Listen, Eric wanted me to take over the care of MacKenzie when he was arrested. But I'm a single guy and I work construction. I thought foster care was better—you know, two parents, a family atmosphere. I'm still convinced it could be. But not with those people."

Missy stared at him awhile longer.

"I didn't tell you all this before now because I wasn't sure. And I didn't think anyone would believe me because of my past."

"Because you have a criminal record."

He nodded.

"Lots of people have made mistakes. Relatively speaking, your brush with the law is minor. You haven't had any trouble since then, have you?"

"No," he said a little too quickly. But he realized she could discover the truth with one phone call. "Okay, that's not the truth. I was arrested. Yesterday."

"Yesterday?" Missy looked at him with alarm.

"Yes, but it was all a misunderstanding. They released me, no charges. Look, I'm not trying to get anything out of this. I just want what's best for MacKenzie."

"I do, too, Travis. Truly I do. If you had something more concrete—"

"They're selling MacKenzie's things online."

"What?"

"One of the other foster kids said that whatever presents I bring to MacKenzie, the Stovers take them and sell them online. The clothes are expensive—designer stuff. The toys, too. They don't care about her."

"That's a fairly serious charge. Do you have any proof?"

"No. But you could ask the boy—Wesley, his name is. He's about twelve."

"I will. Is there anything else—anything besides your suspicions?"

"Wesley also said the Stovers are mean to MacKenzie, that they take advantage of the fact she's a scared little girl."

"Could Wesley be jealous of MacKenzie?"

"I don't think that's it." Travis struggled to keep his voice even, to not lose his temper. Missy was just being thorough. She was looking at all the angles. God only knew what the Stovers' lawyers would try to claim. They would dig through Travis's past and try to discredit him. And it wouldn't be that difficult.

He needed facts.

"I'll talk to him," Missy said. "Alone. I have to admit, whenever I'm there, the parents hover. And they always herd the other kids outside or into another room, like they don't want me to talk to them."

Travis nodded. Maybe Missy would at least look into his complaint, even if she didn't completely believe him.

"Why were you arrested? Do you mind my asking?"

Hell, yes, he minded. Because he didn't have a satisfactory answer. But he needed to keep Missy on his side. "They thought I kidnapped someone," he said with a laugh. "But when they talked to the supposed victim, she set them straight."

"And they never filed charges?"

"No. They didn't have any evidence." So long as Elena didn't have a change of heart, they never would.

Elena. He needed to talk to her. Maybe she'd cooled off toward Daniel by now. But he wanted to make sure his actions hadn't resulted in some long-term condition. The problem was, he didn't even know how to get in touch with her. She'd never given him her number, and why would she? Despite what her parents thought, he and Elena weren't… Wait. Her parents. How many Elmer Marquezes could there be in Houston?

Once he was sitting behind the wheel of his truck

in the parking lot outside Missy's office, Travis took out his phone and called Information.

"Is that Elmer Marquez, M.D.?" the operator asked.

M.D.? As in doctor? "I'm looking for a home number. On Sandpiper Lane."

"I'll connect you."

Elmer had never mentioned what he did for a living. Somehow, the subject never came up. But how had he gone from cane fields to being a doctor?

As the phone rang, Travis almost lost his nerve and hung up. He'd vowed he would stay out of Elena's life. But he also wanted her to see reason. He couldn't stand the thought that she might trash her career out of some misguided need to defend him.

Rosalie answered with a cheery *"Hola!"*

"Rosalie, it's Travis Riggs."

"Travis! How nice to hear from you." She sounded as happy as if he were a long-lost son coming back from the dead.

"Yes, it's nice to talk to you, too," he said politely. "I'm sorry to bother you—"

"Oh, it's no bother!"

"But I really need to get in touch with Elena and I wondered if you might have her cell phone number."

"Of course I do. But why would you need that when Elena is sitting right here? I'll put her on."

Travis heard some muffled noises. Like maybe Elena and her mother were arguing? But in the end, Elena did take the phone. "Hey, Travis."

"So, I guess you're not at work."

"No…I'm taking a leave of absence."

A leave of absence. That didn't sound good. "Elena, seriously, you aren't going to quit your job, are you? I can't have this on my conscience. There's no room."

"I don't know. Daniel gave me his word, then broke it."

"Because he was trying to protect you."

"No. Because he was angry at you. His ego couldn't allow him to let you go without being punished. So he lied to me. The SWAT team, that huge show of force—it was all to punish you, not to protect me."

"It was a natural reaction to everything that had happened. Emotions were running high." He couldn't believe he was defending Daniel Logan, not after the heated words they'd exchanged. But what he told Elena was true. If he ever got his hands on the man who'd murdered Tammy and put Eric through hell, he wouldn't have a good handle on his emotions, either.

"Daniel won't allow his employees' emotions to dictate their behavior. He's always going on about how we have to keep our heads on straight no matter what is going on around us. Yet he doesn't practice that himself."

"He made a mistake."

"He abused his power. I don't like that. I'm giving myself some time to cool off, that's all. I don't know whether I'm going to quit or not."

She sounded pretty upset. Her voice cracked when she spoke. The last thing he wanted to do was upset her further. "Okay. I get it. But I feel responsible. Maybe I didn't physically hurt you, but it seems I messed things up."

She actually laughed. "Think of it this way. You *shook* things up. It's easy to get too comfortable, too complacent, if you never have to struggle. Maybe I am ready for a change." She lowered her voice to a whisper. "And my parents are thrilled to have me living at home like the old days."

Of course. Elena didn't have her own place. Her job included room and board.

"Well, I wish you the best. Goodbye, Elena." *For about the fourth time.*

"Did you talk to MacKenzie's social worker about the Stovers?" she asked before he could disconnect.

"Yeah, just now. She was at least interested in what I had to say, but she said I need something more concrete than a feeling."

"What would you need?"

"Proof that they're selling MacKenzie's toys and clothes—that would be useful."

"I could help with that," she said brightly. "Send me a list of everything you believe they might have sold."

"Seriously?"

"Seriously."

"Can I tell it to you, instead of writing it down?"

"Oh, right. You and computers don't get along. Okay, tell me."

"Zulily dress, pink and black stripes, size 6. Gap Kids jeans, size…"

"Wait a minute. You know this off the top of your head?"

"Yeah. I have a very good memory." Since he seldom wrote anything down, he *had* to have a good memory.

"That's impressive."

He thought it would be a damn sight more impressive if he could type on a computer with some degree of proficiency.

It took about fifteen minutes for them to complete the list of clothes and toys MacKenzie had received since going to live with the Stovers.

"Give me a few minutes. I'll get back to you."

"Okay. Thanks." A few minutes? What could she possibly do in that time?

He checked his watch. Damn, he really needed to get to work. He'd been neglecting the job he'd been hired to do. He had one thing going for him, and that was his professional reputation. He could at least try to preserve that. Hard to believe that yesterday he'd been ready to throw that all aside. He still would—if it would help Eric. But it wouldn't.

When he got to the house in Bellaire, the first thing he thought about was Elena—the frenzied drive from River Oaks with Elena in his trunk, her throwing the wrench at his head, carrying her kicking and screaming in through the back door. He actually smiled—what a spitfire she was! Any other woman would have been cowering and crying over his harsh treatment of her, but she'd come up swinging.

Today he had a couple of crews working—a stonemason to repair the fireplace, some guys to polish the more minor scratches out of the hardwood floor. They were both there, two trucks, four guys, waiting for him to unlock the door. He hadn't meant to make them wait—he'd pay for that, since the crews charged by the hour.

He screeched to a halt in the cul-de-sac and hopped out. "Sorry I'm late, guys."

They didn't seem bothered. The glass on the front door had been broken and patched with plywood. Had the police done that while hunting for Elena?

One more thing for him to repair.

He unlocked the front door and they all started dragging their equipment in. First tool to get plugged in was the radio, tuned to a Spanish-language station and set at top volume. Next came the power chisels and the drum sander, and all was right with the world. Travis went to work repairing the master bath sink.

The space was filled with memories of his time with Elena, too. The room seemed melancholy without her vibrant presence. He went still.

Damn, he had feelings for the woman. Real feelings, not just a passing physical attraction. She was such an incredible force of nature, like no woman he'd ever known. Even Judith, whom he once considered the love of his life, paled by comparison.

After all these years, to want someone so totally unattainable seemed really unfair.

Then again, when had life been fair?

The work he was doing was messy and noisy, but he kept at it, because as long as he was focused on it, he couldn't think about his mistakes or what was missing from his life. He didn't take a break until it was time for lunch. He'd make a run for tacos or pizza—that would keep the crews happy.

As he headed out of the bedroom, he checked his phone. He skidded to a stop—he'd missed a call from Elena. How in the hell? Must have been the noise. At least now he had her number. He started to call her back, but Leo, the stonemason, called to him.

"Hey, boss? Someone here to see you."

Now what? "It's not a cop, is it?" He wasn't dumb enough to believe he was totally out of the woods as far as the kidnapping went. If Daniel Logan could figure out how to make charges stick without Elena's help, he'd do it.

"Not unless they're making cops really different these days," Leo said with a lascivious grin.

Travis made his way toward the front door. She was standing uncertainly in the entryway. "Elena?"

CHAPTER ELEVEN

TRAVIS HELD THE door open for her, but she hesitated. "I tried calling, but you didn't answer."

"How did you know…" He didn't say it out loud, but surely she knew what he was thinking. How did she know where he would be? And how did she know how to find this house? She'd been locked in the back of his truck coming and going.

His puzzlement must have shown on his face. "When I called Daniel from here, he tracked down the signal. A team came here looking for me, but we'd already left. I just asked Celeste for the address."

That explained the front door. At least they'd patched it. That was nice.

"How resourceful of you. Come in. Sorry I didn't hear my phone ring. It's kind of loud in here. But you didn't have to come all the way over."

"Truthfully, I needed to get out of the house. My mother is hovering and asking too many questions about why I'm not at work."

Travis resisted doing the same. She already knew

his thoughts on the matter of her job. No sense belaboring the point.

"I have some news. Mitch Delacroix from Project Justice got all the information you could possibly need to prove who was selling what."

"Seriously? You're working with Project Justice?" Oh, wouldn't Daniel love that? Elena using his foundation for Travis's personal business?

"Not exactly. I asked Mitch for help but only during his time off. Turns out he had today off. He found the items you told me about. All of them. On eBay. All listed by the same seller. This person made no attempt to hide his identity. John Stover."

"That's him! That's the foster father's name!"

She handed him a folder. "I've got all the documentation here. If you take this to the social worker, she can present it to the judge at the adoption hearing."

"Elena, I don't know how to thank you." For the first time in forever, he felt something close to hopeful. He might actually be able to do it—to stop those awful people from taking MacKenzie away forever.

She smiled so sweetly that his heart almost stopped. "I was happy to do it. That gives you a little breathing room. Now I can help you with the Project Justice application."

"Um, don't you think that's a moot point now? Any application I fill out will go directly into the circular file. Not only did I kidnap the founder's assistant, I upset the applecart so thoroughly that she can't come back to work."

"It's worth trying. And stop trying to take the blame for this problem between Daniel and me."

He would drop it for now. "Elena, I don't want you to think I'm ungrateful, because I'm not. I'm just puzzled. Why are you doing this? Why are you helping me? I'm sure there are lots of more deserving people for you to help—people who haven't—" he lowered his voice to a whisper "—people who haven't kidnapped you."

Leo and his helper chose that moment to stride through the foyer and out the front door. "Lunch," Leo announced. "Back in a few."

Travis realized the sander, which had been grinding away upstairs all morning, had also gone silent. The truck belonging to the floor crew was gone, too. He'd waited too long to make a pizza run.

He and Elena were alone in the house.

"I'm helping you because you got to me, okay? And because I need to keep busy or Mama will enslave me in the kitchen, making *pastelitos* for Thanksgiving."

Travis knew *pastelitos*—little puff pastries filled with meat. "For Thanksgiving?" That struck him as funny—such a Cuban dish for the quintessential American holiday.

Elena shrugged. "It's what we do."

"Every family has its traditions, I guess. We used to eat Jell-O on Thanksgiving, so I have no room to criticize. Listen, I need to take these papers to the social worker. Soon as my crews get back from lunch. I can't leave the house open, and I can't lock them out."

She looked at her watch. "When will they be back?"

"An hour or so. But maybe when I'm done with that…we could work on the application. The library's open late tonight."

"No need for that. I've got my computer in the car. We can do it now. And…maybe some of that lasagna's still in the fridge?"

He'd forgotten about the lasagna. "Yeah. Sure."

"Be right back."

She ran to her car—she was driving her father's SUV—and fetched her computer.

What was going on here? He felt as if he'd fallen into some alternate reality, one in which he and Elena had met some other way, that he'd never snatched her off the street and stuffed her into his truck.

While he put the lasagna in the microwave to heat, Elena settled onto the carpet in the living room and turned on her laptop.

"Want me to bring in a chair?"

"That's okay. I don't mind sitting on the floor." She patted the space next to her. "Ready when you are."

He lowered himself to the floor next to her, careful not to touch her. "How does this work?"

"I'll ask you the questions, you'll answer them and I'll type them into the form." She had a cell phone gadget on her laptop that allowed her to go online. In moments, she'd pulled up the hated form. "Full name?"

"Travis Brandon Riggs."

"Date of birth?"

They went through a long list of identifiers—social security number, current address and previous addresses, his relationship with the incarcerated individual, his personal reasons for wanting this person to be free.

That question stopped him. "I want him to be free because he's innocent," Travis said. "Do I need another reason?"

"Absolutely not. In fact, that's the reason Daniel looks for."

"What other answer could there be?"

"Oh, a lot of people want Project Justice to help because they love someone, because they miss them, because their children miss them. But the only reason that really matters is that they're innocent."

Travis nodded.

The questions got harder after that. He had to come up with the chronology of events leading up to Eric's arrest, the main evidence against him, the verdict on all counts named in the indictment, the sentence, where he was incarcerated, his prisoner number.

Travis was able to provide it all. At one point,

Elena looked at him, frowning. "You have your brother's inmate number memorized?"

"Yeah. I told you I have a good memory."

"That's not just a good memory. That's freakish."

He shrugged. "I'm lucky that way, I guess. But I'd trade the memory in a second if I could get a better handle on reading and writing."

"I know this is nosy of me, but did you get special education in school? I mean, clearly you have some kind of learning disability."

"Oh, yeah, that was a treat, getting stuck in special ed." He got mad all over again just thinking about the way he was teased, the cruelty some kids could stoop to and the fact that nobody stopped them. Eric tried to stick up for him once. Big mistake. He still had a slight bump in his nose, the only flaw in his otherwise perfect face. "In all fairness, even if any of those teachers could have helped me, I wasn't willing to let them. I just wanted to get to age sixteen so I could drop out. As you probably know, I don't always make the most reasoned decisions."

"Well, no, you don't." Thankfully she dropped the subject of his learning problems.

They took a break when the lasagna was ready. The floor guys returned while Travis and Elena were in the middle of lunch. Leo gave Travis a curious look but said nothing, just headed upstairs with his helper. He supposed it was a little odd for them to see the boss man sitting on the floor having lunch with a beautiful woman.

"You've got to give me this recipe."

"Are you allowed to cook Italian? Being Cuban and all?"

She nodded enthusiastically. "Well, not me. But I would give the recipe to Mama. She likes to branch out sometimes. She can make a mean stir-fry. And you should taste her baba ghanoush."

That was never going to happen, because despite what this looked and felt like, he and Elena would never really be friends. For whatever reason, he had become her project, her charity case.

Just like he'd been for Judith.

Judith had been drawn to him for all the wrong reasons. Yes, they'd had a strong mutual attraction. She was wealthy, educated, refined—everything he wasn't—which made her seem exotic in his eyes. She'd found his work-roughened hands and his sheer physicality a welcome change from the soft, rich boys she was accustomed to.

How often had she called him a diamond in the rough? At first he'd taken it as a compliment. Later, he'd realized what the term really meant. Judith hadn't fallen in love with him, but with the man she thought he might become with her tutoring.

They'd married way too fast. Maybe she'd done it to thwart her parents, who were every bit as pushy as she was. All he knew was, it didn't take long before brawn and good sex weren't enough for her. She'd wanted him to make a success of himself. She'd wanted to take him to parties and family dinners and be able to brag about what a catch he'd turned out to be.

But he'd bristled at her attempts to change him. He didn't want to earn his GED, didn't see the point in it. He hadn't wanted to dress differently, or have his hair cut by some snotty hairdresser, or go into management at some gargantuan construction corporation. He didn't want to "better himself."

At one point, he thought she'd finally seen the light and accepted him for who he was. But actually she'd given up. She'd found herself another studly "project" but hadn't bothered to inform Travis that their marriage was over.

Elena wasn't as snobby as Judith, but clearly she'd left her humble beginnings far behind. She was a doctor's daughter, and she worked for one of the richest men in the country. He would never be her equal.

She was helping him, and he truly was grateful for that. But if two people were going to get involved, they should start on equal footing. So far Elena had done all the giving, and he'd done all the taking. How could he give back? What did he have that she needed?

Then there was the fact that he'd kidnapped her. How did anyone ever overcome something like that?

"We better get back to work," he said gruffly.

She nodded. As soon as he cleaned up the dishes, they resumed their positions on the floor and Elena opened her laptop.

Before they could get to the next part of the form, Elena's phone rang. She dragged it out of her purse and squinted at the screen. A puzzled look crossed her face.

"Something wrong?"

"It's Daniel."

ELENA'S STOMACH SWOOPED. Should she pick up? She didn't trust herself to talk to her boss without losing it; her emotions were still too close to the surface where Daniel Logan was concerned.

What if he'd found out she was using her contacts at Project Justice for her own selfish interests and those of Travis Riggs?

"Aren't you going to answer it?" Travis asked.

"Should I?"

"Yes, of course! Y'all need to work through whatever's bugging you and get things back to normal."

She hesitated another moment before answering, because curiosity got the better of her. "Yes, Daniel?" She was irritated that her voice cracked.

Travis stood and moved to the other side of the room, giving her some privacy. He picked up a scraping tool and began working on some peeling decals on the front windows.

"Elena. Thank you for taking my call." Daniel sounded oddly formal. Normally he didn't waste time on polite salutations. He simply issued orders and expected her to follow them.

She said nothing, just waited for him to tell her why he'd called.

"I've been going over the Eric Riggs case," he began.

"Oh?"

"You know I don't like being backed into a corner, and I had every intention of forgetting all about Eric Riggs."

"But you couldn't," she said softly.

"No. His brother might be a lowlife bottom-feeder, but that's not Eric's fault. The case kept nagging at me. Even after you were back safe, I just kept thinking about Eric and his little girl, whom he'll never see again if something isn't done."

Elena's heart thumped wildly behind her sternum. At one time she had predicted Daniel might be unable to resist following up on the Riggs case, but that was before she'd argued with him. Now, she was frankly surprised that he would concern himself. His grudge against Travis was strong enough that Elena had figured he wouldn't do *anything* to further Travis's cause, even if the cops had used rubber hoses to beat a confession out of Eric Riggs.

"So, is Project Justice going to take on the case?"

From the corner of her eye, Elena saw Travis go still. Obviously he could still hear her side of the conversation. She'd have put the phone on speaker and let him hear the whole thing if doing so wouldn't have alerted Daniel that she wasn't alone.

"I'd like to work on the case, yes," Daniel said.

"There were so many holes in that trial, so many mistakes made during the investigation. I can think of at least five directions the cops could have gone and didn't because they were so sure right from the start that Eric did it."

"That's fantastic!"

"No, wait, not so fantastic. Number one, I can't officially take on the case without an application. The foundation has pretty strict rules about that."

"That's not a problem. In fact, we—that is, Travis is working on that now. You should have it by the end of the day."

Daniel didn't ask how Elena knew this. "Okay. Second problem—I don't have any investigators to spare. We've got a backlog. Since Eric isn't on death row, his case can't take priority over some others that are more urgent."

"So when would you get to it?"

"Probably not for three months or so."

Damn. "Eric's daughter might be adopted by then."

"I can have someone from my personal legal team look into that. Since it's not directly related to the criminal case, it doesn't have to go through the foundation or follow the established protocol. We can treat it as a separate matter."

"You would do that?"

"Of course. I don't want an innocent man to lose his little girl. But there's something Travis should do if he wants to prevent the child from being adopted.

Because even if the current foster parents aren't approved, there are three other couples waiting in the wings to adopt her."

Elena hadn't known that, and she doubted Travis did, either. Even if the judge threw the book at the Stovers for selling MacKenzie's things online, it would only buy them a little bit of time.

Probably not enough.

"What does Travis need to do? I'm sure he'll do anything!"

"I'm sure he'll do anything, too," Daniel said drily. "But what he needs to do is petition the court to adopt MacKenzie himself. I understand that's what Eric wanted."

"Oh. I'm not sure… He said…" She lowered her voice. "He said he didn't think he'd be an appropriate guardian. You know, because of his, um…" She dropped her voice. "His criminal record."

"Elena," Daniel said sharply. "Is Travis there with you?"

She'd never wanted to lie so badly in her life. But she couldn't very well lie to Daniel when she had made a big fuss over Daniel lying to *her*.

"Yes, he's here."

Long silence. "What the hell is going on with you? No, never mind. None of my business what you do when you're not on the clock."

Thank God. Because she didn't know how she could explain it to him when she didn't understand it herself.

"Maybe Travis isn't an ideal parent," Daniel said, getting back to business. "But as the girl's closest noninstitutionalized relative, he'll have a shot. He'll have to prove he can take care of her, of course. Does he have the means for childcare? He needs to live someplace with a separate bedroom for the child."

"I'm sure he can make the necessary arrangements."

"Okay. If he's agreeable, have him contact Abel Koontz. He's the family lawyer who works with my estate lawyer. Do you need his number?"

"No, I've got it. Thank you, Daniel. I don't know… It's very gracious of you to help. There aren't any strings attached, are there?"

"No, Elena, no strings. I'm going to try to help Eric because it's the right thing to do and not for any other reason." With that he hung up.

If he had insisted she forgive him in return for helping Travis, would she have done it? Maybe. Already she could feel herself softening toward Daniel. He was trying to make things right, after all. He'd had to swallow a boatload of pride to call her.

Travis had given up all pretense of scraping windows. He stood only a few feet away, his arms folded. "What was that about?"

Elena stood up so she could look Travis in the eye when she gave him the news. "Daniel said that Project Justice will take on Eric's case."

Travis looked as if he didn't dare hope. He was still suspicious. "Are you sure?"

She nodded.

"Elena, that's…that's…" He couldn't find the words. Instead, he pulled her into his arms and kissed her. She was stiff with surprise at first, but after a second or two she softened, melting against him, her mouth greedily kissing him back.

A loud banging in the next room was an unwelcome reminder that they weren't alone. He pulled back.

She smiled mischievously. "You're welcome. Oh, Travis, I forgot to tell you. It's not all good news." She squeezed his hand. "Project Justice has a backlog. Three months. And there's more bad news." She told him what Daniel had reported about all the other couples waiting to adopt MacKenzie.

Travis sagged slightly. "I should have expected that, I suppose. MacKenzie is a sweet little girl— who wouldn't want to have her as their daughter?"

"If you can stop the first adoption, it will at least buy you some time," she pointed out.

"But then what? What if the next couple in line is worse than the Stovers?"

"Travis, there's one thing you can do. You can adopt MacKenzie yourself. Daniel has a family law attorney standing by, waiting to help you do that."

Travis was already shaking his head. "I can't do that. I'm a bachelor living in a tiny apartment, I work all the time….How would I take care of her? I'd have to move to a bigger place and even then—"

"Do you want Eric to lose his daughter?"

"Of course I don't."

"Then stop throwing roadblocks in front of yourself! If you love MacKenzie, you can figure out a way to be a father to her. All these reasons you don't want to adopt her are just excuses, because for some reason you don't think you're worthy enough to be a dad. Why, because you aren't some fancy lawyer? Because you're lousy at reading? Because a bunch of stupid teachers said you'd never amount to anything? What are you afraid of? Why don't you prove them wrong?"

Travis stared at her, his jaw hanging open, obviously shocked by her outburst. She was shocked herself. She wasn't even sure where those accusations had come from.

Even if she was right about him, it wasn't her place to say such things.

She looked away. "I'm sorry. Sometimes my mouth gets ahead of my brain."

In all the time they'd been together, he'd never looked at her with such hostility. Even in those few moments before he'd kidnapped her, and he'd been pretty angry then.

Finally he found his voice. "I think you've helped me enough."

"But the application—"

"I can finish the rest on my own. Email it to me."

"Okay," she said in a small voice. Clearly she'd touched a nerve. "I'll send you that lawyer's phone number. You can use it or not." She retreated behind her laptop to do as he'd asked.

Why was she going so far out of her way to help him, anyway? He hadn't asked her to. He'd told her several times that he wanted her out of his life. But she'd convinced herself he didn't mean it.

Apparently he did.

She'd thought that after what they went through, they'd forged some kind of bond. But it must have been all in her head.

"I just sent the form to your phone," she said, but when she looked up he was gone. He'd retreated to some other part of the house.

This was for the best, she reassured herself. She'd jumped on board Travis's cause because it was easier than what she really ought to be doing, which was figuring out some things about her own life.

Elena turned off her laptop, closed it and got to her feet. This was it, then. She wouldn't ever see Travis again.

Her eyes filled with tears. What was the matter with her?

But deep down, she knew. She was falling for Travis. Falling in love like a schoolgirl. But she was going there alone.

CHAPTER TWELVE

TRAVIS STARED AT the lawyer's number on the screen of his phone for a long time—so long, in fact, that his breakfast of eggs and sausage got cold.

He had finished the Project Justice application last night after he'd knocked off work for the day. The only part he and Elena hadn't finished was a personal statement about why he thought his brother's case deserved the attention and resources the foundation could give it.

With Elena doing the typing, they could have knocked it out in a few minutes. Instead, Travis had been forced to go to the library—the main Houston library, which was open late—load the form on to the computer there and painstakingly type out his statement one excruciating word at a time.

It wasn't just the spelling that flummoxed him. Just getting the words from his brain to his typing fingers was a struggle. A teacher had once explained to him that writing was more difficult for him than most people because he'd done so little of it, and the connections in the brain that were formed from doing something over and over had never been created. The older he got, the less malleable his brain was and the harder it would be to ever make those connections.

When he was done, and the library was about to close, he asked one of the librarians to look over the two paragraphs he'd written. She kindly corrected a couple of misspelled words, fixed some commas and added a word he'd left out completely.

"There. I think you're good," the thin, gray-haired woman had said, patting him on the shoulder as if he were a child. He asked her for one more favor—to email the form to Project Justice. As exhausted as he was, he didn't trust himself to type in the address correctly.

"Project Justice," she said as she effortlessly typed the letters and numbers. "Is that the company that helps people who are in prison but shouldn't be?"

"Yes, that's right."

"Well, good luck. I hope they can help you. And if you need any more assistance with the computer, I'm here most evenings."

"Thanks." He was touched by her helpful attitude. He'd never asked a librarian for anything. Previously, his only experience with them was when they told him to be quiet or kicked him out of the school library for causing trouble. Maybe Elena was right about some things—like it was possible he made things more difficult for himself than they needed to be. He did tend to live his life more modestly than he had to. He was an excellent contractor and craftsman, and he could have grown his business and made more money if he'd wanted to. But he hadn't challenged himself to be a big success—maybe because, in his head, Eric was destined to be the successful one.

He wasn't "that Riggs boy" anymore. There was only so much he could blame on a learning disability, one that plenty of people overcame, or so he'd been told. He'd made his life what it was.

For years he'd been so consumed with Eric's issues that he hadn't thought much about his own life. It was time to take stock. At age thirty-three, he was the owner of his own company. Sure, it didn't pull in the big bucks, but he paid his bills and he employed a number of people, helping them to take care of their families. With a little effort, he could take on more work, employ more people, move into a higher income bracket.

Discounting the past few days, he hadn't been in any kind of trouble since getting out of jail almost ten years ago. He was in good health, he paid taxes, he got along with his neighbors, most of whom he never saw.

But his personal life was a disaster. Or, rather, it was nonexistent. He'd been close to Eric and his family, but he really didn't have any other friends, and since Judith, his love life had been limited to occasional one-night stands that didn't have a ghost of a chance of lasting longer than a condom or two.

He'd convinced himself that he didn't like people very much. He preferred to be alone, working with his hands. He understood wood and concrete and steel.

But Elena liked him. Or at least she'd liked him a little, until he'd told her to get out of his life. MacKenzie liked him, too, although it was hard to tell, as she was not effusive with her emotions. Still, sometimes she wanted to sit in his lap or hold his hand.

For a moment, he allowed himself to think about what it might be like to have full custody of MacKenzie.

He wouldn't be her father. He could never replace Eric and would never want to. But could he take care of her? At least better than those horrid Stovers?

He would have to move into a new place. His studio apartment didn't have a separate bedroom for MacKenzie. And he would have to arrange for childcare after school and on holidays. He could enroll her in day care, he supposed, but that would mean foisting her off on strangers again.

Some type of nanny would be better, but that could be costly. Still, he could swing it. He'd been offered bigger jobs—more profitable jobs—than his usual, but he always turned them down, telling himself he didn't really want the hassle.

But maybe he was afraid, like Elena said. Afraid of challenging himself because he didn't want to grow and he didn't want to fail.

Her comments yesterday had stung. But now

that he'd had time to let them sink in, he wondered if she might be right.

THE NEXT MORNING, Travis woke up early, dressed with particular care and headed straight to the social worker's office to show her the evidence he had against the Stovers. Maybe what they did wasn't exactly criminal, but it was morally indefensible. The only way Eric had of showing MacKenzie he loved her was to buy her presents, and her foster parents had taken them away.

Missy's office opened at eight-thirty. It was eight-fifteen when Travis pulled into the parking lot. He had fifteen minutes to kill.

He pulled out his phone and studied the email Elena had sent yesterday with the lawyer's phone number. His finger hovered over the number, highlighted in blue on his phone screen. One touch, and he could put the call through.

Maybe he wasn't the best-qualified guardian in the world. But why not let an unbiased expert make that call? He dialed Koontz's number.

IT WAS THANKSGIVING DAY, but Elena wasn't feeling the spirit of gratitude. Her mother was in a frenzy of cooking. So many things to be done. She'd invited a bunch of "family"—very distant relations, if they were even related at all—for dinner because she loved to cook for a houseful of people.

Elena was all too willing to help. If she kept her

hands busy and her mind occupied, maybe she could stop thinking about Travis. Ever since his harsh dismissal last week, she'd been crying on and off.

She had talked to Daniel twice, but she wasn't ready to go back to work. She hadn't had a vacation in years; maybe she was just tired and needed a rest.

Or maybe she would resign—not to spite Daniel, though. She'd been feeling restless even before the kidnapping. Accepting a job as Daniel's assistant had been impossible to turn down, and she'd enjoyed it a lot at first. She was good at anticipating and meeting his needs.

But she wanted something more. She had a degree in business, and she'd always thought that someday she would run her own company. She had successfully launched the Logan Oil day care center—she'd submitted a budget, located the physical space, overseen the renovation, hired people—and sometimes she'd wiped sticky fingers and changed diapers.

She liked being in charge of something, she realized. But what?

She would have to make some decisions soon. Daniel had said to take her time, but he could only be so patient. He needed an assistant.

Rosalie had put Elena to work getting some stains out of her good tablecloth and napkins. She stood at the sink using cold water, soap and a soft brush on a gravy stain. "I thought you didn't like this tablecloth because it was so hard to get the wrinkles out."

"Well, it's still nice." Rosalie sat at the kitchen

table going through her recipe file and making a shopping list. "Are there enough of the cloth napkins? I'm counting fourteen."

"Fourteen! Mama, where will we put them all?"

"Cousin Marietta is bringing a friend. I couldn't say no. The children can sit at the picnic table on the covered porch. The weather is supposed to warm up and be nice. Easy on the tablecloth. You're about to scrub a hole in it."

She was. The stain was gone and probably had been for some time. She rinsed it well and took it outside to hang on the clothesline to dry. Her mother abhorred electric clothes dryers and refused to have one in the house, although she'd come to terms with the washing machine. Jury was still out on the dishwasher.

Fourteen people. At least five of them were kids; Elena carried a stack of stoneware dishes—the ones from her childhood that were indestructible—out to the covered porch. It was still a little chilly out there, but the sun was out and in a couple of hours, when dinner was served, it would be comfortable.

She spread a colorful tablecloth over the picnic table, one she remembered from many Thanksgivings ago, when *she* was relegated to the children's table. She made short work of setting out plates and silverware. She wondered where the covered dish was that was shaped like a turkey. Kids always loved that. Usually Rosalie filled it with beans and rice.

She set the dining room table for nine. It was going to be crowded.

Let's see, her parents, her aunt, uncle and herself made five. Then there was Tanta Maria's *abuela,* her grown quasi-cousin Marietta, Marietta's friend and… Who was that last person?

"Mama, who's the fourteenth person?" Elena called to her mother in the kitchen as she dragged the card table inside from the garage.

"I don't know what you mean, fourteenth person. It's all the usual ones, plus Marietta's friend."

"So, it's you and me and Papa, Tanta Maria and Cesar, Marietta plus her friend and the five kids—that's still only thirteen."

"Right. Thirteen is an unlucky number to have at dinner." Rosalie crossed herself.

"Okaaay…so who is lucky fourteen?" And why was her mother acting so cagey?

"Elena, I think your father's calling you. You promised to keep an eye on him and that meat smoker—honestly, he is going to burn the house down with that thing."

Uh-huh. "Mama, you're not trying to fix me up, are you? Because the last time you did that, I wound up almost kissing my own cousin."

"I forgot he was a cousin! Anyway, he was a second or third cousin, and don't hold that against me the rest of my life."

"Whoever it is, you can just un-invite him. If

you're worried about thirteen at the table, I'll eat in my room."

"Don't be silly. Go on—see what your father wants."

Great. Just great. As if she didn't have enough to worry about, now her mother was foisting unwanted potential boyfriends on her.

Her father wasn't really calling, but Elena went out to the backyard anyway. Elmer and her uncle Cesar—not a real uncle, but as close as one—were standing guard over the smoker.

"There's my girl," Elmer said with a smile.

"Hey, *pequeña,* how's my favorite honorary niece?" Cesar asked.

Elena gave Cesar a hug. "Pretty good," she answered automatically, because to answer truthfully would be a real downer.

"You still working for the billionaire?"

Elmer made a hissing noise and slashed a finger across his throat.

"It's okay, Papa. I'm taking a leave of absence. I might be ready for a change. I know, it seems stupid to leave a job that's so cushy and pays so well, but..."

"She's mad at her boss," Elmer said. "He lied to her."

"Ah. So it's a matter of principle," Cesar said.

"Sort of," Elena agreed.

"Principle doesn't keep you warm at night, *pequeña.* In this economy, for the right salary, I could overlook a whole lot of principle."

Elena smiled and shook her head. "I'm still mulling things over. Hey, Papa, Mama is setting me up again. She invited someone to dinner, but she won't tell me who."

"Don't look at me. I don't interfere in your personal life."

"So she didn't say anything to you?"

"Not a word."

Elena groaned. Whoever the poor schmuck was, she couldn't un-invite him at this late hour. He probably had nowhere else to go.

The rest of the dinner guests started arriving at around noon. There was lots of hugging, lots of rapid Spanish, exclamations about how Elena was prettier every time they saw her and how much the children had grown.

Elena ate it all up. Ever since going to work for Daniel, she hadn't seen as much of everybody because she worked such long hours, and even when she wasn't working, she was on call. She might actually miss the frenetic activities associated with Daniel's busy schedule—arranging meetings, planning parties, making reservations for hotels and limos and haircuts and massages.

But she would enjoy this time off while she had it. She would look at it as a gift. She would spend time with her "cousins"—the people who'd helped them when they first moved to this country and had become as dear as any blood relatives.

And she would enjoy the simple gathering, so different than Daniel's expensive parties. No designer table toppers or silk table linens, just a crepe-paper turkey and some greenery from the backyard that Rosalie had woven into a garland. No live music, but the cheery Christmas carols coming from the music channel on TV made her smile.

By the time the turkey was done, the mystery guest hadn't shown and Elena was beginning to hope he never would. But just as Rosalie called everyone to their respective tables, the doorbell rang.

"I'll get it!" screamed little Maria, who at seven was the youngest member of their party. She was already hyper from snitching marshmallows from the bag while Elena topped the candied yams.

Elena retreated to the kitchen, ostensibly to bring another dish to the table. She wondered if it was too late to plead a migraine and escape to her room. No, her mother would see through that in a second. Elena had never suffered migraines. So she gritted her teeth and braced herself. Then she heard a familiar voice.

"Thank you for inviting me, Rosalie."

"There's always room at the table for one more, Travis."

EVEN AS TRAVIS greeted his hostess and shook Elmer's hand, his eyes scanned the living room, then the dining room for Elena. He was taking a huge risk coming here. He had no idea how Elena would receive him. She might dump a bowl of gravy over his head, and he wouldn't blame her. He'd treated her rather harshly when they were last together.

Where was she?

"Elena," Rosalie called over her shoulder. "Your friend Travis is here. And he's brought homemade cornbread. Travis, did you make this yourself?"

"Yes, ma'am," he answered, still scanning the room for Elena.

Finally, she appeared at the kitchen door, holding—oh, dear God, she was holding a gravy boat, filled to the brim and steaming hot. Was his unpleasant fantasy about to become reality? But then he focused on Elena herself. She looked like a Latina angel, her golden-brown hair tousled around her face like a halo, her features natural with just a hint of makeup.

For a couple of seconds, he couldn't breathe at all. The rest of the room receded into the background, and everyone went quiet. It was a cliché, he knew, but now he understood what it meant when people said "time stood still."

Then she smiled, and everything went back to normal. Except his heart. It started beating twice as fast as was healthy.

"Hello, Travis. How nice that you could come."

Nice for her? Or for him?

He almost hadn't come. In fact, when Rosalie had first called him, he had thanked her for the invitation but answered it with a definitive no. Elena likely hadn't mentioned their argument, so her mother would have no way of knowing how awkward it would be for them to spend the holiday together.

"Where will you spend Thanksgiving, then?" Rosalie had asked.

"I'll...I'll probably go to a bar and watch the football game." The football game was a matchup between the UT Longhorns and the Texas A&M Aggies.

"No! You can't do that! On Thanksgiving, you're supposed to be with friends and family."

"I wish I could. But my brother is in prison, and my niece is staying with a family that won't let me near her."

"You find family where you look for it," Rosalie admonished. "When Elena, Elmer and I arrived in this country, we had only the clothes on our backs. We left behind our older son, our parents, brothers and sisters, most of whom we will never see again. But there were people here who reached out to us. They fed us, put a roof over our heads, helped us find jobs, taught us English. Our first Thanksgiving we went to the house of total strangers, and we ate the most wonderful meal we'd ever had in our lives. The people who helped us became our new family.

"Maybe you're not in need the way we were, but everyone needs family. I am offering the Marquez family to you. Sit at our table. Break bread with us. Thanksgiving is the chance to be grateful for all the things we have in our lives, not a time to feel sorry for what we've lost."

So she'd shamed him into saying yes. He might have to face Elena's displeasure, but that was infinitely better than having Rosalie scold him again. She might look like a nice, middle-aged lady, but he wouldn't deliberately run afoul of her.

Elena was another matter. He didn't particularly relish the thought of her ire directed at him. She'd been remarkably tolerant of his poor behavior in the past, but at some point she had to get her fill. Then he had no idea what might happen. He'd been treated to a woman's temper once before and would have lost his front teeth if he hadn't ducked fast enough. He already knew Elena could throw a wrench.

"We were all just sitting down at the table, so you're right on time," Rosalie said. "Here, take this seat." Rosalie proceeded to organize everyone exactly where she wanted them. She and Elena would be closest to the kitchen; Travis was next to Elena. He shouldn't have been surprised—Elena's mother was clearly playing matchmaker.

Too bad she was doomed to disappointment.

"Elena, make introductions while I bring the rest of the food in."

"Of course. Travis, this is my Tanta Maria and Uncle Cesar, and my cousin Marietta…." She went around the table and everyone greeted him cordially. They asked the usual polite getting-to-know-you questions about his work and how he knew Elena. Elena didn't help out, leaving it to him to manufacture the details and match his story to what they had already told her parents.

An elderly woman dressed all in black was introduced as someone's grandmother. Apparently she didn't speak English, because every so often she would tug on the sleeve of her granddaughter and ask questions in whispered Spanish, gesturing and pointing at Travis. She didn't seem especially pleased to be sharing her table with him, because she referred to him as an opportunistic interloper with a look of bad news about him, and then called him a *comepinga,* which he couldn't translate exactly, but he knew it was a bad thing

The meal was everything a man could wish for on Thanksgiving and then some. In addition to the promised *pastelitos,* which were like nothing Travis had ever tasted, Rosalie had baked the enormous turkey to perfection. The dressing had walnuts, raisins and peppers in it, and the result was surprisingly tasty. All the customary dishes were there—mashed potatoes, corn on the cob, candied yams—which Rosalie emphasized had been Elena's doing—cranberry sauce and three kinds of pie for dessert.

He hadn't had much of an appetite that week, and even when he felt like eating, he'd had little time to fix anything, what with all the trips he'd been making to the Social Services office, the lawyer's office and the place where he had to take a lie detector test and have his fingerprints taken, just to make sure he was who he said he was. It was nice to take a break from all that and bask in the love and warmth of Elena's family.

Elena herself, however, had little to say to him. She didn't seem angry.... More resigned, and maybe a little curious about why he'd accepted the dinner invitation when a week ago he had so clearly kicked her out of his life.

He wanted to explain it to her, but he had to get her alone first, and privacy was at a premium with this crowd of friends and relatives. Even the patio and backyard were filled with screaming kids and a couple of dogs that might or might not belong there. He hadn't seen a dog on his first visit.

As soon as the meal was over, most of the men and some of the women slipped into the living room to watch football. The grandmother retired to one of the bedrooms to take a nap. It was probably time for Travis to leave.

He stacked a few dishes and tried to take them to the kitchen, but Rosalie predictably wouldn't allow it. "Travis, haven't we had this discussion about guests and dishes?"

"Now, Rosalie, last time we talked, you said to treat you like family. And families help clean up after a meal."

"Fair enough, and I'll let you next time, okay? But really, didn't you say something about wanting to watch football?"

Sure, he liked football as much as the next guy, but he didn't have any particular loyalty to either school.

"I probably should go——" he tried, but Rosalie clicked her tongue and shook her head.

"We both know no one is expecting you today."

"Mama!" Elena sounded horrified. "If he wants to leave, let him."

"He doesn't want to leave—he's just trying to be polite. But there will be plenty of leftovers later."

"He's probably tired of us by now," Elena argued. "He's not used to being around so many people. Maybe he'd like to have part of the holiday to himself."

Rosalie considered this. "Well, perhaps you should take a walk, Travis. It's a beautiful day, and you could have some peace and quiet for a few minutes. Elena, take him outside and show him how to get to that nice jogging trail behind our house."

"Oh, um…" She looked at Travis uncertainly.

"A walk sounds like just the thing," he said. "Elena, I'd love it if you could show me the trail."

She hesitated a few moments, and then wiped her hands on the dishcloth she'd slung over her shoulder. "Okay, but I don't want to leave Mama with all these dishes——"

"Nonsense." It was Tanta Maria. "I'll help Rosalie clean up. I don't like football, and it will give us a chance to catch up. You two young people go have fun."

Fun. Probably not an apt description of the mood between himself and Elena.

"Okay." Elena handed the towel to her aunt. "Let

me get a sweater. I'll meet you on the front porch."
She shot her mother a look that could only be described as venomous before she left the room to find her sweater.

Travis grabbed his jacket from the coat closet and went to the porch to wait for her, and she appeared a couple of minutes later. Had she brushed her hair? Swiped on some lip gloss? He was jazzed to think she might have primped, even a little, for him.

"The jogging trail is this way." She headed for the corner.

It was a pleasant neighborhood. Lots of people were outside enjoying the weather—kids tossing the football, moms with babies in strollers, people walking dogs.

She stopped at the corner. "The trail is right down there, at the corner of that fence. It runs for about a mile around the park."

Suddenly he realized she wasn't going to walk with him. She'd turned back toward the house.

"Elena. Where are you going?"

She stopped. "I figured you'd had enough of me and my family."

"Not you. Walk with me."

She hesitated and then nodded. "Okay, but only to keep my mother off my back."

They walked in silence for a few minutes. Elena had her arms crossed, her shoulders hunched as if it were cold, although it had to be close to seventy degrees.

"So, what are you doing here?" she finally said. "I thought you were done with me."

"I'm pretty sure you've noticed your mother is a little bit hard to say no to."

"Yes, she is, but I don't for a minute believe you couldn't have come up with a suitable excuse. Or you could have just said no, told her you and I had no chance of becoming a couple. You're not some shrinking violet."

She was right—he could have found a way out of this. "I guess the truth is I wanted to come. I wanted to see you again."

"That's not how I saw it last week. I think your exact words were, 'You've helped enough.'"

"So, I wanted to see you again to apologize. You touched a nerve. I acted like an ass, and I'm really sorry. I owe you this tremendous debt of gratitude, and instead I treat you like—"

"Stop. You were right to be angry. I don't have any right to psychoanalyze you. Whatever your choices regarding MacKenzie, I'm sure you have good reasons."

"Yeah, well, I came here to tell you something in addition to apologizing. I took the folder you gave me to the social worker. She's going to launch an investigation into the Stovers. And she's already removed MacKenzie from their home."

"Travis, that's wonderful! So you stopped the adoption?"

"Probably. Postponed it, at least. But I realized

you were right. There are plenty of parents out there—nice parents, good parents—who would want to adopt a sweet, pretty, well-behaved child like my niece. But even the nicest parents aren't going to want to give her up once Eric gets out of prison. So I talked to that lawyer of Daniel's. I applied to adopt MacKenzie myself, and the lawyer seems to think I have a chance."

Elena's reserved manner vanished in a heartbeat. She smiled as if she'd just grabbed the brass ring on the merry-go-round. "That's wonderful!" Then she did something really unexpected. She hugged him.

CHAPTER THIRTEEN

TRAVIS PUT HIS ARMS around Elena, relishing the feel of her softness against him. She smelled like a fresh breeze with a hint of roasted marshmallow. Her hair was soft as a kitten against his cheek. God, she was so warm and vibrant, so alive, and it made him realize that for a long time, he'd been…well, if not dead, then certainly living less than a full life.

That was going to change. Once he had responsibility for MacKenzie—if he did—everything he did would have consequences for him and for her, as well.

He didn't want to release Elena, but eventually he had to. The embrace was becoming awkwardly long. He either had to let her go…or kiss her. And the last time he'd kissed her, he'd nearly lost control of himself.

He let her go.

"You're going to be a great dad, you'll see."

"I'll be her uncle Travis no matter what the adoption papers say. She has only one daddy. And maybe, just maybe, the adoption won't even be necessary."

"Have you heard something?" she asked eagerly. "I hate being out of the loop."

"No one is being too chatty with me, either. I mean, just because Project Justice took on Eric's case, that doesn't mean I'm anyone's favorite person. I told them pretty much everything I know in the application—"

"Did you get it sent in?"

He nodded. "I finished it that night. It took a while. A librarian helped me. Honestly, I can't believe I never asked one for help before. She was really nice. But I'd convinced myself I had to go it alone, that it would somehow…I don't know, diminish me to admit I couldn't do something by myself."

"We all have hot buttons."

"Really? What are your hot buttons?"

She thought for a moment. "I hate it when people abuse their power."

"Is that why you're so mad at Daniel? Because he threw his weight around?"

"Yes, exactly. You know that saying, with great power comes great responsibility? Normally, Daniel doesn't take advantage of people just because he can. But he wanted his revenge against you and he got it, never mind what I wanted, even though I was the supposed victim."

"You're not still thinking of quitting your job, are you?"

"I don't know. I've been doing a lot of thinking. Just because someone is really good at a job doesn't necessarily mean it's the right job for them. I want something more."

"More than living in a mansion, driving fancy cars…? Most people would kill for your job."

"I know. And I don't want to seem ungrateful. Daniel has done a lot for me and my whole family."

"Your family?"

"My father got a job working in one of Logan Oil's fields in Louisiana. The Logans wouldn't have known we existed, except there was an accident. My father was trained to be a doctor. He took quick action and saved a man's life. Daniel's father was so impressed that he helped my dad get the certification he needed to practice. After the senior Mr. Logan died, Daniel continued to take an interest in our family. He helped me get into college and gave me my first job."

"But you don't want to keep working as his assistant simply out of gratitude—is that it?"

"Something like that. Maybe I'm deluding myself. I don't even know where I'd go or what I'd do. All I know is, I feel this…this *yearning* to do something important. To make a difference."

She'd sure as hell made a difference in his life. If not for her, he wouldn't have a sliver of a chance at stopping MacKenzie's adoption and freeing his brother.

That was how things had started with Judith. She'd referred him to all her rich friends for their home repairs, then she'd filled out the papers he needed to set up his business. Then she'd decided that wasn't good enough, and she'd pushed him into applying for a corporate job with a large home builder—which, thank God, he hadn't gotten.

"Maybe you should just talk to Daniel," Travis said. "Tell him what you just told me. He probably has another job somewhere that you'd like better."

"Maybe," she said without much enthusiasm.

They walked along the path through the park in companionable silence for a while. Finally Elena spoke again. "Have you worked out childcare for MacKenzie?"

"First I have to figure out where I'm living. Have to find a place with a separate bedroom for Mac-Kenzie, near a good school." Eric's house was just sitting there, empty, but there was no way he could expect MacKenzie to live in the house where her mother was murdered.

"Then I have to find day care for after school, holidays, teacher in-service days, a month at Christmas… Oh, sorry. Didn't mean to dump all that on you. It's just… There's a lot on my mind right now."

"What about a nanny? If someone could care for MacKenzie at home, it might be less disruptive than taking her to yet another place—"

"I'd like that. But the cost is…well, not something I can cover. My business does okay, but not enough for that."

"I could do it."

"What?"

She'd stopped in the middle of the path. A teenage boy on Rollerblades almost ran her over. "No, really, I could. I love kids. In fact, one of the things I really missed working at Daniel's was that I wasn't around kids. I used to run the day care center at Logan Oil."

"You'd trade your job as a billionaire's personal assistant to be a nanny working for minimum wage?"

"We could try it out. I'll have to make a decision about my assistant job eventually, but maybe not until the end of the year. And if I took care of MacKenzie, it would have the added benefit of getting me out of my parents' house for several hours every day, which, believe me, would be a huge blessing for all of us. I don't know if you noticed, but my mother can be a tad overbearing."

Travis's head spun. If he had responsible day care in place, he could get MacKenzie right away. Missy said they could expedite him as a foster parent while all the adoption stuff got sorted out. That way, he wouldn't have to rip MacKenzie out of yet another home at some later date once he got everything settled.

Hell, what was he thinking? Elena couldn't be his nanny. For one thing, he was having a hard time keeping his hands off her even now.

"You could get an apartment with a spare bedroom," she went on, "and I could live in. You wouldn't have to pay me beyond room and board."

"Wait a minute. You would work for me…for free?"

"For room and board. I mean, it's just temporary, right? Then you'll have time to explore all the child-care options and pick the best one. Travis, this is a great idea!"

Travis let himself imagine what it might be like to have a bigger apartment, to have MacKenzie living there, to have Elena with them, sleeping under the same roof. The fantasy felt suspiciously like a family.

He shook his head. "No, no, Elena, this can't work."

"Why?"

"Because I…I couldn't live in the same apartment with you and not… It would drive me insane, okay?"

"Am I that annoying?"

"Not annoying. Alluring. Sexy." Did he have to paint a picture for her?

"Oh. Oh…." She started walking again. She wouldn't look at him.

"Surely this doesn't come as a big surprise to you."

"Well, yes, it sort of does."

"I kissed you. Twice."

"I thought I kissed you." She almost squirmed, she was so uncomfortable talking about it.

"You might have started it, but I finished it. I liked having you in my arms. A guy like me, well, how often do I get to kiss a classy Cuban goddess like you?"

"I don't know. I guess that's something that's yet to be determined." Finally she peered at him through her lashes. "Cuban goddess, huh? That's stretching it."

"I don't think it is."

They had almost completed the circular path around the park. He had to get this thing settled now. He wasn't going back inside the Marquez house, where he was likely to get sucked into another round of pie and football.

"Elena, I came over here today because I didn't like how we said goodbye. But we've fixed that now. I've apologized. And now I'm going to leave—for good this time. Because if I don't… I mean, I can't just be friends with you. I can't be your employer. I can't let you live with me or take care of MacKenzie. You get that, right?"

"Because you don't think we could—"

"We can't. You're not thinking straight. You went through a trauma. You're at a crossroads. That's no reason to make reckless decisions. And throwing in your lot with mine—that, dear Elena, is reckless. So I'm gonna leave you now. Again. I won't come back."

She stopped walking again. "You can't just—"

He kept walking. He had to. No matter how she tempted him. He would drive over to Eric's house and mow the lawn, something he did every week or so. The physical activity might keep his mind off what he was walking away from.

Elena made a strange sound, somewhere between a groan and a scream. "You can't just decide that!

Don't I get a say? I know my own mind. But I guess you don't trust my judgment, either. First Daniel, now you."

"Goodbye, Elena. Tell your mother thanks."

"Oh, no you don't." Elena ran to catch up with him, and then turned to face him, walking backward. "Do you have any idea what kind of hell she'll put me through when you don't come back? And if I tell her you're never coming back? She'll think I did something to drive you off."

"I'll tell her you didn't."

"You think I won't take you up on that offer? I've got your phone number. I'll make her call you. And *you* can explain."

He turned that possible conversation over in his mind. *Nope. The outcome wouldn't be pretty.* "She'll just have to understand."

"Understand that you're being unreasonable?"

"Understand that it could never work. Tell her about how I threw you into a truck and kidnapped you. Tell her that. You think she'll want you to have anything to do with me if she knows the true story of how we met?"

"I'm not sure. But my father would kill you. So that secret is never coming out. Never."

Maybe she was right about that. He couldn't afford to have anyone wanting to kill him, not if he expected MacKenzie's adoption to go through. Although Missy was on his side, her opinion could change if she sensed anything the slightest bit hinky with Travis. Her first responsibility was to MacKenzie.

No drama, Missy had said. He needed to look as stable as possible.

Elena put her hands on her hips. "Do you make it a habit to sabotage your happiness?"

"Do you make it a habit to tell people how they ought to live their lives? I will *not* be your charity case, your do-gooder project."

"That's not—" She stopped. The hurt expression on her face nearly did him in.

He softened his voice. "I'm not trying to be hurtful. I just need for you to understand why I shouldn't be part of your life."

"You keep saying that. But here you are."

"Quitting you is kind of like quitting smoking. Maybe it takes a few tries, a few backslides, before I succeed."

"Fine. Walk away. I won't call you again. I can't guarantee what my mother will do, but I'll try to impress upon her that she needs to drop it."

"It's for the best."

"Whatever. Give me your phone."

He pulled his cell phone from his pocket and handed it to her. "Who are you going to call?"

"No one." With dexterous fingers, she quickly tapped the screen. "I'm giving you my cell number. *Por si las moscas.*"

It took a moment for Travis to translate. "For the flies?"

"It's a Cuban saying. It means 'just in case.'"

They were almost back to the Marquez house. He was trying to come up with the words to soften his abrupt departure when he noticed Elena was no longer focused on him. She was staring past him at something in the street.

He looked where she was looking and immediately saw what had shocked her. Someone had spray-painted his truck. Even with the previously colorful paint job, the new addition stood out in shocking relief.

"You'll never get her," Elena read out loud.

"I can read it," he snapped.

"I didn't say you couldn't!"

"You didn't tell me about the jealous boyfriend."

"Travis, I don't have a jealous boyfriend. Or an unjealous boyfriend, either."

"A stalker, then."

"No, I don't have any stalkers. I haven't dated anyone in a long time, and no one has shown any interest."

"I find that hard to believe."

"Travis, I don't think this is about me at all. I think it's about MacKenzie."

Oh, God. That possibility hadn't even occurred to him. "In front of your house?"

"Maybe someone's been following you."

That thought sent a chill up his spine. Someone following him, keeping tabs on him.

"The Stovers must be pretty mad that you ratted

them out," Elena said. "They've lost MacKenzie, and they might lose their other meal tickets, as well, if Social Services takes the other foster kids away."

"You think they might try to get back at me? Make sure I can't adopt her, either?"

"I wouldn't rule it out. You better be careful. They might try to dig up dirt on you or goad you into something."

"Or maybe they just want revenge. Obviously they know where I live. And now they know where *you* live."

Elena issued an unladylike snort. "I'm not afraid. People who express themselves through graffiti are too chicken to confront anyone face-to-face. They feel powerless, and scary-sounding anonymous threats are the best they can do."

"Well, I wouldn't bet your safety on psychological statistics. You should be afraid. Be careful. Tell your parents to be careful, too. Lock your doors. Don't answer the door to strangers. Stay alert."

"Travis, I had to go to bodyguard school before I could work for Daniel. I know the drill. I'll be careful."

"Okay. Damn, I'm sorry to bring this onto your doorstep."

"It's okay."

He unlocked his truck.

"Wait. Aren't you going to call the police?"

"They won't come, not for vandalism."

"It's more than vandalism. It's a threat."

"No. I don't want any official record of any problems involving the police. Better if I act like it doesn't bother me."

Elena looked around nervously. "You think he's watching?"

"No. He's long gone." He hoped. "Goodbye, Elena." If he hadn't already been convinced he didn't belong in Elena's world, this little incident did the trick. He was *not* going to endanger Elena and her family by allowing the Stovers to think he cared for her.

"YES, I THINK this place is wonderful," Missy enthused as Travis showed her around his new digs. He'd always thought the next time he moved, it would be into his own house, a little slice of real estate to call his own. But buying a house took time: contracts, inspections, insurance, loan approvals... All that stuff took weeks Travis didn't have. So he'd resigned himself to yet another boring, white-walled apartment. A two-bedroom right in his own complex had been vacant and available.

But Thanksgiving Day, on his way home from mowing the lawn at his brother's house, he'd spotted a yard sign that piqued his interest: Rent to Own. And it was in the front yard of a cute little two-story structure with a wraparound porch. "Lease today— move in tomorrow."

The house was in his brother's old neighborhood, Timbergrove, but on the other side of White Oak

Bayou, where the houses were more modest frame cottages from the 1950s.

He'd gone the next day to look and decided it was perfect. It needed some work, too, which meant he could get it at a good price. When he'd told the owner he was interested in buying the house as is, but renting it until the sale closed, the owner was amenable. They'd quickly settled on terms and signed some papers, and by Tuesday he was moving his stuff in. He'd called Missy on Wednesday morning, eager for her to see how serious he was about making things good for MacKenzie.

"This is her room, see?" He opened the door to the second-largest bedroom. It had lots of windows. "I haven't bought the furniture yet, but I will. Maybe today."

Missy laughed. "For someone who had to be dragged kicking and screaming into the father role, you're remarkably enthusiastic."

"I have to admit, the idea has grown on me. But I'm not her father. I'm Uncle Trav. Her father will be coming home."

"Has she visited her father in prison?"

"We've managed it only a few times. Getting the Stovers to cooperate is almost impossible. I schedule the visit, but then they call and tell me MacKenzie is sick or something has come up. They won't let *me* take her to visit, God forbid. But Eric won't be a stranger. They talk on the phone. He writes her letters. She remembers him."

"You're a good uncle."

"I try."

He was surprised at how much he wanted to adopt MacKenzie, when two weeks ago he'd been adamantly opposed to the idea. He supposed he owed a good part of his attitude change to Elena. She'd forced him to take a good, hard look at himself, at his life and his motivations for declaring he couldn't be a fit guardian. He'd been startled to realize she was right. He was afraid—afraid he wasn't up to the task. Afraid he wouldn't be as good a father as Eric was, or that he would somehow inadvertently do some damage to that poor fragile child.

He was still afraid. But he'd realized that shouldn't stop him from trying to do what was right.

"Do you have childcare worked out yet?" Missy asked, checking out the bathroom.

"There are three day care centers within a couple of miles," Travis replied. "I'm going to check them out tomorrow."

"Have you thought about a nanny? I only ask because MacKenzie might feel more secure dealing with just one caregiver in her own home. Day care can be wonderful, don't get me wrong. And socializing with other children is great. But day care has its own problems. For one thing, if your child is sick, you can't leave them at day care, and then what do you do?"

"I guess I would stay home with her," Travis said. But what would he do if he *had* to go to work?

Someone had to supervise his work crews. Jobs had to get finished on time if he wanted to get paid. "I'd love to have a nanny—"

"I know, it's expensive. My own kids are in day care as we speak, so I understand, believe me."

But he had a perfectly good candidate for a nanny, at least a temporary one.

It didn't help matters that everywhere he looked in the house, he pictured Elena. She'd planted that seed in his mind—that she could be MacKenzie's nanny. He saw her pushing MacKenzie on the tire swing that he planned to hang from the big tree in the backyard. He saw her fixing sandwiches in the kitchen. He saw her helping him paint the living room, which currently was a particularly revolting shade of mustard yellow—and that had absolutely nothing to do with childcare.

"Well, as soon as you work all that out, you can bring MacKenzie to live with you."

"I… Really? What about… I thought maybe my background would make things more difficult."

"It's different when you are the child's next of kin and her biological father is willing to surrender his parental rights to you. I've gotten to know you pretty well, Mr. Riggs, and I know you'll take good care of MacKenzie. You won't do everything perfectly—no one does. But you're stable and responsible and clearly you love your niece. Wow, this is just a great house."

"Thanks." But the word came out as a squeak.

He could have MacKenzie in a matter of days. "I...I might have the nanny thing worked out. A family friend volunteered to take care of MacKenzie. She has experience managing a day care center, and she loves kids."

"That sounds great. Let me know. I'll get out of your hair. I know you have work to do."

"Thanks, Missy, you've been great."

As Missy had pointed out, he needed to get to work. His crews were reliable, but they tended to get lazy and move a little slow if he didn't make an appearance every so often. The bank was breathing down his neck to get the house finished, because they wanted to put it on the market in January. Lots of people started to think about moving after the holidays were over.

But he lingered for a few minutes after Missy left, walking from room to room, opening some of the boxes.

Hell, who was he kidding? It might take him weeks to work out childcare—unless he called Elena.

She would never let him hear the end of it. He'd been the one to firmly insist they had to stay away from each other. And he was going to cave in yet again and drag her back into his life.

At least the Stovers didn't know the location of this house, he reasoned. And if Elena was living there in the spare room, it would be easier to ensure her safety. He hadn't heard a peep out of the Stovers since the graffiti incident; he hoped that would be the end of it.

Ah, hell, he knew he was going to do it. He should have erased her from his contact list when he was determined to stay out of her life. But he hadn't, and he was still one phone button away from hearing her voice.

He pushed it, his heart beating furiously. He'd never felt like this calling a woman before—not even his ex-wife when he'd been in his greatest throes of lust.

"Hello?" It was a man's voice.

What the hell? "I'm trying to reach Elena Marquez."

"Travis? Travis Riggs?"

Oh, God. He knew who that was. "Yes, it's me." Travis injected as much arrogance as he could into his voice. "Where's Elena?"

"This is a company phone, and she returned it to me this morning. She resigned, but I'm sure you knew that."

Oh, hell. "I thought she was just taking a leave of absence."

"Never mind. What the hell are you doing calling her? If you're harassing her, so help me I will hang you up by your—"

"I'm not harassing her. I know it sounds a little crazy, but we became friends."

"You expect me to believe Elena got friendly with a man who kidnapped her?"

"She's pretty amazing that way."

"We'll see about that." Daniel disconnected.

Damn it to hell, now what? Daniel would call Elena and give her the third degree, probably chew her out for being gullible enough to associate with an ex-con kidnapper, and, really, could he blame Daniel?

He wanted to warn her, but it was probably too late. Daniel was no doubt calling her on her new cell number—one Travis didn't have.

There was nothing he could do.

CHAPTER FOURTEEN

ELENA EXAMINED THE ancient Subaru and tried to put on a happy face. Uncle Cesar was letting her use it for free—it belonged to his daughter, who was away at a private university where they didn't allow freshmen to have cars. All she had to do was pay for insurance. She was going to need some kind of transportation to go for job interviews and such.

Daniel hadn't taken the news well that she wanted to resign. He'd blamed Travis, and he'd been dubious when she'd insisted Travis had tried to talk her *out* of quitting.

"The whole kidnapping thing did wake me up," Elena had tried to explain. "I've gotten way too comfortable here. Spoiled, even. I don't even have to buy my own toothpaste! I feel like I was in a cocoon, and now I'm a butterfly and I need to…migrate."

He hadn't appreciated her analogy. He kept asking what she wanted—shorter hours? More pay? An assistant?

"Didn't you ever want to make your mark in the world? You started your first business when you were sixteen."

"You have plenty of time to make your mark," he'd argued, but her mind was made up. He'd given her her final paycheck and accepted the phone, the computer and her keys.

"I know it's a little old and battered," Cesar was saying. "And it's nothing like those fancy cars you drove at your old job, but it'll get you where you need to go. The engine's all tuned up and it has new back tires. The air-conditioning is out, but you won't really need that for a while."

"It's wonderful, Uncle," she said. "I'm so grateful you're letting me use it. But won't Angela want it when she comes home for Christmas?"

"The kind of grades she's making, I wasn't going to give her the car back, anyway. Maybe in the summer."

Poor Angela. She'd never been the most studious girl, and Elena gave her points for getting into college at all.

She gave Cesar a hug. "Thanks. Can I take her out for a spin?"

"Anytime you want. It's all yours now."

As she walked around to the driver's side, she spotted her mother standing on the front porch, her arms crossed over her ample bosom.

"I'm going to drive around the block." Elena waved to her mother, but her mother didn't wave back. She just kept staring, her expression decidedly…angry. What was going on?

Elena closed the car door without getting in.

"I have to go, Elena," Cesar said. He'd probably noticed the expression on Rosalie's face and didn't want to tangle with her.

"Yeah, okay. Thanks again." Elena marched up to the front porch. "Mama? What's wrong?"

"How could you bring that man into our house? How could you let him eat at our table?"

"What, um, what man are you talking about?" But she knew. Who else could it be but Travis?

"You know who I'm talking about. That horrible man who *kidnapped* you. You never even told us what happened to you. Don't you think we have a right to know?"

"Mama, Mama, calm down. It's not what it seems."

"Did he or did he not throw you into the back of his truck and hold you hostage for more than twenty-four hours?"

"Who told you?" Oh, God, she hoped the story hadn't somehow leaked to the press. An official police report had probably been filed, but she had a feeling Daniel had found a way to hush it up, mostly to save her any embarrassment and save him from having to explain why he'd claimed his assistant was kidnapped when it appeared she hadn't been.

"It doesn't matter who told me. It's true?"

"It's true," she admitted. "But it was an act of desperation. His brother was going to lose his little girl for good—he just wanted someone to listen to him.

That was all. And he didn't hurt me. He took very good care of me—he made sure I had something to eat and that I was warm—"

"Did he touch you?"

"Touch me? Oh. No, of course not." She tried not to think about the kiss. "He was a complete gentleman."

"A gentleman kidnapper."

"Yes. I've forgiven him for what he did, and I want you to forgive him, too. He's a good man."

"*Estas comiendo de lo que pica el pollo!* He's a criminal! And this isn't the first time he's been in trouble. Mr. Logan said—"

"*Daniel* told you this?" She couldn't believe it. He'd tattled on her.

"Well, yes. He called wanting to talk to you. I guess he was upset because Travis called your old phone, looking for you." Rosalie lowered her voice. "If your father finds out about this, he's going to have a stroke."

Travis had called her? Despite being furious with Daniel, her heart lifted at the realization that Travis had opened the door between them again. She simply couldn't help herself. He was making it pretty damn hard for her to believe him when he said he wanted to stay out of her life, but she didn't care. She knew he was feeling a pull toward her just as she was drawn to him.

"I don't care what Daniel says, and I don't care what Travis did in the past. I can tell he's a good man who cares about his family, and I'm not stupid or naive. Excuse me." She walked past her mother and into the house, found her purse and dug out her new cell phone. It was a basic model, nothing like the fancy phone she'd used working for Daniel. She'd thought it was important to return that one to him with all of the phone numbers and data intact.

But she'd carefully copied down a few numbers and entered them into her new phone—including Travis's. She wasn't sure why she'd thought that necessary when she had no expectation that she would ever talk to him again.

Now she was glad she'd done it. She went into her bedroom, closed the door and dialed him without hesitation.

"Travis Riggs," he answered. Obviously he wouldn't recognize her new number.

"Travis? It's Elena."

He said nothing for several seconds. Then, "Elena, I'm so sorry. I—I called your number—"

"I know what happened. Daniel answered, and he wasn't too pleased you were calling me."

"To put it mildly. I think he blistered my eardrum. I guess he told you?"

"Worse. He talked to my mother. Ratted me out. I was ready to forgive him for the SWAT team incident, but now I'm really angry again."

"How did your parents react when they learned you'd been kidnapped?"

"My father doesn't know, thank God. But my mother... She knows what it's like to be judged unfairly. A lot of people were dead set against letting Cubans live in this country just because we managed to get our feet onto American soil before the Coast Guard caught us. We faced some pretty ugly attitudes. My mother should know not to judge someone—"

"Elena, she's just trying to protect you. No one wants their daughter associating with a criminal."

She took a deep breath, trying to clear her head. "Forget about all that. Travis, why did you call?"

"Oh. Well, I was going to talk to you about being MacKenzie's nanny. But there's no way now."

"I'll do it. I need to put some distance between myself and my parents."

"You haven't even met MacKenzie."

"Of course, you'll want to see whether she takes to me or not. She's a traumatized little girl and probably wary of strangers. I understand. But I think we should try."

She could almost hear Travis thinking on the other end of the line.

"Once I have childcare worked out," he said after a moment, "the social worker says I can at least get temporary custody of MacKenzie. She's not in a great situation now. They removed her from the Stover home and she's in some kind of temporary shelter place, like an orphanage or something. I keep seeing scenes from *Oliver Twist* in my head."

"Then let's do it! On a trial basis," she said quickly. "You can fire me anytime you want. Or if you find someone better, or you find a day care that you love—I'll understand. Meanwhile, at least you won't have to worry about her safety. I only have a few things. I can move in immediately."

"You're incredible, Elena. I never met anyone as open and forgiving as you."

That was odd. She would bet those were not the adjectives that came to mind when most people were asked to describe her. She'd been working on her resume earlier today and looking over some letters of referral she'd accumulated. *Professional. Efficient. Pleasant. Organized.* Those were the words people used to describe her. And sometimes, *brutally efficient* and *ruthlessly organized.*

That wasn't necessarily the kind of praise she wanted to live up to.

She realized Travis was waiting for some type of response from her. "Something about you makes me want to be open and forgiving, Travis. Don't ask me to explain it better than that. I can't."

TRAVIS WAS A mass of nerves as he waited for Elena. He'd spent the previous day furnishing both her room and MacKenzie's and feverishly unpacking, rushing from the work site to Ikea to his new home and back. He wanted everything to be perfect. With

Elena here, he could get MacKenzie by the end of the week.

He had to focus on MacKenzie's well-being and put aside his misgivings about Elena's decision to help him.

When a battered, red car pulled to the curb in front of his house, he was surprised. He'd expected to see Elmer's SUV, and he'd been worrying about Elena's lack of her own transportation. He wanted her to be able to pick up MacKenzie from school or take her to the park or the doctor or wherever, but his budget wouldn't stretch to cover a second vehicle.

His surprise quickly gave way to a host of other feelings at seeing Elena emerge from the car—relief that she hadn't changed her mind and sheer delight over her beauty, her grace, her bouncy step and the smile on her face. She wasn't just happy— she was happy to see him.

His heart swelled, and for a few startling moments he didn't recognize what he was feeling. Was he having a heart attack? No, way too pleasant for that.

Travis opened the door before she could ring the bell. "Elena." That was when it hit him. That alien feeling was happiness. He was genuinely happy for the first time in…well, maybe years. Before Tammy's murder he'd been relatively satisfied with his life, but it was like he'd had a glass ceiling over his emotions, not allowing them to soar too high, careful not to take too much joy in life. But he couldn't contain the feelings Elena brought out.

She stared at him for several heart-stopping seconds, and he wanted more than anything to take her in his arms and kiss her. But that would be sending the wrong message. Elena was now his employee—and he would pay her a salary, never mind that she'd offered to do it for free. He'd asked Missy what would be an appropriate amount, and it wasn't beyond his means.

Salary or no salary, he absolutely could not take advantage of the fact that he and Elena would be sharing a roof. Plus, he didn't want to confuse MacKenzie. Poor kid was probably confused enough.

"This house is great!" Elena finally said, breaking the spell. She wore jeans and clogs and a gauzy top that was perfectly modest, even as it teased his senses by what it didn't show. Her hair was pulled back in a no-nonsense ponytail and she wore hardly any makeup. She looked different than that polished, sophisticated woman he'd first met at the River Oaks mansion, but no less appealing.

"Thanks. I've been working night and day on it to get it ready. This is the living room." He took her on a quick tour of the downstairs, which consisted of the living room, dining room, a kitchen that hadn't been updated since the 1960s, a half bath and a screened-in porch.

Upstairs were the bedrooms plus two bathrooms. He was particularly proud of how MacKenzie's room had turned out. He'd bought her a twin bed with a bright pink quilt and some ruffly pillows, a small

desk and chair—not that a kindergartener had homework, but she might like to sit there and draw pictures or look at a picture book, he reasoned. Then
there was a shelf for her toys. He'd bought a couple
of stuffed animals and a doll to get her started, but
he didn't want to overwhelm her. He would let Eric
direct the rest of his toy purchases.

He'd also bought a fuzzy throw rug with a car-
toon kitten on it. The saleswoman had assured him
that every little girl would love it.

"This is so cute! You did this?" Elena looked
around, as if she expected him to be hiding an in-
terior designer somewhere.

"I tapped into my inner Martha Stewart, what
can I say? The lady at Ikea helped. This is the bathroom. You and MacKenzie will have to share—I
hope that's okay."

"It's fine."

"I mean, I'd be happy to put you in the master
bedroom, and then you could have your own—"

"Don't be silly. When I was a kid, I had to share
a bathroom with four people. It's no big deal sharing with one little girl."

He held his breath as he showed Elena her room.
He'd bought an old-fashioned iron bed he'd spotted
at a garage sale and outfitted it with a new mattress
and box spring, crisp white sheets and a patchwork
quilt his grandmother had made. He'd had the quilt
in storage for his entire adult life, too sentimental to
part with it even though he had only vague memo-

ries of his mother's mother. He was pleased to be able to put it to good use. He'd also bought a dresser and nightstand, painted white with china knobs, and a small bookshelf.

"I'm sure it's not what you're used to…"

"It's wonderful."

"Yeah, but at Daniel's house and at your parents'—"

Elena's smile vanished. "Don't speak Daniel's name. He is dead to me."

"Isn't that a little melodramatic?"

She thought for a moment, worrying her lower lip with her teeth in a way that made his stomach clench with desire. "Okay, maybe he's not dead. But he's real sick."

"So you'll do it? You'll be MacKenzie's nanny?"

"Are you kidding?" The smile returned. "I've got all my stuff in the car. I'm moving in—try and stop me."

Dear God. Elena was moving in…today. Now. He'd thought he would have another day or two to prepare himself. He'd thought she would want to think it over before committing.

"Are you okay?" she asked, all soft concern. "You look like you swallowed a bug."

"I'm…fine. It's all just a little sudden. Everything's happening so fast. I'm not sure I'm ready."

"Of course you're ready." She stood very close to him, looking up at him with those molten brown eyes, her lips plump and moist and slightly parted, her breasts rising and falling as if she was out of breath. If he didn't know better, he would think…

"I'm ready," she whispered.

That was when it happened. He lost it—he lost the thread of self-control he'd desperately been holding on to. She was in his arms and his mouth was on hers, claiming her, branding, conquering.

This kiss was nothing like the first tentative kisses they'd stolen, Travis thought dazedly. This one was fueled by passion and heat and a need for Elena that had been building for weeks.

And here they were, alone in the house, neither of them in any hurry to be somewhere…and a brand-new bed with fresh sheets only a few steps away.

He tried to grab on to some sanity when Elena worked her hands under his blue knit shirt—one of his nicest, which he'd put on just because she was coming over. "Elena, wait, wait, we can't—"

"I am so tired of people telling me what I can and can't do. Do you want me?"

"It's not that simple."

"It's a yes-or-no question. Do you want to make love to me or not?"

"Of course I do!" he said perhaps a little too enthusiastically. "But…but we're not teenagers. We can't just—"

"Who says we can't?"

"Your father will kill me," he blurted out, because it was the first excuse that came to mind.

"My father won't know." She crossed her arms

in front of her, grabbed the hem of her blouse and pulled it over her head. His heart almost stopped seeing Elena's breasts in nothing but a shell-pink bra edged with lace. She saw his expression and smiled lazily, and he was a goner.

"You're too good for me...."

"That's a bunch of *mierda* and you know it. It's just sex. No one's going to demand you make an honest woman of me, okay?" she said with a laugh, but that was exactly what he was thinking—that Elena was the kind of woman a man made a commitment to, not one to be tumbled casually on a whim.

Although this didn't feel like a whim. It felt important. Significant.

"Stop overthinking, Travis. For just a little while shrug the world off your shoulders. Forget about everybody but you and me. It's okay to do that."

He wasn't sure it was okay, but he was beyond any ability to deny Elena. How could he say no to one of the best things to ever come into his lousy life?

They fell onto the bed. The sheets still had that "new" smell, since he hadn't had time to wash them. The quilt was as soft and fresh-smelling as the day he'd taken it down from the clothesline and vacuum-packed it. The pillows were brand-new, too—stuffed with fluffy down.

But none of it smelled as good as Elena, whose scent still reminded him of cinnamon and nutmeg, the most decadent pastry in the case. She'd managed to drag his shirt over his head, and now she was pressed against his bare chest. He pulled the elastic band off her ponytail, and her hair fell in a thick, glorious cloud around her face and then his face as she kissed him.

He wanted her naked. He flicked open the bra clasp in the middle of her back; maybe he hadn't learned much in high school, but his misspent youth had at least taught him how to gracefully remove a girl's bra.

She rose up far enough that she could wiggle out of the undergarment and toss it aside. Her breasts felt exquisite pressed against him, but he wanted to see them. See all of her. He'd imagined her naked countless times since they'd met, but he was willing to bet the reality would be even better.

Elena wasn't a tiny thing, she was tall and curvy in all the right places. Still, he was probably twice her weight, and he easily flipped her onto her back, then stood up and pulled her to her feet.

"What…?"

"I just want to see you."

"Ohhh." She smiled seductively and struck a pose, pouting and twisting a strand of hair around her finger.

"All of you," he clarified as he sat on the edge of the bed to remove his boots, keeping his gaze firmly focused on Elena.

She kicked off her clogs and made a show of slithering out of her jeans, turning away from him and wiggling her cute bottom far more than was strictly necessary. When she stood in front of him wearing only a pair of pink bikini panties, his breath whooshed out of his lungs.

How in the hell did he get so lucky that this amazing creature was giving herself to him?

She crooked a finger at him. "Stand up."

He followed orders. If she'd told him to walk across hot coals barefoot, he'd have done it, no questions asked.

Elena went to work on the button fly of his jeans, and he found himself wishing there were more than five buttons.

When she was done, she made as if to finish undressing him, but there was only so much of her sweet brand of torture he could take without losing what little control he still clung to. So he shoved the jeans and his boxers down and kicked them aside.

He knew she was looking at him. At *him,* the part of him that was hard as concrete right now. He could feel her hot gaze on him, and once again he found it hard to breathe.

"Damn, Travis. If I'd known what you were hiding—"

"What, you think I should wear it on the outside from now on?" But all joking aside, he was a big guy in more ways than one—big enough that he'd destroyed more than one condom.

Oh. Hell.

"Aren't you going to take my panties off?" she

said playfully, but then the smile abruptly fled her face. "What's wrong?"

"Nothing. It's just—I don't have any protection. And there's no way I'll risk—"

"No worries, I've taken care of that." She searched around the room for something—her purse, which she'd dropped on the floor near the door. After rooting around in it, she came up with a string of three small square packets.

"What are you doing with condoms in your purse?" he blurted out.

"These were in the stuff I brought from Daniel's house. I couldn't leave them lying around, certainly not in the bathroom or my bedroom—my mother snoops. So I hid them in my purse, which I guard like a pit bull."

She set the condoms on the nightstand. "Now, where were we?"

Second thoughts crept back into his brain. What if the condom failed? What if he got her pregnant—what would they do then?

"You're overthinking again, Travis." She led him back to the bed. How had she known? "Now finish undressing me. Please."

How could he say no? He would just have to be extra careful.

He hooked his index fingers under the elastic of her panties and slowly lowered them along her thighs, revealing a small, neat thatch of curls a few shades darker than the hair on her head. Also revealed was an obvious bikini tan line—and what a teeny-tiny bikini it must have been.

At Daniel's, she'd probably had the use of a swimming pool and servants to bring her a fresh, icy cocktail whenever needed. Or maybe not—did servants do stuff for other servants?

No swimming pool here. So many things she'd given up because of him.

He couldn't think about that now. He pushed those thoughts to the back of his mind and filled his head with thoughts of Elena and only Elena—her incredible golden skin, her strong but feminine hands and perfectly manicured nails, painted a whimsical lime green. Even the sound of her breathing turned him on, and he enjoyed hearing her sharp intake of breath when he pressed his mouth just to the side of her pubis.

Oh, yeah. That's what he was going to do. He sat her on the edge of the bed and knelt on the floor in front of her.

"Whoa, wait a minute…" She laughed nervously.

"What, you're chickening out now?" He kissed her knee. Lord help him, even her knees were sexy. And he didn't really think she was changing her mind. She just liked it better when she got to be bold and sassy and unpredictable, and he was the one who was unbalanced.

She made no further objections, but she was tense as she waited to see what he would do. He spent some time just kissing her knee, making little circles with his tongue. Eventually, as she relaxed, he nudged her legs open and moved to kissing and licking the inside of her thigh, sometimes alternating with his fingers, brushing the tips lightly, getting closer and closer to the center of her pleasure.

The scent of her—not the cinnamon scent, but something far more womanly and intoxicating—tickled his nose. The scent of desire. At last, he moved his mouth between her thighs.

By now she had opened her legs wide for him. The lips of her femininity were moist and pink, and he teased them open with his tongue.

It had been a long, long time since he'd pleasured a woman in this way. The few sexual liaisons he'd had in recent years had been quick and perfunctory, emotionless. Strictly a release. This... This was something completely different. He was a little surprised he remembered how.

He didn't operate entirely on memory. He let Elena's moans and sighs guide him, quickly learning which strokes she liked, how fast, how hard. She clasped her hands behind his head—maybe just for balance, but maybe to make sure he didn't escape.

He thought about escaping—bringing her to the brink of climax, then stopping, waiting until he was inside her before he brought her all the way. But she wouldn't let him.

When she finally reached her peak, she became a wild thing, a creature of passion rather than reason. Her cries echoed in the almost empty room.

Eventually she let go of him and fell back on the bed. "Travis. That wasn't fair."

"Oh, you're going to claim I took advantage?" He lay down beside her. They were diagonal on the bed, but since she'd already made a wreck of the covers, it didn't matter. He propped his head on his hand so he could watch her. He played with a lock of her hair, and then used the ends like a paintbrush to tickle one of her large, rosy nipples. She laughed and swatted his hand away.

"You don't like that?"

"I'm real sensitive right after I...you know." She blushed, perhaps embarrassed by the strength of her passion.

"I know," he said with a wicked laugh.

"You think that is funny? What you do to me?"

"I think it's great, but I don't kid myself. You can bring me to my knees and make me cry like a baby anytime you want."

"Think so? Let's find out." And just like that, she was up and straddling him, allowing his erection to press against her mons without entering her. Meanwhile she treated him to long, hot, wet kisses, deep kisses, so deep he could swear she touched his soul.

He couldn't resist touching her breasts. They were just the right size, exactly filling his hands, and her nipples reacted to every caress, hardening to pebbled peaks.

She was driving him wild. If she kept this up, he

would never get inside her. Then again, maybe that was the best thing.

He never used to be this worried about fathering a child by accident. But since deciding to take responsibility for MacKenzie, he couldn't be casual about it any longer.

Elena didn't allow him to brood about remote possibilities for long. She grabbed one of the condoms and opened the package.

"Are you sure?"

"What do you mean, am I sure? You think we can undo everything we've done in the past twenty minutes?"

She had a point.

Her hands trembled a bit as she smoothed the latex over him, giving him the idea that she wasn't as experienced as her earlier boldness had made him believe. That pleased him. Though he was as liberated as the next guy regarding a woman's sex life, he still wanted to feel as if he was at least a little bit special, not just one in a long line of conquests.

"There. I think we've got it."

"I hope so, because if I don't bury myself inside you in the next fifteen seconds I'm going to lose my mind."

"Yeah, but what a way to go crazy."

Elena might believe she was calling the shots, but Travis needed to be on top. It wasn't a macho thing; he just needed to be in control so he lasted longer than two seconds. Once again, he maneuvered her onto her back. Without hesitation she opened herself to him like a flower to the sun.

His stomach whooshed just before that magical moment, the one right before he made that most intimate contact. This was so incredible. Did she even realize the gift she was giving him?

Then she welcomed him inside, and he sank into her depths, filling her with as much of him as she could handle. He tried to take it slowly, let her get used to him. He couldn't bear the thought of causing her pain. But she didn't *look* like she was in pain as she raised her hips to meet him, encouraging him to go deeper still.

He could have ended it anytime. He was that primed. But he bit his lip and made himself hold on, wanting to give her as much pleasure as he took. He wasn't sure if she would climax again so soon after the first time, but given the way she was breathing and the glazed look in her eyes and the little noises in the back of her throat, she enjoyed the hell out of their coupling.

Biting his lip no longer worked. He resorted to biting his tongue—in between kissing Elena—until he couldn't hold on one more second.

His climax was the way he imagined the birth of a star might be: cataclysmic. Galaxies colliding. Epic amounts of energy changing form. By the time it was over, he couldn't tell where she began and he ended, they were so tightly entwined. They breathed in unison, inhaling great gulps of air. Their sweat mingled. His face was buried in her hair.

"Well," she said once she'd caught her breath. "I'd say this bedroom is officially broken-in."

CHAPTER FIFTEEN

ELENA SPRAWLED ON her new bed, an exhausted but satisfied heap. Her legs were tangled with Travis's. Her head leaned against his shoulder, their fingers entwined.

They'd barely spoken since their no-holds-barred lovemaking. Words didn't seem necessary, and anyway she didn't want to break the spell. No one knew they were here. For a little while at least, this was their private cocoon. The rest of the world might as well not exist.

From somewhere, a phone chimed. Wasn't hers, so it had to be his. *Damn it.*

"Damn it," he murmured, echoing her thoughts, and she grinned as he forced his body to an upright position and hefted himself off the bed. She turned to her side and watched him moving around, finding his jeans, digging into the pocket, all while completely and unabashedly naked.

He glanced at the screen. "Yeah, Leo, what's up… What? Whoa, slow down, my Spanish isn't *that* good….Oh, hell. I'll be there as soon as I can. I'm, like, half an hour away."

"What's wrong?"

"A pipe burst in the house I'm working on. My painters came back from lunch and found water everywhere. They managed to get the water turned off, but the place is flooded." As he recounted the conversation to her, he pulled on his clothes as quickly as he could. "I'm sorry, Elena. I'm so sorry but I have to go take care of this."

"Of course you do." She popped out of bed and started putting her clothes on, too.

"You don't have to rush around just because I do. You can stay in bed if you want."

"Without you? What fun would that be? Anyway, I'm not in the habit of lounging in bed in the middle of the day. I'm coming with you."

"Why would you do that? It's not going to be any fun."

"Maybe I can help. I'm *very* good at crisis management. I've dealt with everything from home repair emergencies to medical crises to the trickiest logistic snafus."

"If you want to come, I won't stop you, but taking a girl with me to work isn't how I like to show her a good time."

"You already showed me a good time." She grinned at him, and he grinned back.

"You are one in a million."

She finger-combed her hair and pulled it back into the elastic, stepped into her clogs and grabbed her purse. She was ready before him, but only because he had to put on work boots and tie them.

"How am I going to explain you to my crew?"

"Why do you have to? You're the boss. But if you feel compelled you can tell them the truth—your niece is coming to live with you, and I'm the nanny you just hired." She ducked into the bathroom and grabbed every towel she could get her hands on. "Do you have mops and buckets at the house?"

"Yes. Elena, you don't have to—"

"Maybe it's not as bad as it sounds."

"It's bad, all right." The floors upstairs had just been refinished, and the carpeting downstairs was brand-new. Now he would have to do it all over again.

"Don't borrow trouble 'til you see the situation for yourself."

"Okay, Mary Sunshine." He grabbed his keys, locked the house and they both climbed into his truck.

"What's the insurance situation?"

"I have insurance," he said impatiently.

"A washing machine hose burst at my parents' house a few months ago, and insurance covered it."

"It's not the money that worries me—it's the time. I promised the house would be done by the first of the year."

"So, you can hire an extra crew if you have to. I know dozens of qualified, bonded and insured craftspeople. Who's your insurance company?"

"Securex."

"Good, I've worked with them before." She was already scrolling through her phone contacts. Ah, there was the one she wanted. Dave Brewer answered on the second ring.

"Dave! It's Elena Marquez."

Travis looked over at her suspiciously.

"Elena?" Dave said. "What can I do for you? Does Mr. Logan need something?"

"Actually, this isn't for Mr. Logan. A friend of mine, a contractor, is a client of yours. He's had a plumbing incident at a property he's working on and he needs to file a claim—fast. He's working against a deadline. We're on our way to the property now— we don't know the extent of the damage yet."

Suddenly she realized Travis had pulled over to the side of the road and turned off the engine.

"Do you have his policy number?" Dave asked.

She looked over at Travis questioningly.

"Hang up the phone," he said. "Now."

"I'll call you back, Dave." She disconnected. "Travis. What?" His severe expression alarmed her.

"I appreciate you wanting to help." He sounded as if he was struggling not to raise his voice. "But you don't have to rescue me. My foreman has already called my insurance agent. I know how to handle this type of crisis, okay? I didn't just start renovating houses last week. I'm happy to have your company, but that's it."

"Oh." She'd obviously done something to offend

him. "Okay. I guess I'm just in the habit of jumping in and handling problems."

"That's no longer your job. Maybe Daniel needed someone to keep his calendar and pick out his ties, but I don't."

"Got it. But…I've built some goodwill with a lot of service providers. No reason you shouldn't benefit from it."

"Great. If I need your help, I'll ask."

Whoa. Apparently she'd hit his hot button again.

Elena's phone rang. She checked the screen and groaned. She wasn't ready to talk to her mother yet. But if she put it off, it would just get worse. She answered. "Hello, Mama."

"Elena, where are you?"

"I told you. I'm taking a new job as a nanny to Travis's niece."

"You're living under his roof?" She sounded as if this might be worse than learning Elena had joined a devil-worshiping cult.

"In his spare bedroom, yes. It's a perfectly customary living arrangement. Lots of people have live-in nannies. You didn't object when I moved into Daniel's home."

"That was different. He's a billionaire and he's married. And that house is huge. Travis is a bachelor."

She wasn't going to have this argument. She waited in silence.

"What am I going to tell your father?" Rosalie finally asked.

"Don't tell him anything. Just…tell him I have a new job and I moved out."

"But he's going to want to know the details."

"Tell him if he has to know more to call me. I'll think of something to tell him." She disconnected before Rosalie could offer up any more arguments.

She wouldn't lie to her father. But she prayed he wouldn't find out about the kidnapping. She couldn't bear the thought of what might happen.

"I don't want to be the cause of you fighting with your parents," Travis said.

"It isn't the first time we've argued, and it won't be the last. Please don't worry about it." But she knew he would.

Travis had pulled his truck through the gated neighborhood entrance; the security guard waved him through. He made a couple more turns and ended up parked at the end of Marigold Circle.

Elena grabbed the towels she'd brought with her, and they both headed for the front door. A Hispanic man met them before they even got to the porch.

"Glad you're here, Travis. It's worse than I thought."

"Worse how? You got the water turned off, right?"

"Yeah. But after I looked around a little, I realized it wasn't just a random pipe burst. Someone got in here while we were at lunch. Where the pipes are still exposed in the bedroom—they hit them with a sledgehammer or something. And they left a message."

"A message?"

"Spray-painted on the wall."

Elena's stomach tightened with apprehension as the three of them made their way up the stairs. They entered a large bedroom, where two men were working to sop up water. One had a mop; the other was on his hands and knees with towels. The towels were already soaked, so the ones Elena had brought would be welcome.

Elena's eyes were drawn to the hole in the wall. The pipes inside were bent at odd angles, mangled and broken. But Travis wasn't even looking at that. His gaze was riveted on the wall behind her. She turned to look.

"I will destroy you," the two of them read at the same time. A chill ran down Elena's spine.

"It's definitely the same guy," Travis said. "Same color of paint, and the letters look the same. Although I guess all block letters look the same."

"And he's escalating."

"Drew," Travis said decisively to the guy on the floor. "Get some Kilz and cover that graffiti. Pablo, get a pipe cutter and cut out the damaged portion of the pipe."

"Travis," Elena objected, "you have to call the police."

"No. If Social Services finds out someone is threatening me, I'll never get MacKenzie."

"But the insurance claims adjuster will be here soon, right?"

"We'll say the water got turned on by accident. If they deny the claim, I'll deal with it. The damage isn't that bad. I think this floor will be okay once it dries. I might have to sand and refinish it again."

"There's more damage downstairs," Pablo said.

Elena and Travis trooped downstairs. Pablo led them to a study, where water pooled in what looked like a newly carpeted floor. It was still dripping down a set of built-in bookcases.

Elena's phone was already in her hand. "I know a good company that does water extraction. I'll—" She froze as Travis shot her a look that hit her like a bowling ball. "Right. I'll just go sit on the front porch and wait for you." She dropped the last towel she'd been holding and walked out of the room.

She didn't agree with Travis's decision not to involve the police. The vandal was getting bolder and more destructive. What if his actions escalated? What if he targeted MacKenzie?

Even if the Stovers weren't violent, they could do serious damage to Travis's business.

But it was Travis's call. She exited the house and sat down on the front porch steps, intending to stay out of his way. Still, she wondered: at what point did a hot button become too hot?

A couple of hours later, the problem was under control. The insurance guy came and went. Judging from all the smiling going on as he left, Elena guessed the damage would be covered. Finally Travis grabbed his jacket and joined Elena on the porch.

"I told you it wouldn't be that fun coming with me. You ready to go?"

"Anytime. And it might have been a little bit fun if you'd just let mc help."

"I hired you as a nanny. You don't have to help with anything else."

"I know I don't *have* to. I *want* to help. That's what friends do."

"But you're not...um..."

"Were you getting ready to say I'm not your friend? Really?" She climbed into the passenger seat and slammed the door.

"Of course you're my friend," Travis said when he joined her inside the truck.

"Good. Because if you'll think back a couple of hours you might remember me doing something that strangers or acquaintances or business associates usually don't do."

"I know. I'm fully aware of everything you've done for me, Elena. Believe me. Acutely aware. That's the problem—you've done so much that I don't deserve—"

"Why don't you deserve it?"

"You *know* why. I didn't just kidnap you. I caused a rift between you and your boss. You're fighting with your parents because of me.... Hell, I came into your life like a hurricane and wrecked it!"

"Wreck-It Riggs. Maybe I should call you that from now on."

"By all rights, you shouldn't even like me."

"But I do. And just because I want to help you handle a problem here and there doesn't mean I think you're weak or incompetent. I just like to be useful, okay? So take a deep breath, stop being so suspicious of my motives and let me lend a hand. I know. Tell me what I can do to help you get ready for MacKenzie. *That* seems like something in a nanny's job description."

Travis took a few deep breaths. Then he nodded. "The social worker is coming on Monday. I still need to address some safety issues at my house. Then I need to go grocery shopping so I have a fridge full of nutritious food—oh, hell. I still need to buy a refrigerator. And I have to be out of my apartment, too. They were pretty nice about me breaking my lease because they have a waiting list, but only if I move out by Monday."

"I can do the refrigerator and the grocery shopping. And I can pack boxes and carry them around. Stop looking at me like that. It's not a big deal. I *like* being helpful."

In truth, she hadn't felt so alive in a long time. Travis would never admit it, but he *needed* her. Well, he required *someone* in his life. No one should have to handle his problems completely on his own. He needed her to help his niece. And he just needed her, period. She'd never met anyone as isolated as he was.

The way Travis was looking at her, she knew he was trying to think of a reason not to let her pitch in. It obviously went against his grain. He was used to going it alone, the lone warrior. Travis against the world. Finally, though, he nodded. "Okay. But we haven't discussed your salary. Yes, I'm going to pay you. Nothing like Daniel was paying you, I'm sure, but something approaching fair."

She started to argue, but she realized his pride would not budge on the matter of a paycheck. "Whatever you think is fair. I have no clue what nannies earn, but remember, you're giving me a place to live, as well, so take that into consideration."

"I have." He suggested a weekly salary that was about one-fifth of what she'd earned at Daniel's. But it was enough to cover her incidentals and keep her gas tank filled.

"That sounds fine," she said with a smile. "Now, then. What kind of refrigerator would you like me to buy?"

He quoted the dimensions he wanted, obviously having measured the space earlier in his new home—*their* new home, she thought with a little thrill. He'd also apparently committed them to memory. She typed in the figures on her phone.

"Freakish," she murmured.

CHAPTER SIXTEEN

WHEN TRAVIS GOT HOME late Sunday night, he could hardly believe everything he and Elena had gotten done over the weekend. He'd gone over the house inch by inch to make sure there was nothing that might be dangerous for a child or adult; he'd checked over the wiring and electrical outlets, even opening a wall or two to peek inside. He'd checked for any nails or splinters in the woodwork that might snag small hands or feet; he'd tested for lead paint and asbestos. He'd put textured decals in the tubs, good locks on all the windows and doors, installed smoke alarms in every bedroom and a couple downstairs.

He'd bought MacKenzie some new outfits, because he feared she would arrive at his place with only the clothes on her back. An alarm company was scheduled to come first thing in the morning to install a security system just in case the Stovers showed up, although he'd kept his new address unlisted. Of course, the way the Stovers had found him before was to follow him—how else could they have known he was going to Elena's for Thanksgiving?

Or the address of the house he was working on—
that wasn't even written down anywhere.

So he was being careful not to let anyone tail
him, and he'd cautioned Elena to also be aware and
to call the police if she suspected someone was following her.

But maybe the Stovers would give up soon. It was
like Elena had said; people who scrawled things
with spray paint usually did so because they were
too afraid to confront someone directly.

His crew had repaired the water damage, replac-
ing the carpeting and a few of the hardwood floor
slats upstairs. He'd also had to replace some drywall,
patch and paint, put new glass in the front door, but
it all looked good as new. He'd reported the vandalism to the security gate. The guard there swore he
hadn't let anyone in who didn't belong. But clearly
Stover had observed Travis working on the house,
and he had to have gotten in somehow.

Anyway, the security system was installed and
working at that house, and he was now the only one
with a key.

He was bone-tired, but with Elena's help he'd
done everything on his list. He had the last load of
stuff in the back—some miscellaneous tools and
lumber from his storage unit at his old apartment.
He'd turned in his keys. Now he looked forward
to coming home to Elena. This was probably their
last night alone in the house. One more night to resist temptation.

There had been no repeat of the stormy passion from Friday. Although he sensed Elena wasn't completely against the idea, he was trying not to give in. His plate was full, what with his new responsibilities as the guardian of a troubled little girl. But even if the timing hadn't been bad…for Elena's own good, he had to discourage the idea of a romance between them.

It was Judith all over again. Judith, with her classy background and lofty education, who always knew what to wear, what to say and which fork to use. Judith, who'd fallen in love with Travis's potential but not with the real him. No matter how hard she'd tried to remake him, he had stubbornly remained the same old Travis—a man of simple tastes, basic needs. Good with his hands, hopeless when it came to fine wines, foreign films and schmoozing the "right people."

Granted, Elena hadn't once put him down for his lack of education. Her efforts to help him appeared far less self-serving than Judith's. But the differences between them couldn't be swept under the rug.

He was grateful to Elena for offering to take care of MacKenzie and for all her help documenting the Stovers' theft, putting him in touch with a family law attorney, refusing to press charges. But gratitude was not a proper foundation for a relationship.

Relationship. He couldn't stand that word. Judith had gone on and on about their *relationship* or lack thereof, and her wonderful *relationship* with her new lover who was another "diamond in the rough," but one who was willing to improve himself, according to Judith, anyway. Clearly Travis didn't know how to have a relationship, and that seemed to be something women wanted.

All that said, he couldn't stop the way his heart thumped whenever he thought about coming home to Elena.

The lights were on, glowing warm and welcoming as he pulled into the driveway. In the dark, the house really looked like something special; he couldn't see the cracked and peeling paint. He'd done some tree trimming and very basic landscaping that morning so the place wouldn't look like a jungle. He smiled just remembering Elena pitching in to help, on her hands and knees yanking out weeds that were almost as big as she was. She wasn't afraid of hard work, that was for sure.

He grabbed the bag with the few last purchases he'd made on his way home—curtains for Elena's room, some colorful dish towels for the kitchen, some eco-friendly cleaning products to replace the harsh chemical ones he'd had before.

As he opened the front door, a delicious smell greeted him. Wait a minute. Elena *said* she didn't know how to cook.

"Hey!" She appeared at the door to the kitchen, smiling. "Welcome home. Have you eaten?"

"No, but I hope you didn't wait for me." It was

after nine o'clock. "You don't have to fix my meals, you know. That's not your job."

"Oh, I didn't actually cook. It's frozen enchiladas. They'll be ready in about five minutes."

He joined her in the kitchen, where she was putting a salad together. A half glass of red wine sat on the counter next to a big salad bowl. "Would you like some wine?" she asked when she saw where his gaze had traveled. "Or a cold beer?"

A streak of alarm rushed up his spine. "Wine? Beer? We can't have that in the house!"

"We can't? Oh. For tomorrow. Actually, I don't think they mind if you have a little wine or beer around, but if you're uneasy about it, we can put it in my car trunk tomorrow morning."

Travis took a deep breath. "I'm probably being paranoid. But I just want everything to be perfect."

"I know. It will be. I washed all the towels and put them back in the bathrooms, and the fridge and pantry are overflowing with more healthy foods than you can shake a stick at. Oh, and I bought a first-aid kit. I thought that might be a good thing to have— bandages, antibiotic cream, children's aspirin. It's in the master bathroom."

"I never even thought of that."

"It's on the list the social worker gave you."

He hadn't looked at the list—Missy had gone over it with him, and he'd committed it to memory. Or so he thought. "Did I forget anything else?"

"No, I think everything else is covered."

He made himself relax. He had done everything he could. If some uptight state bureaucrat decided he wasn't a fit guardian after all this… He didn't even want to consider the possibility.

"Thank you, Elena. I think I will have that beer." He opened the door of his brand new fridge. A six-pack of Samuel Adams was nestled among a jungle of fruits and vegetables, milk, cheese, eggs, orange juice, condiments and whole-wheat bread. He pulled one out of the carton, closed the fridge and used a drawer handle to pop off the cap.

God, how long had it been since someone had prepared a hot meal for him? He could get used to this in a hurry. A very pleasant sensation bloomed inside his chest. It came from the realization that someone cared for him.

Eric cared about Travis, of course. But the last few years, they'd both been focused solely on Eric and his issues. Eric had often expressed appreciation for all that Travis did, or at least tried to do.

But this… This was something different.

"What can I do to help?" he asked. "Set the…" No, the little kitchen table was already set. His old stoneware dishes looked a lot better matched up with place mats and colorful plastic water tumblers. She'd even put a candle on the table, which made him wonder. Was he being seduced?

"Not a thing. I have it all under control."

"You always do," he said with a grin.

The oven timer went off. Travis served up bubbling, melty-cheesy enchiladas while Elena scooped salad into bowls and added dressing and croutons. Soon they were seated at the intimate table, enjoying their meal and talking about their day like a married couple.

What a fantasy. Almost more potent than the fantasy of having her naked and in his bed. Almost.

"I almost bought frozen lasagna," she said with a teasing smile. "But I knew it wouldn't be as good as the stuff you served me when I was your hostage."

"Please, Elena. I'm trying to forget that ever happened."

"Oh, come on. It has to be the cutest meet ever."

"What?" She thought it was cute that he went temporarily insane and assaulted her?

"Just imagine what a great story we'd have to tell our grandchildren. If we ever got married and had children. And grandchildren."

What the hell was he supposed to make of that? Then he realized she might be tipsy. "How much of that wine have you had?"

"Enough to give me stupid-mouth, apparently. Sorry. I was just being silly."

He started to agree with her, but he realized she was blushing. He could tell even in the candlelight. She was embarrassed. So he let it pass, even as his traitorous imagination conjured up a picture of him and Elena in their seventies, gray-haired and wrinkled, with toddlers all around them. Toddlers with Elena's dramatic coloring.

Elena would still be beautiful when she was old, of that he was sure.

"So what time is the social worker coming tomorrow?" she asked, thankfully breaking into his reverie.

"Ten. And if everything is good, she'll bring MacKenzie over later in the day."

"Does MacKenzie know? You talked to her on the phone yesterday, right?"

"I didn't mention it. I didn't want to get her hopes up in case it didn't work out."

"How do you think she'll take it?"

He shrugged. "Honestly? No idea. She seems to like me, but she doesn't express much emotion."

"I think she'll be happy here."

"As happy as she can be without her real parents," Travis said glumly. "I don't know if she'll ever recover from losing both of her parents so abruptly. Before Tammy's murder she was a different child—cheerful, a real chatterbox. Always laughing. She's a ghost of what she was before."

"Has she been to therapy?"

"Eric paid for her to see a pricey child psychologist. My guess is, though, that the Stovers didn't always take her. They might have found some way to cash those checks themselves. It never occurred to me to be suspicious about that until recently, when the other stuff came to light."

"So, once you have custody, you can try again."

"Yeah. I will. But the best therapy in the world

would be to get Eric out of prison. Do you really think Project Justice will make it happen?"

She nodded. "They will. And they might get to it sooner than three months. That's just an estimate."

"I feel like I should be doing something—like talking to Eric's neighbors. The police said no one saw anything, but I find that hard to believe."

"Sometimes people just don't notice things. It's a constant challenge with murder investigations. Either they don't see anything or they remember incorrectly. Human memory is very fallible. Except yours, of course."

"I forgot the first-aid kit."

"How much did you spend for the stuff in that bag?" she asked, pointing to the plastic bag he'd dropped on the floor when he'd walked in.

"Fifty-two dollars and eighty cents. Why?"

She gave him a penetrating stare. "Freakish. You have a freakish memory."

"You say that like it's a bad thing."

"No. It's a good thing. Amazing, really. But you can't expect everyone to remember things like you do."

"Okay. But we'll never know what people do or don't remember if they aren't questioned. And I'm convinced the police didn't question the neighbors. Or if they did, none of them saw Eric returning in the middle of the day—which is what the police claim happened—so their statements were buried."

"Definite possibility." She reached out and rubbed

his upper arm. "I love it that you're so devoted to your family."

"Don't make me out to be a martyr," he said gruffly. "Eric and MacKenzie are all I have."

"Not true. You have me." She blinked at him with a bright smile, which faded when he didn't smile back. "Oh, dear. Stupid-mouth strikes again."

"No. I mean, I'm not sure what you mean by that."

"By what? Stupid-mouth? You know, when I say things that only an idiot would—"

"I know what stupid-mouth means. I'm just… I do have you. You're in my kitchen, you're sleeping in my house, you're…you're…"

"Having sex with you?"

"Yeah." Every time he thought about that, it blew his mind. "I'm still trying to figure out why."

"Does there have to be a reason? Maybe just because I want to. Isn't that good enough?"

"No. It doesn't make sense. Even Stockholm Syndrome should have worn off by now."

"Do you actually think you're not likeable?"

Did he? "I don't think I'm *un*likeable. I just think it's unlikely that *you* would like me."

"Well, I do. Get over it," she snapped. "I like you, and I'm annoyed that ever since we had sex you've been treating me like I have the plague. Did I do something wrong? Have I offended you?"

"Elena, of course not. It's just… You're my employee. I don't want to take advantage."

"What, you think I'm going to accuse you of sexual harassment?"

"No, but that doesn't mean it's okay for me to do it."

"Travis…" She sighed. "Forget it. My mother said I'd lost my mind," she muttered as she took her plate to the sink.

"I think she's a smart woman, your mother."

"And I'm an idiot, apparently." She'd turned on the water to rinse her plate, but she was just standing there, leaning against the sink. *Oh, God.* Her shoulders were shaking. He'd made her cry.

"Elena—"

"Just shut up, okay? Everything you say makes it ten times worse."

Makes what worse?

He opened his mouth, intending to apologize, then clamped it shut again. She'd told him to shut up. But she hadn't told him he couldn't *do* something. He stood and went to her, putting his hands on her shoulders. When she didn't try to shake him off, he reached past her to turn off the water and then put his arms around her and pressed his face into her hair. They stood there for a long time.

"I wanted tonight to be special." Her voice was thick with tears. "You said you'd be home for dinner."

He *was* home for dinner. A late dinner. If he'd had any idea Elena was preparing a nice meal for him…

"I mean, you were late, but that's okay. I didn't mind that."

"It *was* special."

"But clearly you don't... I mean, am I making a fool of myself? You have to tell me the truth."

"About what?" Why were women so confusing? Why didn't they just say what they meant?

"I have feelings for you. Really strong, um, positive feelings. And I need to know if you feel anything for me or if you're just being polite."

Polite? "I'm not polite. Of course I have feelings for you. How could I not? But—"

"Stop thinking," she said. "I can almost hear the gears in your brain. Stop thinking and just feel. And for God's sake, take me to bed before I have to humiliate myself further by begging."

He was helpless to deny her. She had fair warning, after all. He scooped her into his arms like a gallant knight carrying his ladylove to the castle keep, and he carried her all the way upstairs—to the master bedroom this time. Bigger bed.

She giggled, reminding him that she was under the influence, but he was past caring about that. This amazing creature was his—for tonight.

He set her down only long enough to take off her clothes. She wasn't wearing much—a Mexican shirt, a gauzy skirt that slid right down her legs along with her panties. She was already barefoot. The bra disappeared, and then she was working on his clothes.

"Shower," he said. "I've been working all day."

"Do I look like I care?" She made quick work of the buttons on his shirt. "Unless you want me to join you? I'll scrub your back."

He nearly swooned, picturing Elena naked and slick in the shower. No, he was too turned on. Making love in the shower seemed like an activity that required finesse, perhaps a more leisurely approach.

He wasn't feeling leisurely.

"Never mind the shower. I need you now." He'd been in denial about how powerfully he wanted her. But ever since he'd tasted the forbidden fruit…

"Mmm, me, too."

Travis practically ripped his own clothes off. They fell onto the bed, shoving blankets and pillows out of the way. He was kissing her everywhere, filling his hands with her breasts, and she had her hands on him, around him. And then he was squeezing her bottom and she was teasing his chest hair with her teeth and licking his nipples.

No woman had ever done that to him before—treating him like a giant lollipop. But she was every bit as crazed as he was.

"Now, Travis. Please," she whimpered. "I've been thinking about this all day until I was almost batty with it."

"I don't want to hurt you."

She laughed hysterically. "Hurt me?"

She was so soft and delicate, and he was so… well, hard. He was afraid of losing control. "What about—"

"Right here." She had the condom in her hand already out of the package. He thought the condoms were in *her* room.

"I put a few in here while you were gone, okay?" she said, answering his unasked question. "I'm not trying to hide the fact that I planned for this. Hoped for it, anyway."

With a smile and a kiss he took the condom from her and managed it himself. He was afraid of losing control if she did it.

She had him on his back and didn't intend to let him up. Not that he couldn't have reversed things any time he pleased, but this felt good. It was her seduction, after all; he'd let her see it through her way.

She wasted no time straddling his hips and gently guiding him home. But once he was poised to enter her, she didn't mess around. She enveloped him, a hot, tight, wet sleeve. The air whooshed out of her lungs as she lowered herself completely, allowing all of her weight onto him.

"Ah, Elena." She was so perfect. So perfectly formed. He could almost span her slender waist with his big hands. Her bottom was soft to the touch but with the underlying muscles of someone who was fit.

And her breasts… He could write a sonnet about them. Maybe he would learn how to write better just so he could do that. Even as he plunged inside her, he felt this odd urge to give her something special, something meaningful. As the pressure buil in his loins, his heart expanded, too, and during those few, unguarded seconds when they became one, he let her in.

As she got closer to coming, she swung her head from side to side, her beautiful hair flying every which way. Their sexual dance grew more frenzied. Travis's thrusts were faster, harder, deeper.

Then she screamed. If he hadn't already been on the verge of his own personal earthquake, it might have scared him. Instead, he joined her with a cry of triumph that echoed through the whole house.

Her scream devolved into semihysterical laughter. Moisture dropped onto his chest, and he realized she was crying. Laughing and crying at the same time. *Wow.*

After what seemed like a long time, but was probably only a few seconds, she calmed. Her frenetic breathing slowed, and she slumped against him as if she was exhausted. Her skin was coated with a light sheen of perspiration.

"Sorry," she whispered with a giggle. "I'm so sorry. I hope the neighbors don't call the police."

He wrapped his arms around her, smiling so widely his face hurt. If anyone heard them, he doubted they would mistake the sounds they'd made for anything but shouts of passionate ecstasy.

The last time they'd made love, there'd been no time for enjoying the afterglow. They'd been forced to leap out of bed and deal with that blasted broken pipe.

Tonight was different. Here they were, pleasantly buzzed from their wine and beer, relaxed and satiated. It was late—no one was going to call. He hoped she would spend the night with him.

After a few minutes, Elena stirred and shifted, moving from on top of him to beside him. She was nestled under his arm, her head pillowed on his shoulder, her hair covering them both.

"I still need that shower," he said.

"No, you don't," she said firmly. "Please don't leave. If you leave, you'll get all sensible and bristly again. Just…stay here."

She didn't have to twist his arm. "Not going anywhere." If she wanted them to go to sleep like this, all wrapped around each other, still sticky with each other's body fluids, he wasn't going to argue.

Travis wasn't sure what lay ahead. But until the sun rose tomorrow, she was his and he was hers, and nothing and nobody could come between them.

CHAPTER SEVENTEEN

MONDAY MORNING DAWNED gray and gloomy, the sky dark with impending rain. The forecast was for thunderstorms. But Travis tried not to let that bother him. He might have MacKenzie today.

He woke up early, slipping out of bed while trying not to wake Elena. She'd stolen all the covers from him during the night; now she was sprawled on her stomach with the blankets heaped around her, one arm dangling off the edge, one foot hanging off the other edge.

A king-size bed would be a necessity with this one, he thought with a grin.

Once he'd showered and dressed, he went downstairs, started the coffeemaker and cleaned up the previous night's dishes. He gathered up the open bottle of wine and the beer and put them in a brown paper sack, then carried the sack to his truck and locked it in the cargo area.

A few fat drops of rain fell on him as he headed back inside, and thunder rumbled in the distance.

He was surprised to find Elena in the kitchen when he returned, pouring herself a cup of coffee.

He sneaked up behind her and kissed her on the side of her neck, and she giggled.

They hadn't had an opportunity to flirt and play like most couples. He hadn't yet had the chance to court Elena, to take her out for dinner and a movie, buy her flowers. She deserved that, and he was going to give it to her.

If she'd have him. If she wanted him that way. Their relationship—there was that word again—was unfolding in such an unorthodox way, he wasn't sure what to expect. He would have to feel his way through it.

"You already did the dishes," she said.

"I was up early. Couldn't sleep. You want some breakfast?"

"I'm starving." She handed him a full mug of coffee, then got another one for herself. "I could make bacon and eggs. Or oatmeal."

Most days, he made do with cold cereal or a couple of toaster waffles. But this *was* their very first morning together—not counting when she was his hostage.

"You sit down and relax. I'll cook. I have to do something to make up for that dreadful pancake I made for you out in the woods."

"It was a pretty good pancake, actually. But I'm happy to have you cook. There's nothing sexier than a man wearing an apron and oven mitts."

He whistled as he worked, quickly putting together a couple of spinach omelets and some toast.

Elena ran upstairs to shower and dress. He was just scooping the second omelet out of the pan when she returned.

"Do I look like a responsible nanny?" She'd put on a pair of conservative beige pants with a ribbed turtleneck. Her hair was pulled back into a no-nonsense ponytail, and it appeared she wasn't wearing any makeup. Her only jewelry was a plain gold watch with a black band and tiny gold hoops in her ears.

The effect was sexy as hell. All he could think about was undressing her.

"You look the picture of responsible nannydom," he answered. She set the table while the eggs cooked. A loud clap of thunder shook the house as they sat down to breakfast.

Elena glanced out the kitchen window. "Wow, it's really coming down."

"Yeah. I hope the weather doesn't stop Missy from coming today." It wasn't yet nine o'clock. They still had lots of time.

Elena took her first bite of omelet. "Wow again. I was thinking how much I'll miss Cora's cooking—Cora is Daniel's Cordon Bleu–trained chef. But if you keep this up, I won't miss it at all."

"I used to make these for Eric." Travis was pleased she liked his cooking. "It was the only way I could get him to eat any vegetables. But don't kid yourself. My repertoire is limited. I know how to fix about five dishes. That's it."

"You've got me beat. Maybe I'll get a cookbook

and learn a few more recipes. I can find out what MacKenzie likes."

"We can all learn together. MacKenzie's not too young to help out. When I was her age, my mom always had me mash the potatoes."

"When I was her age, I would have killed for mashed potatoes," Elena said absently. Then she flashed him a look of alarm, as if she hadn't really meant to say the words out loud. "Sorry. That sounded an awful lot like I was trying to one-up you. 'My childhood was crappier than yours.' I didn't mean it that way."

"The funny thing is I don't consider those times to be crappy at all. Looking back, I know we were poor, but I didn't see it at the time. We were a family, a team. We took care of each other. It pissed me off when Social Services took me and Eric away from my mom. I know they had to—we were living in a car. But it was just temporary. We had food and clean clothes, and we bathed at least every couple of days at a truck stop. It was summer, so school wasn't an issue. I thought we were on vacation."

Elena reached across the table and placed her hand on his forearm. "It sounds like she loved you a lot."

"She did."

"What happened to her?"

"Cancer. It happened while I was in the army. She didn't tell me—didn't want to bother me with it. Eric had just started college—he was oblivious.

By the time I found out and I arranged for leave to come home, it was almost too late. She died less than twenty-four hours after I got home."

"Oh, Travis. I'm so sorry."

He touched her cheek. "Thanks. But it was a long time ago. She left me a letter insisting that I not be sad, that I go out and live my life and make her proud. I didn't exactly do that."

"You're doing it now. Look at how you're running your own business, and how you're trying to help Eric and MacKenzie. Of course she would be proud."

"Yeah, I bet she'd be crowing to all her friends in heaven about how I kidnapped a nice lady who was trying to help me—"

"Travis. Stop. That's over and done, okay?"

Somehow, he had a hard time believing that was true. Against all odds, Elena had forgiven him; he believed that. But he'd gotten off so easy. No charges filed against him, no jail and the victim of his crime had turned into his ally.

Things just didn't work out like that. Actions had consequences. Any minute now, the other shoe would drop.

They finished breakfast, cleared the dishes and cleaned the kitchen together until it sparkled.

"Let's do one more walk-through," Travis said. "Just to make sure we didn't miss anything."

Everything downstairs appeared to be in order. "Maybe I should have bought some pictures for the walls."

"Travis, it's fine." Elena squeezed his hand. "You know the social worker, right?"

"Yeah. She's nice."

"There you have it. She's not going to be looking for an excuse to turn you down. Good foster homes are hard to find."

"Yeah, but I'm a single guy."

"You're MacKenzie's uncle. You're a shoo-in. I remember when my parents applied to be foster parents. The social worker spent about five minutes at our house, asked a few questions. That was it."

"Your parents fostered kids?"

"Just for a short time. Marietta—you met her at Thanksgiving? When she first came to this country, her parents had nothing but the clothes on their backs. Marietta and her sister stayed with us until their parents could get back on their feet. Our Cuban extended 'family' does that for each other. When we arrived in this country, strangers took us in. We return the favor."

"Well, that's nice and all, but your father is a doctor. He lives in a really nice house, and he has a stay-at-home wife. They had you to prove they knew how to raise kids."

"You have everything you need, Travis. Trust me."

He wanted to believe her. But life had kicked him in the teeth too many times—he was afraid to hope that this time could be different.

Upstairs, Travis and Elena went to work making

the bed. Given how severely they'd disrupted the covers last night, it wasn't a simple job.

"You're the most restless sleeper I've ever known," Travis said as they smoothed the bedspread over the sheets. "Makes me wonder what you're doing in your dreams."

"I don't know. I don't remember my dreams. I'm sorry if I kept you awake."

"No worries." She'd have to kick him continuously in the head while singing the "Hallelujah Chorus" in her sleep all night long before he'd even think about complaining about having her in his bed. "Where are those condoms? We need to hide them good."

"The social worker isn't going to snoop in your nightstand."

"You never know." He folded up the three remaining condoms from the string Elena had stashed in his bedroom and tucked them inside a box of bandages in the bathroom.

"Travis," Elena said from the bedroom, "do you hear that?"

"Hear what? Is she here?" It was a quarter to ten. Missy could arrive any minute. He stepped back into the bedroom to find Elena standing near the foot of the bed, her head cocked and brow furrowed, listening.

"I hear water dripping."

Oh, God. Not another plumbing disaster. What were the odds? Then another possibility occurred to me, one much more likely given the fact it was raining like Niagara Falls out there.

They followed the sound of trickling water down the hall, checking Elena's room first. Nothing appeared amiss. Likewise, the bathroom seemed in good working order, no leaks.

When they entered MacKenzie's room, the problem became evident. Water was pouring through the ceiling onto the hardwood floor. Apparently the roof leaked.

Why today? Why did it have to rain *today?*

"Oh, *Dios mío,* it's like a shower coming out of the ceiling!"

Travis didn't stop to admire his new fountain. He rushed down to the garage to find a bucket. "Grab some towels!" he yelled over his shoulder.

"I'm on it," she yelled back.

By the time he returned with a mop and bucket, Elena was on her hands and knees sopping up the lake with a stack of the brand-new towels he'd just bought. He set the bucket under the leak, but at the rate the water was pouring in, it would overflow the container in no time.

"We need a second bucket," he said. "Can you find something? Maybe a big pot or a plastic wastebasket? I'm going up on the roof to see if I can't stop the water from coming in."

"Travis, you can't go up on the roof in weather like this! It's the middle of a thunderstorm. You'll get struck by lightning and nothing will be left of you but a piece of ash."

"I have to. Missy will be here any minute. If she sees this, I doubt she'll be impressed if we tell her MacKenzie can take a shower without going down the hall to the bathroom."

"She'll understand. Roof leaks happen."

"I can't take the risk." He didn't have time to debate.

In the garage he found a tarp and some bricks; if he could find where the rain was coming in, perhaps he could at least slow down the amount of water getting through.

As he raised his extension ladder and leaned it up against the edge of the roof, rain pelted him, invading his ears and eyes and instantly soaking his clothes. It was cold rain, too. What a bummer if he fixed the leak only to catch a cold and die of pneumonia.

He hauled the tarp and the bricks up, making three trips. Once he was up on the roof, he kept low; the roof's pitch was steep and the shingles were slippery. Falling off the roof and breaking his leg wouldn't help his chances of fostering MacKenzie, either.

It didn't take him long to find the problem. The flashing around the dormer was all bent up. Since it was raining almost sideways, the water was hitting the exterior wall of the dormer and leaking right under the warped edge of the flashing.

The wind was blowing pretty hard, but maybe the tarp would stay put if he nailed the corners down and then used plenty of bricks around the edges.

He draped the tarp over half the dormer, fighting the wind the entire time. One gust filled up the tarp and damn near had him airborne with the tarp as a parasail. But eventually he wrestled the thing into submission.

He suspected this problem wasn't new. In fact, he'd noticed a slight water stain in that corner of MacKenzie's room, and he'd painted it over with Kilz, making a mental note to inspect the roof when he had more time.

Guess he should have *made* time.

When he returned to the bedroom, Elena had the water under control.

"The waterfall has slowed to only a few drops." She sounded relieved. "Were you able to fix it?"

"Only temporarily. It looks like hell, but Missy won't be able to see it from the street. With any luck, she won't want to go out into the backyard."

"The ceiling is bulging a little bit, but it doesn't look too bad."

"Let's just hope Missy doesn't notice."

Finally she looked at him, and her eyes widened. "You're soaked through!"

"That's what happens to people who aren't smart enough to come in out of the rain." He went to his own bedroom to change clothes and towel-dry his hair. He should have gotten a haircut, he realized, as he attempted to comb the wavy mess into some kind of order.

Then he thought about the way Elena ran her fingers through it, the way she grabbed handfuls of it when she was in the throes of passion, and he decided his hair was just fine.

"She's here!" Elena called from downstairs. "Her car is pulling up now."

Travis tossed his wet towel into the hamper, checked MacKenzie's bedroom to be sure there was no more water leaking from the ceiling and trotted downstairs as the doorbell chimed. He opened the door while Elena stood deferentially in the background, as would be appropriate for an employee.

Frankly, in all the panic, he'd all but forgotten she was supposed to be his employee. He'd begun to think of her as a partner.

No, even worse than that: he'd started to think of her as a foster mother to his foster father. Those were dangerous thoughts.

"Travis, good morning," Missy said as she shook out her umbrella on the front porch. "What a day, huh?"

"Yeah, what a day." He let her in and took her umbrella and her raincoat. He didn't have a coat tree or umbrella stand. He'd been doing good to furnish the living room with a sofa and coffee table. So he draped the coat over a dining room chair and set the umbrella next to it.

He quickly introduced Elena, who was all demure

politeness. Missy smiled broadly, though she asked some pointed questions. "Travis said you managed... a day care?"

"Yes, for two years, at the Logan Oil corporate headquarters," Elena answered smoothly.

"Okay. That works." Missy looked around. "Travis, this place is just adorable. I can't believe you found it and moved in so quickly."

"I was motivated. There's still a lot of work to do, but I think I covered everything important—the safety issues," he clarified.

Missy looked everything over carefully. She didn't hesitate to open drawers, cupboards and closets. As he'd predicted, she didn't venture into the backyard, but she did stand on the screened-in porch and look around. She couldn't hide her smile when she saw the tire swing Travis had hung.

"I think she'll love that," Missy murmured, more to herself than Travis.

As she took a tour of the upstairs, the expression on her face told Travis everything—she was pleased with what she saw. They ended up in MacKenzie's room, and Missy clapped her hands together gleefully.

"This is adorable! Who did all this? Ms. Marquez?"

"Travis did every bit of it himself," Elena said.

Missy crossed the room to look out the window, which had a view of the backyard. "Well, it's just charming—"

At that moment, a large hunk of plaster chose to

dislodge itself from the ceiling and plummet to the floor with a deafening bang, missing Missy's head by inches.

For a few heart-stopping moments, they all just stood there. Missy looked down at the plaster on the floor, then up at the gaping hole in the ceiling, which revealed a patch of rotting roof decking through which daylight was visible.

Finally she looked at Travis. "Oh, dear."

Talk about an understatement. "There was a leak," Travis said. "I only found out about it this morning, when it started raining. I did a temporary repair—"

"He went up on the roof in the pouring rain," Elena added.

"And I cleaned up in here. I had no idea the damage was this extensive. The moment the rain stops, I'll have a crew up on that roof. I'll fix it. It'll be good as new."

He brushed some plaster dust off Missy's shoulder. She looked at his hand as if it was offensive, and he stopped.

"I just don't know, Travis. MacKenzie clearly can't sleep in this room until the roof and ceiling are repaired."

"She can sleep in my room," Elena said. "I'll sleep in here, or on the couch, until it's fixed."

Missy looked around thoughtfully. "It makes me wonder what other defects might be hidden…."

"Frankly, Missy," Travis said, "this is an old house. Things go wrong in old houses. What I do know is that it doesn't have lead pipes or asbestos or bad wiring. All of that has been checked. Anything else that goes wrong, I can fix—probably better than most any foster parent you could find."

After a few moments, Missy smiled. "You're right, of course. It's my job to think of worst-case scenarios. Everyone has home-repair disasters and you're better equipped than most to deal with them. You've accomplished a lot in a very short time, and I applaud you. I can finish up the paperwork today and bring MacKenzie over this afternoon."

Travis had to resist the urge to grab Missy and hug her. He'd done it! *They'd* done it. Without Elena's help, this never would have happened. This was only the first of many hurdles, of course. The adoption process would be messy and expensive. But he'd do whatever it took to keep MacKenzie in Eric's life. As her foster father, he could keep Eric's picture in MacKenzie's room. He could talk to her every night about her father, read her her father's letters, let the two of them talk on the phone.

And then Project Justice would do their thing, and pretty soon father and daughter would be re-united....

"Travis?" Missy looked at him with concern.

"What? Oh, sorry. I was just imagining how nice it would be to have a child in this house."

"Missy was just asking if you'll be home this afternoon."

"You tell me what time to be here and I'll be here."

They all walked down the stairs. Travis felt lighter somehow. Like his feet were barely touching the steps. He retrieved Missy's raincoat and helped her put it on. The rain had let up, but it was still cool outside.

She took her umbrella. "I'll call when I have a better idea of when—"

Just then someone honked their car horn—loudly, repeatedly.

"What in the world…?" Elena went to the front door and opened it. Her lips formed a surprised O and her face went white.

"Elena, what is it?"

Then someone started screaming outside. "Elena, you come out here right now!"

Travis knew that voice, except when he'd heard it last, it had been in a much friendlier tone.

"Papa, what are you doing here?"

Sure enough, Elmer Marquez had gotten out of his SUV and was striding up the walkway toward Travis's front door, the storm on his face far worse than anything they'd experienced from the sky that morning. "Elena, I want you out of that criminal's house right now. What do you think you're doing, living in sin with that…that felon?"

"Don't call him that!" Elena stepped out onto the front porch, effectively barring the door from Elmer. "And what makes you think I'm living in sin? I'm a live-in nanny with my own bedroom. There is a difference."

Why now? Why couldn't Elmer have waited another two minutes, and Missy would have missed the whole show?

Missy looked decidedly scandalized. "Who is that man? Do you know him?"

"He's Elena's father. And I take it he's slightly overprotective. I guess he doesn't like it that his little girl is working for an ex-con." At least, he thought that was what Elmer referred to. Unless…

"This man kidnapped you! He threw you into the back of his truck and held you prisoner. You don't call that a felon? And he has a criminal record besides that!"

"Papa, please, can we discuss this some other time?"

"No, we cannot. There is nothing to discuss. Get your things. You are coming home with me."

"No, I am not! I am not a child and you can't order me around."

"You brought this man into our home. You endangered our family."

"He is not dangerous!"

"He kidnapped you!"

"It was a misunderstanding!"

"Are you coming with me? Or will you force me to teach this Travis Riggs a lesson, make sure he never comes near my family again?" Elmer tried to move Elena to the side, but she refused to let him pass.

"Wait, wait, I'll come with you, okay? Give me a second to get my things."

Elmer grabbed on to Elena's arm. "You are not going back inside that house! I forbid it."

"Fine, I'll go with you." She threw a look over her shoulder at Travis—pleading with him to understand? To forgive her?

He wanted to stop her. He wanted to insist that any beef her father had with him, they should deal with it face to face, man to man. On the other hand, he didn't want to drag out this hideous confrontation any longer than necessary. Missy was already horrified.

With a sinking feeling, he watched Elena practically drag her father away from the house.

"Mr. Riggs," Missy said in a stern, schoolmarm voice. "Did you or did you not kidnap that woman?"

He really, really wanted to lie. But she wouldn't take his word for it. She might check with the police and find out the truth. "Yes. But the next morning, I released her. It was an impulsive gesture."

"It was an impulsive felony."

"No charges were filed. Elena understood why I did it. She forgave me."

"Well, clearly her father didn't. That man sounds dangerous."

"He's not dangerous. He's a doctor."

Missy's lips pressed together in a hard line. "My ex-husband was a doctor. Didn't stop him from being dangerous."

Great. Could he think of anything to say that might make things worse?

"I'm sorry, Travis. I've overlooked a lot of things—your criminal record, the fact that you're a single working man. I've tried to make allowances because you are MacKenzie's blood relative and because I'm sympathetic to your wish not to have MacKenzie forever separated from her father. But I can't in good conscience—"

"No, Missy, please don't say it. I can fix this. Elena will calm her father down—"

"You said it yourself—you committed a crime on an impulse. A lack of impulse control is not a desirable trait for a potential foster father to exhibit."

"I guess it isn't." It wasn't as if he could argue the point. "Is that it, then? The decision is made?"

"You can always appeal. Maybe my supervisor will feel differently than I do."

But Travis guessed not.

He watched as Missy walked to her car. She gave him one last sad look before climbing behind the wheel.

Travis should have known it was too good to be true. Ten minutes ago he'd had a beautiful house and a beautiful lover and he'd been about to get custody of his beautiful niece. Now he had a house with a big hole in the roof, with a higher mortgage than he really wanted to pay, and two empty bedrooms.

Without MacKenzie, there was no reason for Elena to come back. No job to come back to. He doubted she would want to live there—they weren't exactly candidates for living together, not when he'd never even taken her out on a proper date.

Hell, why was he standing in the rain feeling sorry for himself? He wasn't the one who was about to lose his daughter. He'd really let Eric down.

CHAPTER EIGHTEEN

ELENA FORCED BACK her tears as her father revved the engine of his SUV and put it in gear. "Papa, you have no idea what you just did."

"I saved you from a life of ruin. That's what I did."

"Oh, what, you imagine that I'm some virgin whose reputation you have to protect, so you can marry me off?"

"A woman's reputation *is* important."

"Well, sorry to disappoint you, but I'm not a virgin."

"I knew it! That man ruined you. He is going to have to pay—"

"No, Papa. I lost my virginity in college. And I've had lovers since then, too. Will you please get your head out of nineteenth-century Cuba?"

He paid her no attention. "I'll ask Cesar to pick up your things. I would do it myself, but I am afraid of what I might do to that man."

That wouldn't be happening, but she didn't argue. She would wait until they got home. Her mother would calm her father down, make him see reason.

Maybe they didn't like Travis. That was their right, their choice. But they couldn't stop her from seeing him. Or continuing to live with him, for that matter, though she had a terrible feeling he no longer needed a nanny.

"The social worker was at Travis's house to approve him as a foster parent. You showing up and acting like a crazy person, making threats—you probably ruined that for him."

"What kind of social worker lets a kidnapper have a child?"

"He would have been a wonderful parent. He was so excited. You should have seen how he decorated MacKenzie's room. And he hung this tire swing in the backyard and he was asking me about what kinds of foods kids like…" She couldn't go on. Her voice was cracking, her eyes filling with tears.

"*Pequeña,* don't cry. That man has brought nothing but trouble into your life. Since you met him you've left your job, you've upset your mother, you've compromised your reputation—where will it end?"

He was wrong. Travis had brought a lot more than trouble into her life. He'd brought something warm and alive and wonderful to her. He'd allowed her to hope and dream and plan, to work toward something really good.

And now her father had spoiled it.

Of course her papa didn't understand. He thought he was protecting her. But did he have to be so…so

Cuban? Elena's mother was actually standing on the front porch, wringing her hands, when Elena and her father pulled into the driveway.

"I told him not to go," Rosalie said the moment Elena got out of the car. "I told him not to interfere, but he wouldn't listen to me. I'm so sorry, Elena. I wasn't going to tell him but he found out some-how—"

"A guy called me," Elmer said as they all went inside the house. "Said I should talk to the police about my daughter's kidnapping. You think I should have just ignored him?"

Elena stopped in the foyer. She had a bad feel-ing about that phone call. "What man? Did he give his name?"

"Actually, he made a point of giving his name. Stover."

"Stover. That jerk," she muttered.

"You know this Stover?" Rosalie asked.

"I know of him. He was the foster father to Mac-Kenzie, the little girl I was going to be looking after. He was doing some bad things—Travis reported him to the authorities and they took MacKenzie away from him. Now I guess he's returning the favor." Stover had probably done some research on Travis, looking for something he could use to hurt Travis's reputation, and he'd found the arrest record.

"You have no concept, do you?" Elena contin-ued. "By showing up at Travis's house acting like a lunatic, you've ruined four lives."

Her mother led them all into the kitchen. She rubbed the top of Elena's back, right along her spine, as she'd done when Elena was a girl, to soothe the pain of a skinned knee or when she'd been teased at school. "What four lives, *pequeña?*"

"Travis's, for starters. He was finally starting to believe in himself, to believe he could make a positive change, that he could do something good for his brother. Now he'll just go back to thinking he doesn't deserve to succeed or be happy. MacKenzie's—she'd have had a happy home with her uncle Trav, someone who truly loves her and wants what's best for her. Eric's, MacKenzie's father—because MacKenzie is going to get adopted before Eric's proven innocent, and he'll lose her forever. And mine."

Maybe it was melodramatic to say her life was completely ruined, but it sure felt like that in the moment. "I know you can't see it, but Travis is a good man. Yes, he has a criminal record. But all he did was defend himself. And, yes, he did kidnap me. But I was never in any danger. He treated me with the utmost kindness and respect. All he wanted was for Daniel to look into his brother's case. All he wanted was to get his brother out of prison, because Eric didn't kill his wife."

"How do you know any of this is true, Elena?" her father asked. It was a reasonable request. All she had on most of this information was Travis's word.

"I know. I am a good judge of character. Everything Travis has told me is the truth. He is a man with integrity. And I think…I think I might be falling in love with him."

It was all too much for Elena. How could everything have gone so wrong, so fast? She felt so helpless. There was nothing she could do to help Travis now except… She could be with him. She never would have left that house in the first place, except that was the most expedient way of removing her father from the scene.

"Elena, please." Her father sounded as if he was about to cry, too. He never could stand her tears.

She pulled herself together as best she could. "Now that we've cleared everything up, I'm going back to Travis's house. *My* house." At least for now. He wouldn't want her to stay there—he'd only grudgingly agreed to let her move in, and only because he was in desperate need of childcare. But she couldn't let him deal with this setback alone, to think she didn't care.

"You can't go back there," her father declared. "I forbid it."

"Elmer." Rosalie jumped to Elena's defense. "Our daughter is a grown woman. You can't forbid her to do anything. You'll only make her more determined. And you're due at the hospital in thirty minutes."

"If you defy my wishes, daughter, I will disown you."

"Elmer!"

"Sorry, Papa," Elena said sadly. "I have to do what

my heart tells me." She walked over to the small table by the front door, where a bowl full of change sat. She fished out a handful of quarters.

"Elena," Rosalie said, "what are you doing?"

"Bus fare. I'll pay you back." She gave her mother a hug and a kiss, and did the same for her father, who grudgingly returned the affection. Then she walked out the door.

FOR THE FIRST few minutes after Elena and Missy left, Travis operated on autopilot. The rain was clearing up. He called his roofing guy, Paulie, and asked him to round up a crew to fix his roof. He went upstairs and cleaned up the mess in MacKenzie's room. Or rather, the room that would never be MacKenzie's. He brought a ladder upstairs and got a good look at the damage. A couple of support beams were rotted; he'd have to replace those. Then a large sheetrock patch, some mud, some paint—he'd been planning to repaint this room, anyway.

He was going to let MacKenzie pick the color. Now maybe he'd just go with white.

Anyway, he couldn't do any of that until the roof was fixed. He put another tarp down on the floor to protect it from fallout during the repair.

It was noon, and he knew he should be hungry, but the thought of food was unappealing. He could get in his truck, check on the Marigold Circle house, but Leo was there and he would let Travis know if there were any problems.

When he realized he was wandering from room to room like a ghost, he stopped and forced himself to sit down and think. What the hell should she do? Did he have any recourse? Maybe once Missy had a chance to think about it, she would change her mind. He could try to make her understand… but hell, there was no getting around the fact that he had kidnapped a woman. It didn't matter that, in her broad-mindedness, Elena had forgiven him. He'd still done the deed.

For the hundredth time, he wished he could go back to that morning when he'd shown up at Daniel Logan's house and choose a different path.

The doorbell broke into his thoughts. What the hell? The way this day was going, it could only be trouble, and he thought about ignoring it. But the bell rang again; whoever was there wasn't going away. He made his way to the door and yanked it open. "What?"

Elena was standing there, looking like an angel. She must have come to collect her things—at least her purse. She'd left with only the clothes on her back.

"Travis. I'm so sorry."

"Sorry? You didn't do anything wrong."

"Can I come in?"

"Yeah. Of course." He stepped aside and she entered.

"It was my father who showed up here acting

crazy. He ruined everything. I should have anticipated that something like this might happen. I never told him the truth about…about how we met—"

"That I committed a felony against you. Let's not sugarcoat it at this late date."

"Whatever. I told you he had a temper. I knew if he found out—if Mama told him—he would explode."

"Still not your fault." God, she was so beautiful. More than anything he wanted to fold her into his arms, to feel her heart beating against his. He wanted to strip her clothes off and bury himself in her and stay there forever.

"If I hadn't volunteered to take care of MacKenzie, if I hadn't pushed—"

"If I hadn't thrown you into the back of my truck. How about that?"

"I just feel so bad about…about all of it. *I* understand why you did it. *I* forgave you. So why can't everyone else?"

"Because that's not how the world works, Elena. People are full of anger. No one wants to forgive anyone for anything. They want revenge. They want to see people pay. The fact that you're so understanding and forgiving, that's great, but you can't expect the rest of the world to hop on board the peace train with you."

"Well, I'm sorry, anyway."

He shook his head. "It wasn't meant to be."

She frowned disapprovingly. "If you say so. Are you giving up? Because I never took you for a quitter."

"I don't think you understand. Game over. Missy isn't going to change her mind."

"What if I talk to her? I could take her out to lunch and take the time to explain what really happened."

Travis shook his head. "I looked into that woman's eyes. Her mind is made up. Even if I did what I did for the most sympathetic reasons, I still have 'poor impulse control.' I still committed a serious crime."

Elena digested this for a few moments. "Are you going to make me move out? It would be extremely uncomfortable staying with my parents."

"Then maybe you should ask Daniel for your old job back."

She flinched. He felt bad for hurting her, but it had to be done. Elena needed to unhitch her wagon from his—sooner, rather than later. Her father was right. She was ruining her chances to succeed on her own by associating with him.

"I know the nanny job is off the table," she said. "But you could use a business manager."

That threw him. "Excuse me? What the hell are you talking about?"

"Travis, you're really good at what you do— building, repairing, renovating. But let's face it, there's only so much business you can carry around in your head. You need someone to organize you, to do your billing, your accounting. Do you even own a filing cabinet?"

"That is beside the point. Me and my freakish memory carry the business just fine. I've been doing it that way for years."

"But wouldn't you like your business to grow? I'll work for free. If I can't significantly increase your income within a couple of months, fire me."

"No."

"Why not?"

"Because you're trying to fix something that's not broken. You're trying to fix *me*. When my ex and I got divorced, I swore I would never be some woman's project. I'm not a diamond in the rough—I'm a plain old rock. And you know what? The world needs rocks. You want a diamond? Look elsewhere."

She stared at him without speaking for a good thirty seconds. "I like rocks."

For God's sake. "Get your things. Get out. Leave me be."

"I don't want to."

"You are the most obstinate woman I've ever met!"

"I've been called worse."

If she wouldn't leave, then he would. Because if he stayed, with her looking up at him with those doe eyes, he was going to cave in and take the temporary comfort she offered. He turned his back to Elena and strode through the kitchen to the garage door, grabbing his jacket on the way out.

Elena trailed behind him. "Wait. Where are you going?"

"I'm doing what I should have done from the beginning. I'm going to find out who killed Tammy. If Project Justice won't do it now, I will." He hit the garage door opener and climbed into his truck.

The brazen woman clearly wasn't going to take no for an answer. She had his passenger door open before he could lock it.

"Elena—"

"Just shut up and listen to me, you pigheaded ass!"

ELENA DIDN'T THINK too long about what she wanted to say. She'd shocked Travis into silence, but it wouldn't last long.

"Maybe last night didn't mean anything to you. Okay, I get it. I'm the one who seduced you, and it's not like you promised me anything. So forget the whole idea of us as a couple. And forget me working for you. It was pushy of me to even suggest such a thing. You've been running your business for a long time, and clearly it's working for you. I made the mistake of visualizing how Daniel would have done things. But Daniel is Daniel and you are you, and I didn't mean to judge you."

"Last night did mean something to me," he objected. "I shouldn't have…knowing there was no future—"

"I don't want to rehash it, okay? You don't owe

me an explanation. I want to talk about what's going on here, right now."

"I told you. I'm going to find the real murderer."

"And how do you propose to do that?"

"Well…I thought I would start by talking to the detective who worked on the case. See if they'll let me look at the case file."

Elena made a sound like a buzzer. "Wrong answer. I can guarantee you the detective will blow you off. The case is solved as far as he or she is concerned, and he has zero interest in anyone trying to prove he arrested the wrong guy. The police don't let civilians anywhere near their notes or evidence. Especially when appeals are still ongoing."

"How do you know?"

"Because I've been privy to how Project Justice works for a while now. Daniel gets involved in all the more difficult cases. And when he's involved, I'm there—taking notes, acting as a sounding board. I understand how cases get solved. If finding Tammy's murderer is really what you're after, I can help. Let me help."

She could tell Travis wanted to object. He couldn't seem to understand why she wanted to help, but she was tired of trying to explain it to him.

"So you don't want anything in return?"

She shook her head.

"Elena, there's no such thing as an utterly selfless act. Everyone acts in their own self-interest. People give to charity so they can brag about it, or at least know they look good to the accountant who does their taxes. If not that, then they do it to feel good about themselves. That's the payoff."

"Okay, if you just *have* to assign me a motive, I want to feel good about myself."

"I think it's more than that."

She made a strangled noise of sheer frustration. "Of course you do."

"You're angry with Daniel. And you're trying to get back at him the only way you know how—by allying yourself with someone he finds...appalling."

Elena shook her head. "That's not the reason."

"Then why?"

She was scared to admit her true motivation— that she couldn't stand the thought of Travis going it alone. He'd spent way too much of his life alone. He might not know it, but Travis Riggs needed people in his life. He needed a child of his own to spoil and nurture. He needed love.

"Can't you just accept that I'm here because I want to be here?" she finally asked. "If I can help you accomplish your goal, why do you care what my reasons are?"

"I don't want you hurt."

"I'm not going to get hurt." At least, not physically. Her heart was a different matter.

"Okay."

"Okay?"

"I can't fight you anymore. You're like the wind—relentless, blowing sand at a rock until the rock wears away. So, tell me. How do Project Justice cases get solved?"

ERIC'S HOUSE WASN'T terribly far from Travis's—it only took about seven minutes to get there.

"I hadn't realized your new house was so close to your brother's."

"I go to Eric's every couple of weeks to mow the lawn, keep it looking decent enough to make the neighbors happy. I passed that 'rent to own' sign probably a dozen times before I really noticed it."

Travis pulled into the driveway of the elegant colonial and cut the truck's engine. A forlorn "for sale" sign, a bit faded now, stood in the yard.

"It's a gorgeous house," Elena couldn't help commenting. "What a shame that someone can't overlook the tragedy and turn it into a happy home again."

"Someone will, someday."

They entered through the front door into a spacious foyer. The place was elegant, but it had an eerie feeling to it. Elena took a quick tour of the downstairs; pictures still hung on the walls. A fan of magazines adorned the coffee table, along with the TV remote control. The dining room table was set.

"It's almost like someone could come home any minute," she said.

"The Realtor hired a stager to come in and make it look good. Not that it helped."

"I think if you don't want potential buyers to

envision the people who used to live here, it might be better to empty the place. But that's just my opinion. I don't know anything about real estate."

"It just seemed so final…clearing out Eric's things, putting it all in storage. I mean, even if he got out of prison tomorrow, he and MacKenzie would never come here to live. Especially since it's possible MacKenzie witnessed her mother's murder."

Elena didn't even want to think about that. Could a child ever fully recover from the trauma of seeing her mother killed right before her eyes?

They entered the kitchen last.

"This is where it happened, huh?" Elena asked.

"Right on the other side of the island. Eric came home from work and found her on the floor there. Stabbed with her own kitchen knife. There was some kind of struggle—a bar stool was knocked over."

Uncomfortable as it was, Elena envisioned the body on the floor, the bar stool lying on its side.

"The knife set is gone now, of course."

"So, an impulsive crime. A crime of passion. Whoever did it didn't come here intending to kill Tammy. Your theory is that her lover did it?"

"I know she was cheating on Eric."

"How?"

"The signs were there—a new hairstyle and she started dressing differently. Evasive answers to questions about where she was all day and why MacKenzie had needed a babysitter. Certain calls on her cell phone that she wouldn't answer if Eric was around. A sudden interest in finances—she wanted to know where all the money was."

"Like she might be contemplating divorce. I take it Eric confided in you, told you all this was happening."

"A lot of it I saw myself, and some I learned only after I told Eric what I suspected. He didn't want to believe she was cheating. He was in heavy denial, or at least pretending to be. He won't speak ill of Tammy and he especially doesn't want MacKenzie ever to hear any suspicion that her mother was unfaithful. That's one reason the cheating never came to light. Eric wouldn't hear of it, and the lawyer thought that even if it was true, it would hurt rather than help Eric's case."

"Her girlfriends would know. Did she have any close women friends, or maybe a sister?"

"No family at all, other than the grandmother. I don't know about her friends. All of Tammy's personal stuff is boxed out in the garage—anything the police didn't keep."

"Personal stuff like what? Clothes?"

"I don't know. We can dig through it if you want."

"I do want."

Elena was glad to see there were only six boxes. If Tammy had owned a computer, the police had probably kept that. Same with a phone. If Tammy had been anything like Elena, she kept all her contacts and her schedule on one or the other rather than on paper.

Elena and Travis dragged the boxes inside, opened them one by one and spread the contents onto the kitchen table—bank statements with canceled checks, credit card bills, receipts, newspaper and magazine clippings.

It was a gold mine. Elena made a pile of things she wanted to take home with her, to study at leisure later. "We can probably find out where she had her hair done, where she shopped, where she had lunch—any of those things might lead to her closest friends. Women tell their hairdressers everything."

"I'm sure the police went through this stuff."

"Yeah, but if they'd already made up their minds about Eric, they didn't look too close. What's this?" In one box, Elena found a huge accordion file. It was stuffed to overflowing with coupons—cut from newspapers and magazines and printed off the computer. "Wow, she was pretty serious about her couponing."

"Yeah, she belonged to some neighborhood coupon club—a group of moms who would get together once a week and trade coupons and free samples. I think it was really just an excuse to socialize. Their kids would all play together."

"That sounds like a treasure trove of gossip. Any idea who the other members were?"

"No clue. Eric might know some names."

In the very back of the accordion file was an envelope with a greeting card. The card was one of those innocuous "Thinking of You" varieties with a picture of flowers in a wicker basket. Inside were several coupons and a handwritten message, *Thought you could use these.* It was signed simply, *J.*

"Now this is interesting. Take a look at these coupons." Handling them only by the edges, she laid them out on the table one by one.

Travis peered at them before saying anything. "Five dollars off on a dozen roses? Get a free sample of Ciro's Chocolate Truffles? Ten percent off all massage oils?"

"Pretty cheap gesture, giving her the coupons instead of the real deal. Probably an inside joke. But I do believe we're looking at a gift from Tammy's lover."

CHAPTER NINETEEN

TRAVIS STUDIED THE COUPONS. "J. That could be anybody."

"But J, whoever he is, undoubtedly left some fingerprints on these items, not to mention DNA when he licked the envelope. The Project Justice lab can help us out." Elena felt tingly with excitement. They'd barely started, and already they had a meaningful lead.

It took only a few minutes to sort through the rest of the boxes. The last one had some photo albums, but they appeared to be from high school and college. Elena stashed the few items she wanted to examine further into a plastic garbage bag, and they returned the rest to the garage.

One life, summed up in six boxes—how sad. Tammy clearly had her faults, but she hadn't deserved what happened to her.

They locked the bag in the back of the truck. Travis started to open the driver's door, but Elena stopped him.

"Aren't we going to talk to the neighbors? We

could see if any of them know J. Or if any of them *are* J."

Travis looked uncomfortable. She knew he didn't want her getting so deeply involved. Rather than give him the opportunity to object, she turned and headed for the next-door neighbor's porch.

They must have rung twenty doorbells. They talked to a few people. Some refused to say anything, some truly didn't even know about the murder and a few tried to help. But none of them knew anything about the coupon club. None of them knew anything, in fact, that was helpful.

Discouraged, Travis and Elena headed back to the truck.

The sound of an electric scooter coming down the street drew Elena's attention. The girl on the lime-green scooter stopped at the curb in front of Eric's house and pulled off her helmet.

"Mr. Riggs? Is that you?"

The scooter rider was a young woman—maybe still a teenager, maybe a little older. She had long dark hair and a tattoo of a butterfly on her forearm.

His hand on the truck door handle, Travis looked blankly at her for a few moments before recognition apparently kicked in and he smiled. "April. I hardly recognized you. You're so grown-up."

The girl smiled back, seemingly pleased by the compliment.

Travis made quick introductions. "April used to babysit for MacKenzie."

"How is MacKenzie? I saw her a few times with that family over on the next block, the ones with all the foster kids. She always looked so sad. The other kids would be playing ball or whatever and she would just sit there."

"MacKenzie still misses her parents, I think," Travis said.

Elena sifted through the questions she wanted to ask this April. A babysitter could be privy to all kinds of information. Left alone in the house with only a toddler, she might have done some snooping. Or seen who was with Tammy when she came and went.

"It was so terrible, what happened to that family," Elena said. "It must have really shaken up the neighborhood."

April nodded. "It was all anyone talked about for months. Of course, my parents wanted to shield me from it. I was only fifteen. But it was all over the TV. Eric was so nice. We just couldn't believe what they said he did. I always figured it was the yardman."

"Jimmy?" Travis asked. "Why would you think that?"

"I heard he'd been in prison. And some people thought… It was probably just gossip. But Jimmy was always flirting with the ladies when he mowed their lawns, and some people thought it went further than flirting. It seemed like he spent a *lot* of time mowing the Riggs's lawn."

Travis and Elena shared a meaningful look. Could Jimmy be the coupon sender, the mysterious J?

"Do you know Jimmy's last name?" Travis asked.

April thought for a few moments. "No. But I still see him around the neighborhood."

"Were you at home the day it happened?" Elena asked.

"I was," April replied. "In fact, I was supposed to come over at three that afternoon and babysit, just until Eric got home. I'd been doing a lot of sitting for MacKenzie that summer. Tammy said her day care wasn't working out anymore. Anyway, when I went over there and rang the bell, no one answered. But I could hear voices inside." April shivered. "They were yelling."

"Could you recognize the voices?" Travis asked.

"Oh, it was Tammy. And a man. But not Eric."

Travis exchanged a look with Elena and then returned his attention to April. "You're sure about that?"

"Positive. Then I heard a loud crash, and the arguing stopped."

"What about Jimmy? Could it have been him?"

April thought for a few moments. "Maybe. I never really talked to Jimmy that much. But it definitely wasn't Eric. I know his voice. I didn't want to interrupt whatever was going on—I didn't want to *know,* so I just went home. I figured Tammy would call if she still wanted me."

Travis looked as if he'd been kicked in the head by a mule.

"Did you say three o'clock?"

April nodded.

"April, did you tell the police about this?"

"No, I never talked to them. I guess they came by the house the next day, but I was gone. My parents didn't want the police questioning me. They convinced me I didn't know anything that could have helped find the killer and I shouldn't get involved. But now... You're saying I could have helped prove Eric was innocent?"

"Eric has a solid alibi up until three-thirty. April, would you be willing to tell the police what you just told me?"

"Of course! I'm eighteen now. My parents can't stop me."

"Great. In the meantime...it would be better if you didn't say anything to anyone. I might be paranoid, but the real murderer is still out there somewhere, and..."

"He would just as soon I keep quiet. Yeah, I get it. No Twitter, no Facebook."

"Thanks, April. I'll be in touch in the next couple of days, okay?"

She nodded and then looked wistful. "I wish I'd done more. What if I'd walked into the house? Maybe I could have stopped—"

"Don't think like that," Elena said. "If you'd

walked in, you might have been killed yourself. You did what you thought was right at the time."

April nodded and gave Travis her cell phone number, then continued on to her house next door.

Elena barely contained her excitement. Could it really be this easy? Could they be this lucky?

"Do you think the police will even listen to her at this point?" Travis asked after they were back in the truck and on the way home.

"You don't have to go to the police. Go straight to Eric's attorney, the one who is handling the appeal. Is he or she someone you trust?"

"I used to. He's a different guy than the one who handled the original trial, an appeal specialist. But why didn't *he* do what we just did?"

"He was probably focused on procedural issues. That's what most appeals are based on. Don't be too hard on him."

"I'll call him as soon as we get home. Hell, what I really want to do is call him now."

"Do it. Pull over somewhere so you don't get a ticket and call him." This was such an unexpected turn of events. Elena had been excited to find that card from Tammy's lover, and that might be an interesting lead for the police to follow. But it wasn't something she and Travis had to worry about now. All they had to do was establish the time of death at three o'clock, and they were on their way to overturning Eric's conviction.

Travis pulled onto a random side street. He spent

some time scrolling through his contacts, looking for the lawyer.

"I'm surprised you don't have his number memorized," Elena said.

"Not so freakish after all, am I? There it is." After a few moments the call connected. "Richard Strauss, please...Travis Riggs...Regarding the appeal for my brother, Eric Riggs...Oh, no. How long?...Well, is there someone else I can talk to? This is kind of important. I might have proof of my brother's innocence...Okay, yeah, I'll talk to her...Next week? Can't we do this any faster? There are people trying to adopt Eric's daughter as we speak...Okay, okay, put me down for eleven next Wednesday. But if she gets any cancellations...Okay." Travis provided his name and phone number, then disconnected.

"It's okay." Elena touched his arm, but that felt so impersonal, so she took his hand. "Next week will be soon enough. There may be other people applying to adopt MacKenzie, but these things take time. No way can they get it done in a week."

"Yeah, but I hate to think of her in that *place*. That shelter or wherever she is."

"I'm sure she's being well cared for. Can you go visit her?"

"No. It's a shelter where they take abused kids, and the location is secret. I guess they thought that was the safest place for her when they removed her from the Stovers'. The only way I can visit her is if Missy brings her to a neutral location, and I don't think Missy is inclined to do that right now. I have to at least let her cool off a few days before I even try. Then there's April. What if she changes her mind? What if something happens to her?"

"Don't let this get you down, Travis. We're still way ahead of where we were a few hours ago. Keep that in mind. You've got a real chance now to get Eric out of prison. And he'll get his daughter back. Focus on that."

"You're right. And I have you to thank. But, Elena—"

"I know. I need to move on with my life."

She wanted to argue. But if she tried to look at things logically, what was keeping them together? From the beginning, one odd circumstance after another had conspired to keep them rotating in each other's orbits. Whether it was desperation, necessity, expediency, a sense of duty... Before she could always come up with a reason to be with Travis.

All those reasons were gone now. Almost with no effort, they'd come up with compelling evidence of Eric's innocence. But Travis could take it from here. He could talk to the lawyer, who would know what to do if he had a brain in his head.

Travis didn't need her anymore.

"There's no rush," he said quietly. "I understand how it could be uncomfortable living with your parents right now, so you're welcome to stay until you find something else."

"Yeah, okay. Thanks."

Just what she wanted: to be Travis's roommate.

Elena didn't understand what was going on. She still wanted to be with him. But apparently he didn't return her feelings. With all the heightened emotions of the kidnapping and the drama of MacKenzie's situation, maybe Travis had simply needed a physical and emotional outlet, and she'd been handy.

Now, with a solution to his problems in hand, it appeared his desire for her had deflated right along with the tension.

Elena would simply have to accept that this chapter in her life was over. She needed to get on with her life—a life without Travis.

She would leave him with one gift, however. Provided Daniel would cooperate.

TRAVIS FOUND HIMSELF pacing from the living room, through the dining room, into the kitchen and back again. It wasn't a very big house.

He should be elated—on top of the world. He finally had the means to prove his brother's innocence, or at least introduce a truckload of doubt. Elena was right—he had some breathing room with regard to anyone adopting MacKenzie. Father and daughter would be reunited, and they could all go about the business of rebuilding their lives.

Of course, he now owned a house that was way too big for his needs. But once he finished fixing it up, he could flip it if he decided he really preferred apartment life.

No, the reason for his dissatisfaction was upstairs in her bedroom, updating her résumé and applying for jobs.

Every time he relived their last conversation, he felt sick to his stomach. Politely asking Elena to remove herself from his life had been one of the hardest things he'd ever done. But it was the only decent thing to do.

He'd sensed that Elena might have stuck around if he'd given her any encouragement. She was a woman who liked to help. She liked to get people organized, to straighten out their lives, and in Travis she undoubtedly saw a great big, blank canvas on which to apply her art. A frigging diamond in the rough.

The fact that they were dynamite in bed was just icing on the cake.

But how long could a relationship last based on such a flimsy foundation? He already knew—a couple of years, tops, based on his experience with Judith.

It would be great at first. She probably could organize his business, maybe increase his bottom line by making his operation more efficient, allowing him to take on more work. They would fix dinner together, and the nights would be paradise.

But then the routine would start to get old. Elena would realize that Travis didn't have the extreme ambition of someone like Daniel Logan, that he didn't aspire to be rich or to impress the neighbors with fancy cars or belong to a country club. Her attention would wander. She would hear about other jobs she was qualified for, high-paying jobs. She would see her friends married to suave, sophisticated, wealthy men, and she would realize how she'd limited her choices.

By then, of course, he would be hopelessly in love with her. Hell, he already was. And when she left him, he would be a broken man.

That was why he hadn't encouraged her.

He would miss her terribly. He'd gotten used to having her around—the sound of her voice, her womanly scent, the way she touched him, so sweet and soft on an arm or a shoulder, when she wanted to offer comfort or encouragement.

But he would survive her departure. He had Eric's release to look forward to. In fact, this house would come in handy when that happened. Eric and MacKenzie could live here with him while Eric got his feet back under him. That would serve to distract Travis from obsessing about the huge hole in his life created by Elena's absence.

In a year or two, it would be much harder to let her go.

He probably should go do some work. Believing that he would be busy welcoming MacKenzie into her new home, he'd arranged for Leo to run things for a couple of days. But now Travis needed to be busy.

He should at least call and find out when the roofing crew would arrive. That hole in his roof wouldn't fix itself.

As he dialed, he heard Elena's footsteps coming down the stairs, and he braced himself for the reaction he had every time he laid eyes on her.

She'd changed into a plain skirt and blouse, a very modest, businesslike outfit, but the color and sheen of the fabric, which was a rich olive green, reflected the light and accentuated her curves in a way that was anything but ordinary. She'd pulled her hair up off her face and added a pair of heels that did wonderful things to her legs.

A less pleasing sight were the suitcases she carried.

"You look fantastic," he couldn't help himself from saying.

"Thanks. I left a few things—I'll come get them tomorrow maybe, while you're working, and I'll leave my key on the dining room table...if that's okay."

Too fast. It was happening too fast.

"Sure, but...can I ask where you're going?"

"I have a couple of options," she said breezily. "Please don't worry about me. I promise I won't sleep in my car."

Of course she had options. She wasn't destitute. She had credit cards and friends with guest rooms.

"You've got my number," she said. "Please, let me know how it goes with Eric and MacKenzie."

"I will. I really hope you all can meet someday. I

think you'll like Eric." But not too much, he hoped. Eric was the kind of man women fell for, hard and fast. Not that he didn't believe Eric and Elena would make a fine couple. But watching the court-ship would be like having his teeth pulled one by one without anesthetic. Watching Elena with *any-body* other than himself was an experience he hoped never to have.

ELENA MANAGED TO make it to her car without break-ing down. It wasn't that she would never see him again. If her plan worked out, she would be there when Travis saw his brother walk out of prison a free man. But this was the end of Elena and Travis, the couple, the team.

He believed this was for the best. She disagreed; but maybe where Travis was concerned, she wasn't thinking straight.

As she made her way to the freeway, she allowed one tear to roll down her cheek, but that was all. She had work to do, and she couldn't do it with a red nose and her makeup smeared everywhere.

The winter sun was already sliding toward the horizon as Elena reached River Oaks, but it wasn't yet full-blown rush hour. All too soon she was turn-ing onto Daniel's street.

When she got to Daniel's imposing front gate, she didn't even attempt to put the security code into the keypad. Daniel changed it every week. Instead, she pushed the intercom button.

"Yes, may I help you?" an unfamiliar female voice asked.

Damn. She'd been hoping to deal with someone who knew her. This woman, whoever she was, probably had heard Elena Marquez was persona non grata around here.

"Hi. I'm Elena Marquez. I have an appointment with Daniel at four." Daniel might have changed the security at his gate, but he hadn't changed his computer password recently. She still had access to his calendar, and she'd given herself the appointment.

The motor hummed as the gates slowly opened. One hurdle down of many to cross, but it was a start.

Out of habit, she almost drove to the garage and her old assigned parking place. Only at the last minute did she catch herself and stop in the drive near the fountain. She checked her appearance in the visor mirror, then got out and stood before the front door. She was five minutes early. Daniel abhorred people who were late, and she intended not to get on his bad side. She rang the bell.

The heavy front door opened, revealing a humorless-looking woman with steel-gray hair cut very short. Thick, black-framed glasses perched on the bridge of her pointed nose, and she pursed thin lips disapprovingly as she surveyed Elena.

"Good afternoon," the woman said, because protocol dictated she be civil. "I keep Mr. Logan's schedule, and I wasn't aware of this appointment."

She looked confused, probably wondering how Elena's name had magically appeared on her boss's calendar.

Daniel had already replaced her. Well, she shouldn't be surprised. It wasn't as if she'd given any indication that she might want her job back.

Elena chose not to explain how she came to be on Daniel's schedule. She just smiled pleasantly.

"Well, right this way. He'll see you in the library."

Daniel had probably decided to hire someone more mature this time, since his previous two assistants' personal dramas had caused them to flake out.

Elena wondered how *this* woman would have coped with being kidnapped. She probably wouldn't have fallen in love with her kidnapper.

The library door was ajar. The woman tapped lightly. "Mr. Logan? Your four o'clock is here."

"Is she, now? Send her in. And, Mrs. Drury, would you see to it that the passwords are changed on all of my computers?"

"Yes, sir." Mrs. Drury opened the door and allowed Elena inside. Daniel sat in one of the wingback chairs in front of the huge stone fireplace reading a newspaper on his tablet. His golden retriever, Tucker, lay at his feet.

Daniel stood. "Elena."

"H-hello, Daniel." Good heavens. She was stuttering.

He indicated that she should take the chair opposite his as Mrs. Drury closed the library door.

"You didn't have to resort to subterfuge, you know." He reclaimed his chair and put the tablet aside on a nearby table. "I'd have agreed to see you. You're the one who's angry, not me."

Oh, he was angry, all right. He might be the picture of civility to anyone who didn't know him, but she saw that muscle ticking in his jaw.

"I'm not angry anymore." She settled into the chair, setting her briefcase beside her. "I overreacted. In my defense, my emotions were running high."

"Understandable, given what you'd just gone through. And for what it's worth, you were right. The SWAT team was too much. I could have called them off well before you and Travis arrived, and I didn't. I wanted to see him suffer."

"And my parents? Did you want to see them suffer, too?"

Daniel shifted in his chair. "I'd convinced myself that you were experiencing some kind of delusion where Travis was concerned, brought on by stress. I thought your parents should know what kind of man had influence over their daughter."

She would not get mad all over again. That wasn't why she was there. This wasn't about her. It wasn't even about Travis. It was about Eric and MacKenzie, two completely innocent parties.

"Aren't you supposed to be nannying?" Daniel asked.

"The job fell through. The social worker found

out about the kidnapping, and she withdrew her approval of Travis as a foster parent. So MacKenzie didn't come live with him."

"Oh. Well…I'm sorry that didn't work out for you."

"Yeah, me, too. That's kind of why I'm here. It's about MacKenzie. She's a very fragile little girl. From what I understand, she wasn't exactly thriving in her former foster home. It was a bad situation. But now she's been put in some kind of shelter for abused children because there's not a spot for her anywhere else, and I'm worried about her."

"A child without a home is a very sad thing. What do you propose I do to help? I don't exactly have any sway with Social Services. Are you suggesting I become a foster parent?"

She smiled at the thought. Any foster kid who came to live with Daniel would feel as if they'd hit the jackpot. "No, nothing like that. You see, MacKenzie's problems would all go away if only Eric were free."

"And he will be, if it's possible. The case is in the queue. Travis got what he wanted."

"And I'm so appreciative. Really. But here's the deal. I've already solved the case. I have a witness ready to testify to the fact that she rang Tammy Riggs's doorbell at three o'clock and heard her arguing with a man who definitely was not Eric."

Daniel's eyebrows rose. "Around the time Tammy was murdered?"

Elena nodded, glad she didn't have to explain. Daniel really had looked into the case, in some detail, if he remembered the particulars.

Now that he was interested, she took her time describing what she and Travis had discovered and how. With every word she spoke, Daniel leaned in closer.

"Then she heard a crash, and the arguing stopped. But no one answered the door, so she left. This witness, April, undoubtedly heard the murder taking place. A bar stool was knocked over during the struggle—that was the crash she heard. And Eric has a solid alibi until three-thirty. We also found this." She opened her briefcase and pulled out a handful of plastic zipper bags. "A card from Tammy's lover. Pretty self-explanatory. His name starts with a *J,* and it might possibly be the yardman, Jimmy LeSalle." Elena had found several checks made out to Jimmy in the papers she'd taken from Eric's house. "He, or maybe his wife, was probably a member of the neighborhood coupon club Tammy belonged to."

"Coupon club?"

Of course Daniel, with his über-wealthy background, probably hadn't ever clipped a coupon in his life. She explained about the club, as she understood it. "It should be a simple matter to find this person. There might be fingerprints or DNA on this stuff, or the handwriting could be identified."

Daniel laid out the plastic bags on a library table and studied them briefly. "It's astounding to me the police never found this, never pursued any other leads. Then again, I guess I shouldn't be surprised, with as many times as I've encountered police apathy or downright laziness."

"April said the police did question neighbors, but her parents shielded her from the investigation. And the card…"

Daniel picked up one of the plastic bags again. "Postmarked a week before Tammy's death. This card was undoubtedly in her personal effects. This coupon file you found was probably given a cursory glance and deemed insignificant."

"It's enough, right? To get Eric's conviction overturned?"

"Maybe. We'd have a shot, anyway. Do you want me to turn this evidence over to whichever of my investigators gets assigned the case?"

"Actually, I was hoping for a bit more. I thought maybe you could talk to the district attorney. Like, now. Today. The sooner we can get the ball rolling, the sooner we can get MacKenzie out of that shelter and into a stable home with her father where she can start to heal."

Elena knew she was asking a lot. Daniel didn't owe her anything, and he did not like to make exceptions when it came to protocol. His foundation was often under tight scrutiny by detractors of every stripe, and any appearance of granting special favors to friends or employees had to be discouraged. He'd already bent the rules a little bit by agreeing to take on the Riggs case to begin with. Now she was asking him to move the case into a priority position.

Daniel was thinking. He gazed into the fireplace, reaching down absently to scratch Tucker behind his floppy ears. Elena resisted the urge to fill the silence with more arguments. She knew better than to interrupt him. He had all the information he needed to make a decision. The fact that he was even considering her request filled her with hope.

Finally, he returned his attention to her. "So, you're asking me for a favor."

"Yes."

"Can I ask you a question?"

"Of course."

"Are you and Travis romantically involved?"

Where had that come from? Daniel didn't usually ask such personal questions out of idle curiosity. Perhaps he was simply trying to understand her motives. She decided to answer the question as honestly as she could. He was definitely making concessions; she should, too.

"I confess, I'm strongly attracted to Travis. From the moment I met him, I sympathized with him. He was in so much pain because of his family members' dire situation. I guess that devotion to his brother and niece got to me."

She expected Daniel to argue with her about Travis's character. But he didn't.

"The attraction wasn't one-sided. We did become physically involved. But for whatever reason, Travis doesn't want me around anymore. Maybe I'm a reminder of something he deeply regrets. Maybe he just doesn't want the responsibility of a real relationship. Maybe he's still gun-shy from his marriage. I don't know. But I've moved out. I know you don't see it, but he's a good man. A really good man."

"So, if the two of you aren't...together, why are you still so involved in his cause?"

Dios, Daniel didn't ask easy questions. "I want to finish what I started. I want to do this one thing, this one really important, good thing for Travis. So few people have truly cared about his welfare. I want him to know what it feels like to have someone do something with no expectation that he do anything in return. That's the best I can do to explain my reasoning."

"So you don't harbor some hope that if you do this grand thing, he'll take you back?"

She shook her head. "It's not like that. I know it's over between us. I don't expect to see him again. Well, that's not true. I do hope to see his face when he finds out Eric is a free man. I want to remember him smiling. But that will be it."

Daniel nodded. "If I do this favor for you—and all I can do is talk to Jamie. I can't guarantee results. Are you willing to do something for me in return?"

"I'll do anything you want me to do." She answered without hesitation, knowing Daniel would not ask her to do anything illegal or immoral.

"Come back to work for me."

For a few moments, she was too stunned to answer. She hadn't expected that. But finally she found her voice. "What about Mrs. Drury? She seems the competent, no-nonsense type."

Daniel groaned. "It's like having my grandmother work for me, and believe me, if you'd known my grandmother, that's not a pleasant thing. I'm terrified of her. She has no sense of humor. She's trying to run my life like an army general. This morning, she actually turned off the hot water heater. She claims cold showers are healthier and will make me more productive. She switched my coffee to decaf without asking!"

Elena couldn't help it—she laughed.

"It's not funny."

"Sorry." Could she go back to work for Daniel? Her anger toward him had tempered; he'd admitted he was wrong and apologized. If she got her old job back, it would solve a multitude of problems, not the least of which she could resume sending money to her relatives still in Cuba. She wouldn't have to find another job, or apartment, or buy a car, or health insurance. But was that just laziness on her part?

"I can see you're not wild about the idea."

"Actually…the idea is very attractive. I was just examining my conscience to see if it would be okay to accept."

"If you could give me a month or two—just long

enough to find a competent replacement—that would help."

She gave it only a moment's further consideration. "Okay. Okay, I'll do it."

CHAPTER TWENTY

THREE DAYS LATER, Elena was back into the swing of her job. It was almost as if she'd never left. Whatever lingering tensions remaining between her and Daniel were dissipating. She admired him too much to hold one or two mistakes against him forever.

But there was still one problem: *She* wasn't the same person she'd been before meeting Travis. Oh, she still performed her job with her usual efficiency. She dressed the same way, ate the same foods, joked around with the security guys.

But at night, when she lay down in her cozy bed with its down duvet and the perfectly controlled temperature, she no longer felt the satisfaction she used to experience. During the day Daniel kept her too busy to think much about Travis. But at night, she literally ached for him.

She would have much preferred to be in Travis's cute little house, even if it did have a hole in the roof, uninsulated walls and creaky floors. Travis would keep her warm, and she could focus on the comforting sound of his heartbeat and breathing rather than house noises.

She recalled the deep timbre of his voice, his Ivory soap scent, the many ways he touched her. She thought about how badly Travis needed chil dren in his life, and how much she wanted to be the woman to bear them. It sounded an awful lot as though she was in love with the man. Seriously in love. And she wasn't getting over it any time soon.

Being the personal assistant to an unspeakably wealthy man who paid all of her living expenses.. It was just too easy, even with the long hours and Daniel's unpredictable expectations.

She wanted passion in her life. She wanted to challenge herself. Set goals and achieve them. Even the prospect of living within a budget and washing her own clothes sounded appealing.

That was it. She'd grown up in the past few weeks. Now she needed to *live* like a responsible adult.

As she showered and dressed that morning, a lit tle bleary-eyed from sleep, she knew she wouldn't stay working for Daniel. She would find him just the right person to be his new assistant. She would pre pare herself, too—find her own apartment, her own car. She would start job hunting in earnest, although she wasn't sure exactly what she wanted to do.

She wondered if there might be a position for her at Project Justice. The important work done there appealed to her. But she wasn't a lawyer, a former cop or a scientist; those were the skills most valued at the foundation.

Finding a job was just one of many challenges

she faced, and the prospect of figuring it all out made her blood race with excitement and anticipation. There was still a big hole in her heart where Travis ought to be, but hopefully she would keep herself so busy, so challenged, that she would have no time to dwell on her loss during the day and would be too exhausted at night to let thoughts of Travis keep her awake.

Daniel was already at the breakfast table when she came downstairs. Normally she beat him by a good fifteen minutes. She checked her watch: no, she wasn't later than usual.

"Good morning, Elena. I trust you slept well?"

"Very well, thank you," she lied. A good assistant never troubled her boss with her personal problems.

"Me, too. I have some space in my schedule around ten-thirty this morning. Come to my office. I have something to discuss with you."

Elena's heart skipped a beat. Could this be something about Eric? She hadn't pressed Daniel for any progress reports. If he said he would talk to his wife, he would do it, and he would inform her of what Jamie's reaction was and what progress was being made whenever he deemed it appropriate. Nagging him would only irritate him.

"I'll be there. Actually, I have something to discuss with you, too." She wanted to give him the news of her resignation before he gave her any good news, so it wouldn't appear she'd been waiting until she got what she wanted before quitting her job.

"I'll look forward to it."

She was so filled with a mixture of excitement and dread, she could hardly eat any of her breakfast, even though Cora had made blueberry crepes, one of Elena's favorites. She just kept swallowing coffee, knowing too much would make her jittery.

Her morning was filled with mistakes—phone numbers misdialed, a lost insurance form Daniel needed to sign, a message for one executive at Logan Energy given to another. But she was so distracted she could hardly answer the phone without stuttering and forgetting commonplace words. When Daniel's ten o'clock video-conferencing appointment wrapped up early, Elena didn't wait around for the clock to actually read ten-thirty. She went directly to Daniel's office, his man cave, and tapped on the door.

"Ready for me?"

"Come on in." He wasn't smiling. What if he had bad news? What if Jamie had scoffed at the idea of Tammy's lover killing her at precisely three o'clock? They were depending on the word of a teenager, after all.

"Hi, Daniel. I hope you won't mind, but I'd like to say my piece first, before yours."

"Okay." He looked worried. "Have I done something wrong?"

"No...oh, no, you've been the model boss. And this is nothing personal against you, but—"

"You're resigning again."

"Yes… How did you know?"

"You're not that hard to read, Elena. I can sense a certain restlessness in you. A vague dissatisfaction that was never evident before."

She was surprised at Daniel's astuteness where she was concerned. For most bosses, if you were a good assistant, you became invisible.

"I had a cat once, when I was a kid," he said. "Her name was Dolly, and she lived indoors all her life. Because she'd never been beyond the front door, she had no interest in running free. But one day, she got out and she was gone for a whole day. I guess she realized what she'd been missing—birds, mice, grass, trees to climb. I found her and brought her back home. But she was forever sitting at the window, looking out, clearly yearning for that freedom she tasted."

"You think I'm Dolly?"

He nodded. "You had a taste of freedom. You want to experience life on your own terms. I get it. And I have no intention of standing in your way."

"Oh, Daniel, thank you. My stomach has been tied up in knots all morning. And I intend to give you plenty of time. We'll find someone really great to take over my job. Someone so great you'll never miss me."

"I doubt that, but I'm trusting you to get me the best candidate possible."

"I will."

Daniel cleared his throat. "I spoke with Jamie

about the Riggs case. She wasn't too happy. Even though it was her predecessor who prosecuted Eric, every time Project Justice overturns a Houston conviction, it reflects badly on her office, and she's tired of it. She doesn't want this to be another public relations disaster."

"So she won't help?"

"On the contrary. She's already handled it…quietly. She brought April in for a deposition two days ago, and she turned over the greeting card and coupons to her own investigators. They found prints on the envelope, and you won't believe who the prints belong to."

"It's Jimmy, right?"

"Wrong. John Stover."

Elena was stunned. "MacKenzie's foster dad was Tammy's lover?"

"Apparently so. His wife was part of that coupon club, so Stover would have known all about it."

"He's a viable suspect, then."

"It's a big leap from having an affair to murder. But there's more. The crime lab took a closer look at Tammy's fingernail clippings and the DNA collected. She definitely scratched someone. Once they get a profile, they'll compare it to Stover's. But even if it doesn't match—even if Stover isn't the murderer—Eric Riggs is in the clear."

"Are you sure? The district attorney will take the word of a teenage girl?"

"She's an honor student headed to Notre Dame—

a credible witness. Her testimony is highly suggestive that Tammy was murdered while Eric was with a client at his office. Now, you know the wheels of justice can move slowly—"

"Of course."

"And it might take some time to get the verdict overturned and officially reopen the case. But I spoke with the governor yesterday and, given the little girl's situation, he's going to grant a full pardon for Eric as soon as possible."

Stunned was far too mild a word to describe what Elena felt. She literally had to grip the arms of her chair to keep from falling out of it. "Oh, my God. *Oh, my God,* Daniel, this is amazing. Thank you!" She flew out of her chair and hugged him, practically climbing into his lap.

Daniel laughed and hugged her back. "Elena."

She came to her senses and extricated herself from him, straightening the tie she'd knocked askew. "I'm so sorry. I forgot myself." She'd never before hugged her boss. It was unseemly.

"It's all right. You're entitled to lose your composure once in a while."

"I have to go tell Travis." She headed for the door, and then realized she was still acting like a lunatic. "Wait. Sorry. I can't just take off in the middle of a workday. Do you mind if I leave for a bit while you're at lunch?"

Daniel grinned. "Go now. I have a feeling you'll be distracted anyway until you take care of this."

She stopped at her room only long enough to change into a pair of jeans and a casual top—mostly because she didn't want to have to explain to Travis why she'd gone back to work for Daniel. He would think she'd sold her soul to the devil. Even though he'd been horrified to hear she'd quit her job because of him, she felt he would still be disappointed in her for changing her mind.

She waited until she was in her car before calling Travis. It occurred to her that he would probably notice she was driving a very nice car—her company car was a red BMW. She hoped he wouldn't ask, because she wouldn't lie outright to him.

When she called his cell, voice mail picked up. "Travis, it's Elena. Call me, please. I need to see you. It's important."

Now that she was in her car, she couldn't just sit there. She decided to drive to Travis's house and see if he might be home. His hours were unpredictable. She had to resist speeding and running through stop signs to get there.

But when she arrived and rang the bell, no one was home. She'd already picked up the rest of her things and left her key, making sure he wasn't home first so she wouldn't have to see him. But today seeing his face would be a pleasure, a memory she would treasure forever.

She dialed his number again. Still no answer.

"Well, that's annoying."

She couldn't just wait there until he returned. That

could be hours. And while Daniel hadn't specified any particular time she should be back at work, she didn't want to abuse his goodwill. He'd gone the extra mile for Eric Riggs. Maybe he'd done it for Jamie, to save the D.A.'s office more embarrassment. But she suspected he'd done it for her.

Then she spotted a couple of guys up on the roof. She got back out of her car and approached. *"Hola!"* When they looked at her, she gave them a friendly wave. "Do you know where Travis is?"

"He's at the big job," one of the men answered. "The house on Marigold Circle."

That made sense. His deadline for having it finished was fast approaching. *"Gracias!"*

The house wasn't far. And somehow it seemed fitting that their final meeting take place at the location where he'd first held her hostage. A couple of trucks were parked in the driveway, but not Travis's. Maybe he'd put it in the garage. She rang the bell, but no one answered. She didn't hear the sound of machinery or hammering or even a radio. She tried the door, but it was locked.

Well, shoot. The guys had probably gone to lunch. She couldn't wait all day. She would just have to give Travis the news over the phone when he finally returned her call. It occurred to her that he might be avoiding her on purpose, but if he didn't want to see her, he would probably just tell her up front.

Disappointed, she turned from the door just as it opened.

She whirled back around to find a tall, dark-haired man in jeans and a T-shirt standing there.

"Oh, hi," she said. "I didn't think anyone was here. I'm looking for Travis. Do you know when he'll be back?"

"He just went to lunch. Should be back anytime. You can come in and wait, if you want. You're... Aren't you Elena, Travis's girlfriend?"

She could understand the mistake. Several of Travis's workers had seen the two of them together. She didn't remember meeting this particular guy on the job before, but construction workers came and went. And they probably gossiped, too. "We're not really... Not anymore. But I still need to talk to him about something." She stepped inside and closed the door behind her. When she turned back to face the man who'd let her in, she was met with a most upsetting sight. The foyer was covered with neon-orange spray paint. Vile words were scrawled on the walls, the tile floor, even the ceiling.

"Oh, no. When did this happen?"

"Just now, actually."

A sense of foreboding hit Elena in the solar plexus. She looked at the man, who smiled at her unpleasantly. She glanced at his hands. Orange paint covered his index finger.

"You're him, aren't you? Stover."

"Right on the first guess."

Dios. She was staring into the face of a murderer. Accusations were on the tip of her tongue, but she stopped herself at the last moment. Stover probably didn't know he was a murder suspect. If she tipped him off, he might flee. Instead, she asked, "Why did you let me in? I was about to leave. You could have gotten away with it."

"Oh, I *will* get away with it. And a lot more, too. Travis Riggs destroyed my life. He took away my livelihood, not to mention my future retirement. I won't rest until I ruin him."

Could she brazen it out? "Fine by me. Son of a bitch dumped me. I just came here to return—"

"Nice try, sweetheart." She turned to run, but she wasn't fast enough. He snagged her by the wrist and jerked her toward him. "Destroying his business is step one. Killing his girlfriend? That ought to put a dent in his swagger."

She struggled against him as he tried to drag her toward the back of the house. "You think you won't get caught? The police know who's behind the vandalism."

"I doubt that very much. I made sure there were no witnesses."

"You're not as smart as you think. They'll know. If you hurt me, they'll know it was you." Where was he taking her? If he wanted to kill her, why not just do it here?

She was making it too easy for him. She recalled how little effort it took for Travis to scoop her up and thrust her into his truck; lying there in that dark cramped space with tools digging into her back, she'd had time to think about how to prevent being victimized again. Yet here she was, letting it happen. She dug in her heels, forcing him to drag her. She tried kicking him, and she made contact a couple of times, hitting him hard enough to make him curse. But his hand remained clamped around her arm like a steel vise. She felt something crack inside her wrist and pain shot up her arm like a hot poker.

"Stand up and walk!" he screamed as he backhanded her across the face.

She refused to meekly cooperate. Instead, she bit his hand the way a dog would.

"Damn it! Bitch!" He threw her onto the floor and she fell on her knees, hard. She scrambled to her feet, but he grabbed her by the hair. "You're not going anywhere." He hit her again, with a closed fist this time. For the first time in her life, she literally saw stars. By the time her vision cleared, Stover had thrown her over his shoulder in a cruel parody of the way Travis had held her. Stover had one hand clamped around her thigh, his fingers digging into her flesh. Beating her fists against his back had no effect.

"Where are you taking me?"

"Somewhere I can take my time with you," he replied matter-of-factly. "Maybe get it on video. Send it to Travis as a little present."

No. She could not allow him to do this to Travis. Just when his brother would get his life back, Travis would lose his. He would forever blame himself for Elena's death. If there was video, those pictures would be burned into Travis's brain forever. She could not let it happen.

As Stover carried her through the kitchen, Elena grabbed on to anything she could get her hands on. She managed to snag the refrigerator door, using her good hand to grip the handle with all her strength and forcing Stover to at least slow down so he could pry her lose. She wiggled and kicked and screamed. He punched her leg with his fist, but she'd reached a ceiling as far as the pain went.

"Let go, bitch."

The fridge door came open and she grabbed the first thing she could get her hands on: a bottle of ketchup. As Stover finally pulled her free of the appliance, she whacked him in the head with the plastic bottle, wishing it was glass. Still, it had to hurt.

She heard a door open.

"Hey, who the hell left this door unlocked?"

"Travis!" she screamed. "Help me, please, help me!"

Stover dropped her onto the hard tile floor, and her knees took the brunt of the fall yet again. But no sooner had she hit the ground than he'd dragged her to her feet again. He reached into the sink behind him, and when his hand came back, it was holding a knife.

"Elena!" Travis cried out.

"Don't come any closer," Stover said in a growl.

"Let her go!" Travis bellowed. "Just drop her and

run out the back door. I won't come after you. You can get away."

"What, and miss out on all the fun? I'm screwed now, any way you look at it. I'm going to prison. I might as well have some fun before I go down."

"Travis, go!" Elena screamed. "Don't try to take him yourself. He's a murderer. He killed Tammy!"

Travis's face went slack with shock.

"Don't listen to her," Stover growled. "Stay. I want to see the look on your face when I slit the throat of the woman you love. Ah, you do love her. I see it in your eyes."

Did he? It was ridiculous for Elena to feel happiness bloom in her chest when she was about to die, but Stover was right. She could see love in Travis's eyes. It was all mixed up with fear and horror and murderous fury, but it was there.

"You are going down, you cowardly piece of filth." Travis now spoke with an eerie calmness. "You can do it easy. You can let Elena go, run out the back door and count on being arrested. But if you cut her, if you do any more damage than you've already done, I will kill you here on the spot. And I won't be merciful. You'll die screaming."

Elena could almost feel the indecision pouring off Stover. At heart, he was a coward, preying on women, victimizing children who couldn't speak up for themselves.

He let her go. Her legs were so shaky they didn't

hold her up, and she crumpled to the floor, gulping in air as she released the breath she'd been holding. If Travis had shown up just one minute later, she would still be Stover's hostage.

"You think you can take me?" Stover adopted a fighting stance.

Elena realized he wasn't going to just meekly surrender. He still had a knife. Travis was unarmed.

"You like kitchen knives, don't you?" Travis said. "Your murder weapon of choice. Is this how it happened with Tammy? She was stringing you along. That day, in the kitchen, she told you it was over. You saw your whole future—all that delicious money she was going to inherit from her grandmother—slipping away, and you lost it. You grabbed a knife and before you knew it… Seventeen stab wounds."

"The bitch deserved it. She said she was leaving her husband. Then she laughed in my face and said she would never leave an attorney for an unemployed loser like me."

Good, Travis. Keep him talking. While he's talking, he's not cutting anyone.

"Then you realized you could still get the money—by adopting MacKenzie. Easy enough for you to get her into your home. You were already approved foster parents, and MacKenzie knew you. You also could make sure she didn't tell anyone what she saw that day."

"Well, aren't you the smarty-pants," Stover said.

"Too bad you won't be able to tell anyone. Just how brave are you? Maybe you'll get the best of me. But you're sure as hell gonna bleed before it's all over. Or you could turn tail and run."

Stover had apparently forgotten Elena. He'd dismissed her as a threat. But she'd be damned if she'd let this maniac carve up Travis like a Halloween pumpkin. Stover stood only a few feet from her. She rose slowly to her hands and knees, then to a squatting position.

His attention fully on Travis, waiting for his opponent to make the first move, Stover wouldn't see Elena.

Without warning she launched herself at him, screaming like an enraged tigress and tackling him around the legs.

Travis reacted with the reflexes and ferocity of a pit bull. In half a second flat he was straddling Stover's chest and had the killer's arm pinned to the floor.

"Let go of the knife!" Travis smashed Stover's arm against that unforgiving tile floor. Finally Stover dropped the weapon. "I got him, Elena. Are you okay? No, stupid question, you're not okay. Can you stand up? Can you find a phone and call 911?"

"I'm on it."

Her phone was lying on the floor in the foyer, along with the rest of the contents of her purse, which had dropped and spilled when Stover had grabbed her. She had to dial with her left hand; her right wrist was swollen up like the Goodyear blimp, and any movement of her fingers caused excruciating pain.

"Nine-one-one, what is your emergency?"

"I need the police."

CHAPTER TWENTY-ONE

TRAVIS KEPT CRANING his neck, trying to see Elena. But he didn't dare move. Stover seemed compliant, defeated even, lying still beneath Travis. But if given a glimmer of daylight, he would get free. The knife still lay only inches from Stover's hand, but Travis couldn't help that. He couldn't let go of anything to grab the knife and throw it out of reach. And he damn sure wasn't going to ask Elena to come near this sick animal.

He'd nearly had a heart attack when he'd seen Elena in Stover's grip, a knife at her throat. She'd been beaten; her face had red blotches that would undoubtedly turn into bruises. Her nose had been bleeding, and one of her eyes was nearly swollen shut. The scene was his worst nightmare come to life—exactly the sort of thing he'd been worried about ever since he realized Stover had a vendetta against him.

"Elena?"

She appeared in the kitchen doorway, a phone in her hand. "The police are on their way." The parts of her face that weren't bruised were as white as the primer paint on the kitchen wall. "Do you want me to get some rope or something?"

"No. I'll sit right here until the police arrive." He didn't want to risk Stover slithering out of his grasp somehow. Travis was *not* going to spend any more time looking over his shoulder, wondering how and where Stover was going to strike.

He looked back up at Elena. She was leaning against the door frame, just staring at him. He'd never seen anyone look so frightened. "That was an incredibly brave thing you did—tackling him."

"Well, I wasn't going to let him slice up your pretty face."

"And I wasn't about to let him hurt you. Hurt you more," he amended. "What the hell happened?"

"I guess I interrupted his spray-painting party. He wanted to punish you. By killing me."

If Stover had succeeded, it wouldn't have just punished Travis. Knowing he'd been the cause of Elena's death would have destroyed him for good.

Travis wanted to hurt Stover for what he'd done to the woman he loved. He wanted to bash the scumbag's face in. But he just sat there, holding Stover's arms, waiting to hear sirens.

It seemed to take forever for the police to arrive. Elena met them at the door and calmly, succinctly, told them what had happened, though at times her voice trembled. Given the extent of her injuries, she made a credible witness. No one was going to doubt she'd been assaulted.

"Then Travis arrived. Stover was going to cut him with the knife, but together we subdued him." She pointed urgently to Travis and Stover on the kitchen floor, where two cops were already untangling the two men. For a few minutes things were crazy; paramedics were trying to stop Elena's nosebleed, more cops arrived, yelling at each other and talking on the radio and Stover was screaming his innocence, claiming Elena and Travis were conspiring against him. He tried to make a big deal about the fact that Elena bit him—pretty much the only injury showing on his body.

"Hey," one of the uniforms said, "did you say your name is John Stover?"

"Yeah, what about it?"

"There's a warrant out for your arrest."

"No way, for what? You must have me mixed up with—"

"For murder, Mr. Stover."

Travis looked to Elena, who was now lying on a gurney while a paramedic splinted her wrist. He wanted to go to her, to be with her. But she was surrounded by a force field of uniforms and medical people.

"Can I take your statement, Mr. Riggs?" a young, plainclothes cop asked politely. A detective, he guessed. No cop had ever treated him with such deference before. Quite a switch.

"Yeah, in a minute." He maneuvered his way

through the sea of khaki and blue until he was standing by Elena's side. "Elena."

She turned her eyes to look at him and smiled like an angel. A beat-up angel. "Travis."

"How are you? Stupid question, you're doing horrible."

"No. I'm good. Really good." She was grinning like a fool. Why was she so happy?

"So, Stover killed Tammy?" Travis asked.

"That's what I came here to tell you. His prints were on that greeting card. His DNA was under Tammy's fingernails. Oh, Travis, the governor is issuing Eric a full pardon, even before his conviction is overturned. He should be free in the next few days."

Travis went suddenly dizzy. "Could you say that again?"

"Eric is going to be a free man."

"You got Daniel to pull some strings."

"I did. He…he asked me to come back to work for him."

"No wonder you're smiling."

"No, idiot, that's not why. I'm happy because you love me."

"Uh…" *Damn it.* How could she know that?

"I'm right. Aren't I?"

"Well you don't have to be so smug about it." There was no point in denying the obvious. He'd known he was in love with her on some level, but he hadn't been ready to admit it—until he'd faced the very real possibility that he would have to live the rest of his life without her. Then it had hit him in the face with more force than that wrench Elena had lobbed at him. He very much wanted her with him.

For the rest of his life.

"Now you're the one who's grinning," she said. "I came over here to tell you in person about Eric— just so I could see your face."

"Excuse me, Mr. Riggs," said the polite cop, who'd been hovering nearby, probably making sure Travis and Elena weren't colluding on the facts. "I really need to take your statement now."

"Okay. Let's do it."

The sooner he got through with this, the sooner he could be with Elena. And prepare for Eric's release. But mostly be with Elena. Maybe she could find a more compatible mate, someone with education and sophistication and millions of dollars. But she'd never find anyone who loved her more than he did. He would work his tail off to be the best man he could be, the man she deserved.

And for maybe the first time ever, he believed he could be that man. It was partially his fault that Stover got to her in the first place. But working together, they'd stopped him. They'd captured a murderer.

If they could do that, they could do anything.

ELENA WISHED NOW that she hadn't told her parents what happened—at least until she was released from the emergency room. But her father had called and asked if she wanted to come to dinner. He'd sounded quite conciliatory. But she couldn't come to dinner, not tonight, because the only way the doctor was going to let her out was if she had an MRI and got the all clear. Apparently she'd hit her head pretty hard at some point during the assault.

So she'd told her father why she couldn't come, and here he was, hovering over her. Rosalie had brought a plate full of *pastelitos* and shared them with every patient in the E.R. who was well enough to eat. Meanwhile, her father was pestering the doctors and nurses, making sure she had the best care possible. They put up with it only because he was a doctor himself.

She did look pretty horrible. Even after the nurses had cleaned most of the blood off her face and patched her up, she still could have landed a role in a zombie movie.

"My poor *pequeña,*" her father said for the tenth time.

"I'm okay, Papa," she answered, also for the tenth time. "But do pay attention." She pointed to her face. "*This* is how a person looks when she's been kidnapped by a *bad* man."

Elmer looked down guiltily. "I know, Elena. You would think, after the way I was harshly judged once upon a time, I would understand something about what men do when they are desperate. I take it your feelings for Travis have not changed?"

"If anything, they've grown. You will see. He cares for me, too. He risked his life for me. He could have turned tail and run, called the police from a safe distance. But he was willing to face that knife-wielding maniac when he had no weapon but his hands."

"Then I believe he has made up for any wrong he might have done. We will consider the slate wiped clean."

"And...?"

"And...I apologize for acting like a crazy man and causing trouble for Travis with the social worker."

Elena knew how hard it was for a proud man like her father to admit he was wrong. She squeezed his hand. *"Te amo, Papa."*

"I love you, too, *pequeña.*"

A man clearing his throat snagged their attention. Travis was standing at the entrance to her room. A slow warmth spread through her body at the sight of him; even in her current, sad physical state, she still responded.

Travis and her father locked gazes. "Dr. Marquez," Travis said deferentially.

"Mr. Riggs. I want to thank you for saving my daughter's life." He held out his hand.

Travis took it without hesitation. "It was more of a team effort, really. Elena was incredibly brave."

"Still... I've already apologized for my poor behavior to Elena, but I must say it to you, too. I know

now that what I did jeopardized the well-being of a little girl."

"You were only trying to protect *your* little girl," Travis said gruffly.

"Then I hope we can start over, you and I."

"I'd like that."

Elena's heart felt as if it had grown wings. To see the two men she loved most in the world coming to terms, shaking hands… Well, it gave her hope. Lots of hope.

"Papa, can you give Travis and me a few moments?"

"Of course. I will go find your mother. Last I saw, she had found a patient with a broken jaw and was talking her ear off because the poor thing can't talk back." He nodded one last time to Travis and left.

Travis pulled up the single plastic chair in the room and sat down close to her bed. He took her uninjured hand in his. "How do you feel?"

"Fantastic."

"Liar."

"No, really, I do. Seeing you and Papa shake hands like that… It was the best medicine in the world."

"Will you stay in the hospital?"

"Not if I can help it." She told him about the test results she was waiting for, which only made him look more worried. "I'm fine, really. It's just a precaution."

"Will you go back to Daniel's?"

"It's where I live now. I moved back in, and he needs me."

"I see. I guess you'll be well cared for there."

"Did you have another idea?"

"I was thinking *I* would take care of you. I had this picture in my head of me bringing you breakfast in bed, drawing you a bath, helping you dress and… undress. How are you going to do all the things Daniel needs you to do when your arm is broken? I've got a perfectly good guest room—"

"Okay."

"Okay?"

"That sounds much better than staying at Daniel's. And you're right, I won't be able to do my job. It's okay, though, Daniel has people who can fill in. But you have to promise me something. Two things, actually."

"Anything."

"I don't want you to neglect your work. You've got some spray paint to deal with."

"I promise. What's the second thing?"

"I don't want to stay in the guest room."

"Are you saying you want to live with me? Like, really live together?"

"That's what I'm saying."

"No."

"Oh." She drooped with disappointment. She'd expected some resistance, but not a flat-out no.

"Not without a wedding ring. I expect your father would not look too kindly on us shacking up without the benefit of a marriage license. And, frankly, I don't want to get on his bad side again."

"Did you just… Was that a—"

"A marriage proposal. Yes, it was. I was planning to wait until you were better, maybe take you out to a nice place, get down on one knee, the whole nine yards. I might have even worn a tie. But I can't wait that long for your answer. Elena Marquez, I love you with all my heart, and I'm sorry it took me so long to get to the place where I could admit it, where I could take the risk of going after what I want. But you were right all along. I deserve to be happy like anyone else. And you, Elena, would make me the happiest man on earth—"

"Yes!" she shrieked, earning a stern look from a passing nurse. She giggled giddily. Maybe it was the meds they'd given her, but she suspected it was just sheer, unadulterated joy.

She clamped a hand over her mouth. "Yes," she whispered between her fingers. He didn't have to take her to a fancy restaurant or give her flowers or a big diamond ring. All he had to do was be there for her, just as she would be for him. "We are going to have the most beautiful babies."

"If they all look like you, yeah. A houseful of babies, if you want. And I've been thinking… I'd understand if you wanted to keep working for Daniel. But if you're still set on trying something new, how would you like to help me expand my business? I'm going to have to earn more money to put all those future babies through college."

"Really? I can be your business manager?"

"Full partner. Fifty-fifty. We'll make enough that you can still send money to your relatives in Cuba."

She was so touched that he'd even considered that. But she wasn't too worried about her relatives. Her father sent money to them, too.

"It's gonna be a lot of work," Travis said. "We'll have to get computerized."

"It'll be fun. I can't wait to get started."

"When you're feeling better. No rush."

"I could not feel any better than I feel right now."

CHRISTMAS EVE AT the Logan estate was always a celebration to remember. Usually Daniel threw a big party—invited all the employees of Project Justice and Logan Energy, hired a live band, spent a fortune on decorations. This year, however, he and Jamie had decided to keep the holiday more low-key—just a few friends, a cozy fire, good food and mulled cider.

A few weeks ago, Elena had begun planning a more elaborate affair. But given all that had happened—and the fact that while she recuperated from her injuries, she wasn't up to the complex logistics of a big party—Daniel had opted for the scaled-back affair, something he could trust the imposing Mrs. Drury to handle.

Missy, having calmed down considerably after

the big blowup, had allowed Travis and Elena to visit MacKenzie.

MacKenzie was shy; she hadn't warmed up to Elena right away. In fact, she'd hardly said a word during that first visit, preferring to sit in Travis's lap with her thumb in her mouth and let him read to her.

But this evening, after a bit of legal finagling, MacKenzie had been released into Elena's care, and the little girl seemed happy enough to climb into the Town Car Daniel had provided them. All of her worldly belongings were packed into a tiny suitcase; by the time Missy had removed her from the Stovers' home, she'd had none of the clothes and toys Eric had bought her.

But that was all about to change.

The car pulled slowly up Daniel's driveway, and MacKenzie's nose was pressed to the glass, looking out. "Wow, that's a big house."

"Yes, it is."

"Am I gonna live there?"

This was the most talkative MacKenzie had been with Elena so far. "No, we're just going to a party."

"Will Uncle Trav be there?"

"Yes, he's on his way here now. And he's bringing a surprise with him."

"Did he find my tea set?"

"It's a better surprise than a tea set."

"A pony?"

"No. But Mr. Logan, the man who owns this

house, has some horses. Maybe later we could go visit them."

MacKenzie seemed to be digesting this new reality. She didn't smile, but why would she? In the world she knew, a lot of promises were made but not kept, and any good fortune could be snatched away from her at any time.

Randall opened the car door while Elena helped MacKenzie out of her child seat. Then the two of them walked hand in hand up to the imposing front door. MacKenzie's eyes were huge as Mrs. Drury let them in.

"May I take your coat, young miss?" the rather scary woman asked.

MacKenzie looked suspicious. She cast a questioning glance at Elena. "Will I get it back?"

"Oh, honey, of course you will. Mrs. Drury will just put it in that closet right over there, see? It'll be there whenever you want it."

Reluctantly MacKenzie allowed the coat to be removed and turned over to Mrs. Drury.

Daniel and Jamie were in the living room, where garlands and ribbons and wreaths had transformed the austere lines of the ultramodern room into something much cozier. A fire blazed in the fireplace, and though Houston experienced few nights that were cold enough to warrant building a fire, tonight was one of them. It always seemed a little more Christmassy if it was cold outside.

MacKenzie studied everything, taking it all in.

Her mouth formed an O as she surveyed the fourteen-foot decorated blue spruce. Then she stared at the fire.

"Hi, Elena," Jamie said. Her pregnancy was clearly showing now; she and Daniel had recently announced that their baby was due in May. "Merry Christmas. You're looking so much better. And who have we here?"

"This is MacKenzie, Travis's niece."

Suddenly shy again, MacKenzie turned and buried her face in the folds of Elena's skirt.

Thankfully, no one pushed to get a response out of MacKenzie. Both Daniel and Jamie knew the little girl's tragic history. A few others arrived—Jillian and her husband, Conner, and some of the senior staff from Project Justice along with family members. When two other children arrived, Elena persuaded MacKenzie to play a game with them in another part of the living room, where Elena could keep her eye on the girl, but MacKenzie didn't seem to participate much. She kept looking over at Elena with a worried expression.

Poor thing. The only security in her world right now was a woman she'd met only once before. When one of the servers brought a plate of kid-friendly hors d'oeuvres to the children, MacKenzie ate quickly, almost frantically, stuffing a cream puff in her mouth while holding another treat in each hand.

Elena remembered what it was like to have to compete for food. When she'd been a street kid in

Havana, she'd fought like a scrappy dog sometimes to keep what she'd scavenged.

After a while, the other two kids decided to go outside, but MacKenzie retreated to Elena's lap. She cheered up again when Daniel brought her a hot chocolate, declaring she'd never had one before.

"Anytime you come to my house," Daniel said, "you can have hot chocolate."

"I probably won't come back," she said solemnly.

Elena's heart ached for the child.

"When is Uncle Trav coming?" MacKenzie asked as Elena wiped off a hot-chocolate mustache from the girl's face.

"Soon, I hope. But don't worry. We'll stay right here until he arrives."

"What about if it's my bedtime?"

"Just this once, you can stay up past your bedtime, okay? But not too late, 'cause Santa Claus is coming tonight."

MacKenzie made a sound of derision that no six-year-old should have made. "Santa Claus isn't real. That's just a story."

"Well, I bet Santa will bring you presents *this* year." Elena and Travis had made sure of that. They'd bought her a new tea set and replaced some of the other toys and clothes the Stovers had sold.

When the doorbell sounded, Elena's breath caught in her throat. She was pretty sure who was about to walk in the door.

"Is it Uncle Trav?" MacKenzie asked excitedly.

"It could be."

MacKenzie wiggled out of Elena's lap, unaware of just how good a Christmas this was about to become.

"Remember, I told you he was bringing you a surprise?"

Travis appeared, standing in the doorway, looking luscious in a pair of dark blue pants and a sweater in a deep plum—he'd asked Elena to take him shopping when they'd made plans to attend this party. "I don't want your friends to think you're marrying down," he'd said. No one would think that if they saw him tonight. With his hair trimmed and the new duds, he was easily the handsomest man in the room.

Travis's gaze zeroed in on MacKenzie.

MacKenzie waved, finally flashing a quick, shy smile.

When it appeared Travis was alone, Elena worried that something had gone wrong with their plans. But then someone else stepped around the corner. He was more gaunt than he'd looked in any of the pictures Elena had seen. His skin was pale, and he had one of the worst haircuts imaginable. But the man was unmistakably Eric Riggs.

"Daddy!" MacKenzie shrieked, and then she was running across the room, dodging guests and furniture with surprising speed and agility. By the time she reached Eric, he was crouching down to receive her. She leaped into his arms and he picked her up and swung her around, then hugged her fiercely. Even from this distance, Elena could see he was crying.

"Daddy, Daddy, Daddy," MacKenzie just kept repeating.

Elena joined Travis, and they put their arms around each other as they watched the scene unfold. Elena had tears in her eyes, too, and she saw Travis dab at his eyes a time or two. The rest of the party guests broke into applause. Most of them had known of the reunion Travis and Elena had orchestrated when they'd learned Eric would be released on Christmas Eve.

No wonder Travis had been so desperate to preserve this father–daughter bond. The love between them was special—anyone could see that. It wouldn't be easy for either of them, starting a life from scratch. But with a firm foundation of love, miracles could happen.

"We do good work," Travis murmured in her ear. "I know we can't take all the credit for this, but knowing we helped make this possible feels pretty good."

"Yeah. It does. Merry Christmas, Travis." She pointed to something above their heads, and he looked up.

"Mistletoe. Did you plan this, too?"

"Might have." And they kissed.

* * * * *

LARGER-PRINT BOOKS!

GET 2 FREE LARGER-PRINT NOVELS PLUS
2 FREE GIFTS!

⬦ HARLEQUIN

super romance®

More Story...More Romance

YES! Please send me 2 FREE LARGER-PRINT Harlequin® Superromance® novels and my 2 FREE gifts (gifts are worth about $10). After receiving them, if I don't wish to receive any more books, I can return the shipping statement marked "cancel." If I don't cancel, I will receive 6 brand-new novels every month and be billed just $5.69 per book in the U.S. or $5.99 per book in Canada. That's a savings of at least 16% off the cover price! It's quite a bargain! Shipping and handling is just 50¢ per book in the U.S. and 75¢ per book in Canada.* I understand that accepting the 2 free books and gifts places me under no obligation to buy anything. I can always return a shipment and cancel at any time. Even if I never buy another book, the two free books and gifts are mine to keep forever.

139/339 HDN F46Y

Name	(PLEASE PRINT)	
Address		Apt. #
City	State/Prov.	Zip/Postal Code

Signature (if under 18, a parent or guardian must sign)

Mail to the **Harlequin® Reader Service:**
IN U.S.A.: P.O. Box 1867, Buffalo, NY 14240-1867
IN CANADA: P.O. Box 609, Fort Erie, Ontario L2A 5X3

**Are you a current subscriber to Harlequin Superromance books
and want to receive the larger-print edition?
Call 1-800-873-8635 today or visit www.ReaderService.com.**

* Terms and prices subject to change without notice. Prices do not include applicable taxes. Sales tax applicable in N.Y. Canadian residents will be charged applicable taxes. Offer not valid in Quebec. This offer is limited to one order per household. Not valid for current subscribers to Harlequin Superromance Larger-Print books. All orders subject to credit approval. Credit or debit balances in a customer's account(s) may be offset by any other outstanding balance owed by or to the customer. Please allow 4 to 6 weeks for delivery. Offer available while quantities last.

Your Privacy—The Harlequin® Reader Service is committed to protecting your privacy. Our Privacy Policy is available online at www.ReaderService.com or upon request from the Harlequin Reader Service.

We make a portion of our mailing list available to reputable third parties that offer products we believe may interest you. If you prefer that we not exchange your name with third parties, or if you wish to clarify or modify your communication preferences, please visit us at www.ReaderService.com/consumerschoice or write to us at Harlequin Reader Service Preference Service, P.O. Box 9062, Buffalo, NY 14269. Include your complete name and address.

HSRLP13R

ReaderService.com

Manage your account online!

- Review your order history
- Manage your payments
- Update your address

> *We've designed*
> *the Harlequin® Reader Service*
> *website just for you.*

Enjoy all the features!

- Reader excerpts from any series
- Respond to mallings and special monthly offers
- Discover new series available to you
- Browse the Bonus Bucks catalog
- Share your feedback

Visit us at:

ReaderService.com